Listen to the Silence...

Sally O'Brien

Copyright © 2017 Sally O'Brien
All rights reserved.

Book layout by www.ebooklaunch.com

My body
My voice
My life
My choice

Preface

Freddie took a deep drag on his cigarette as he strutted out of the London Nightclub. Blowing a few smoke rings, he turned to the drunk, bedraggled Linette as she stumbled out through the door behind him.

"Come on love, I'm feeling the need," he urged her.

"Alright, cor fucking 'ell, I've only just bought these shoes," Linette complained as she splashed the red soled, crystal adorned, pink shoes in a muddy puddle. Freddie grabbed her by the arm and led her along the street, laughing as Linette stumbled, barely able to keep upright on the five inch heels.

"Come on Linnie, I've got work in the morning, I need to be in my bed and snoring my little heart out by three or I'll be knackered tomorrow."

"Where are we going?"

"Just down here," he pointed to an alleyway which ran alongside the club. "I know a place, come on."

"Give us a drag of your fag."

"Yeah like I want your lips around my cigarette; the only thing you're sucking is my cock love."

"Charming."

Freddie continued briskly along the alley, pulling Linette behind him and then stopped when they came to a darkened alcove set into the Nightclub wall.

"Come on Linnie, get on with it, I'm fit to burst."

"Anyone would think you never got any." Linette laughed. "We only had a shag last night and we had that threesome about two days ago. You are one horny bastard."

"I can't help myself; it's your dark good looks and compelling nature that just want me to fuck you."

"Really?" a dirty blond, doe-eyed Linette tugged on Freddie's arm and pulled him around so she could look into his eyes. "Do you really think that Freddie?"

Freddie snorted, "Don't be daft; you're a dirty fucking hooker Linette. I fuck you because I can, because you have a good suck and a dark hot minge." He grabbed her hair and began to move her head towards his penis, which he was releasing from its cloth prison. "Now get on it Linette, you filthy whore and make sure you swallow; the last thing I need is dirty underwear. The wife just hates washing cum stained pants." He giggled as Linette got to work, gagging with every thrust of his manhood.

Freddie walked along the High Road, sucking on his bloodied knuckles. Linette had got just a little bit too full of herself after the blowie, talking about feelings and possible relationships. Freddie had started to suspect she may be getting too full of herself when she had stopped charging him for sex, but had decided to make the most of it and then put her in her place if she got out of hand. He was quite sad that he had had to teach her a lesson; she had a pretty face really, even if it was always smeared with make-up and hidden under a ton of slap and false lashes. Linette wasn't looking quite as pretty now that his knuckles had given her a make under, but Freddie was sure she would bounce back; her type usually did. He would give her a mercy fuck when she was able to walk again.

He whistled to himself as he strolled along the deserted High Road, he knew that he would have to hurry to get a taxi so that he could get home to bed as he had a very important meeting in the morning. Freddie looked left and right but could see no sign of any traffic let alone a Taxi, he marvelled at how such a vibrant and busy city such as London could turn into a ghost town, particularly when he needed to get home. Crossing the road, he swaggered along the street and his mind turned to thoughts of a kebab. He knew in London there must surely be a twenty four hour shop open somewhere so he was determined to find one, buy the big dirty meat filled wrap he wanted and then hail a cab home.

When Freddie took his next step onto the tarmac, he heard the sound of a car coming up the road behind him. Hoping it would be a taxi, he turned with his hand in the air, ready to hail his ride home. Bright lights blinded Freddie and the sound of the car engine deafened him in the otherwise soundless street. Freddie tried to take a step back out of the way of the car, but when he did, the car changed direction and headed straight for him. Drink, drugs and tiredness had clouded Freddie's judgement and he was unable to react quickly enough to get out of the way of the screaming metal giant which headed straight for him.

The car hit Freddie dead centre, causing him to fly along the road and end in a crumpled heap on the tarmac. He groaned, touching his head and body as he felt for any damage that might have occurred, aware that the drink was also, mercifully, dulling any pain he may be feeling. He was vaguely aware of the sound of a car engine once again and hoped that it was now an ambulance coming to see to his injuries.

Freddie began to reach for the phone in his jacket pocket but never managed to get hold of it as the car hit him once again, all four wheels going over his body, breaking skin and crunching bone as arms and legs were carried up into the arches by the turning wheels; pummelling Freddie's body, blood bursting from his veins and spurting over the hard cold floor.

Barely conscious, Freddie's last vision was of a woman standing over him; she bent down and put her face right up to Freddie's ear.

"You are a disgusting human being. You use, abuse and violate women in every way possible. People like you should not be allowed to walk on the planet. I hope you rot in hell, you bastard."

A hard kick to Freddie's face was the final blow which put his light out; Freddie would never know of the baby that was growing in the belly of his woman and would never again lift a hand to hurt her. The woman turned and walked away from the scene and from the car which sat, engine idling, Freddie's limbs still entwined in the rear wheel arches. She walked slowly, purposefully and at no stage did she turn to look back on the life she had destroyed. She was determined to focus only on the life she had just saved.

Monday

Session One:

Monday - 10am

"Hi, my name is Helen ... and I am here to kill a baby."

A loud gasp came from the five other women who sat in a circle inside the sparsely furnished room that Helen had just entered. Helen looked at each one closely, gauging their expressions at her comment. Mainly disgust emanated from all of them, although the short haired, tattooed, butch looking lady gave a wry smile.

"Sorry, have I offended?" Helen asked. "I mean, it's why we're all here isn't it?" A black male got up from his chair, ebony skin shining under the harsh strip lighting in the room. He approached Helen and held out his hand to invite her into the room.

"Hello Helen, I'm Marc, I will be leading these sessions. Please, if you could take a seat I would be very grateful." His gentle voice cajoled Helen into following him and she stalked over to the remaining chair in the circle, slamming her backside into the orange plastic.

"Welcome to the cuckoo's nest," she murmured. Marc sat quietly and replaced the clipboard he had put down earlier onto his lap. He raised an eyebrow at Helen, to which she smiled.

"Sorry, go on Marc, I am just being difficult; it's the way I am I'm afraid, you will learn that about me."

"Hey no problem Helen, it's good to know you like to speak, always helpful in these environments."

"Speaking is my forte."

"That's good to hear." Marc cleared his throat, rearranged the spectacles which dominated his face, and began.

"Good morning ladies; my name is Marc Delgado and I am a counsellor and social worker with Olinsbury Council Services. You were asked to attend this week long session of group counselling in a pilot scheme which has been funded by the NHS. Basically we feel that women like you . . ."

"Baby killers," Helen offered.

Marc cleared his throat again, "Women who are going through the process of a termination; may benefit from speaking to others who are going through the same thing. Now I am not here to help you to make a decision, or to counsel you through your decision to have a termination. You have already had one on one counselling before you have got to this stage, is that correct?"

Heads nodded in agreement. "Your one on one counsellor decided that maybe you would gain something from these sessions - whether that be an answer to your questions, a chance to speak through your decision or an opportunity to change your mind; we hope that we can give you the chance to do that. This is a completely new process, never tried before in the United Kingdom, so I don't know if it will help you; there will be questionnaires offered at the end of the week for you to fill in and give your opinions."

"I already know what my opinion is." Helen stretched out her arms and yawned.

"Please, let him speak." A quiet voice emanated from the woman sitting opposite Helen. With a face that Helen could only describe as 'shrewish', the lady was unable to look Helen in the eye, choosing instead to keep her face pointed towards the floor. Helen was of a mind to retaliate, but the sadness which was etched on the woman's face caused her to hold her tongue.

"Sorry." She said and sat back. "Carry on Marc."

"Thank you Helen. Like I say, I am a facilitator only; just here to help the process run through smoothly. The object of these sessions is for you to do the talking. Tell us about your life, how you got to this stage, what your intentions are and how you intend to move on from this difficult time in your life. Being able to voice all of these things may help you to make an informed choice about what you really wish to do. The sessions will run for three days as there are six of you. On the fourth day you are all scheduled for a termination as per the appointments you were allocated when you first attended the Women's Health Clinic. On Friday, after the termination clinic has been run, you have the opportunity to return to this room and see each other once again; talk through your feelings and hopefully come to terms with the decisions you have made. Do you all understand?"

Heads nodded once again in agreement. "Now we have kept the group small as we don't have many days and we want to give you as much opportunity to talk as possible. This is how I would like the sessions to progress; one of you speaks, then we break for refreshment and reflection. On our return we will discuss what has been said. If anyone wishes to offer an opinion or words of advice, please feel free to do so with impunity. It's very important that people speak the truth if this process is to work."

"You make it sound like we are at an Alcoholics Anonymous meeting. We're not talking about giving up drinking; we are stopping the life of a child."

"Helen if you wish to remain quiet or leave the room then you are welcome to do either."

Helen made to leave.

"But we really would like you to stay," said Marc. "Just give it a try Helen. One day. If it's not helping then you don't have to return tomorrow."

"I know you." Helen spat.

"Do you?" asked Marc.

"Yeah, you live down the same road as me. You're the perfect couple, you and the wife. Aren't you?"

"I am not here to talk about myself,"

"Have you never seen me before?" Helen enquired.

"I'm sorry, no."

"Well it is a long road," Helen nodded, "But funny how I know you and your perfect house, beautiful wife, two cars outside, freshly painted front. Yet you have no idea who I am. I walk past your house when I go to the shop, I put my bins out on the same day as you do, but you don't see me; why is that?"

"Helen, I am not here to discuss my life, my home, my wife or my personal life. I am here merely as a facilitator. If you wish to discuss this with me later on . . ."

"After class?"

"Then you are welcome to approach me."

"Oh sorry," Helen flicked her hair, "Let's get on with the child killing then."

"It's not a child."

Helen and Marc looked at the woman who spoke. She was a beautiful woman in her mid-twenties, leonine hair framing a perfectly made up mocha coloured face. "It's just a bunch of cells, not human; not yet."

"How many weeks are you?" Helen asked.

"Just five, it's not even the size of a peanut yet."

"Well good for you, I'm twenty weeks, so I have a fully formed child in *my* stomach." Helen snapped at the woman; standing up and pushing in her clothing to she could reveal the swelling of motherhood. "See, here's baby," she sang.

"Helen, please sit down." Marc continued quietly. "You are?" he asked the now chaste woman.

"Amelia," she answered.

"Amelia is a beautiful name; it's nice to meet you." Marc looked around, "Maybe we could all just start by saying our names. It would help to break the ice, I will start . . . again." He chuckled. "Hi, my name is Marc." He pointed towards Helen.

"Hi, my name is Helen . . .," she answered in a sarcastic tone, then pointed to Amelia.

"Hi, I'm Amelia," She said, pointing her finger at the shrewish girl.

"I'm Jane," she said to the floor.

"I'm Lorraine, lesbian extraordinaire." Said the woman to Helen's left. She put up her arms and flexed the biceps on each arm, which had tattoos depicting naked women thereon.

"Hello Lorraine," Marc said.

"Verity Roebottom," a forty something, handsome woman smiled at the last member of the group; a very young girl with long blond hair and the brightest blue eyes; she could have stepped straight out of a cartoon movie.

"Alice Carter," she said, her voice sounding as young as she looked; not yet mature, still child-like.

"Hello Alice."

"Hi."

"It's nice to have you here."

"Thank you."

Helen snorted with laughter, but remained wordless.

"Well now we know everybody's name, I think we should begin. Does anybody wish to start?"

All heads remained still and all the women avoided any eye contact with Marc.

"Alice?"

"Yes."

"Do you think you could begin?"

"I could try," Alice agreed.

"Well that would be lovely," Marc smiled. "Whenever you're ready Alice; take all the time you need."

Hi, my name is Alice . . .

"Hello, my name is Alice. I'm fifteen," she blushed. "I don't really know what to say."

"Alice, I'd like you to just talk about your life, what led up to the pregnancy. How you feel about things and why you have made your decisions. Anything else you want to say, there is plenty of time." Marc turned to the rest of the group. "I would ask if we could show each other respect and not interrupt. This will be a very hard thing to talk about; we don't want to make it harder for each other." He glanced briefly in Helen's direction; she ran her fingers over her lips and motioned zipping them together.

"Do you feel ready Alice?"

"I think so."

"Ok, try again."

"Ok, well, yes, I am fifteen; still at school, I will be taking my GCSE exams next year. I'm five weeks pregnant," Alice bit her lip and looked ashamed. "It wasn't meant to happen, I honestly did use protection; condoms. I'm not sure what happened." Alice took a moment to pause; everyone else remained quiet, willing her to continue. "Well the story is that I am quite popular with the lads at school, I've had loads of boyfriends; oh I haven't slept with them all, Kieran was my first, but I have been out on dates. I've been taken to the cinema, roller skating, the park; all crappy places by little boys who don't really know what they're doing and are only really after one thing. I was quite sick of it actually, I just wanted to get on with my school work and study hard, I'm going to be a teacher when I'm older; I love children and think I could be a really good nursery teacher." She smiled and looked at her hands, "That's bad isn't it? Saying that I love children and yet I'm here to get rid of one."

"We are not here to judge you Alice; you may speak your mind." Marc reassured her.

"Thanks, yeah I do love children, but I'm a child myself, I've only been doing GSCE'S for a year and I've still one more year to go, then I've got to do A Levels and then University, there definitely isn't any space there for me to bring up a baby. It's not just that, it's Kieran; we could never have a baby together, not for a long time. You see he's a teacher; he's my teacher."

Gasps and knowing nods came from around the room.

"It's not like that," Alice defended. "It all started at the beginning of this year. Like I said, I was sick of young lads taking me out on dates, I think girls mature a lot quicker than boys; they were all still playing computer games and football, only just wanting to know what it was like to kiss a girl or touch her. I was way beyond that; I help my mum to look after my younger brother, I cook and clean. I don't feel like a child anymore; I've been having periods since I was eleven and I think almost from the day that they start you begin to feel like you're a woman.

Kieran was, is, my form tutor. He's twenty six, just finished his teaching course and this is his first year teaching any students. He's a bit green around the edges, doesn't really know how to handle all of us kids; we've been giving him a pretty hard time. I don't think he's really cut out to be a teacher, or maybe he should be teaching younger kids."

Helen yawned loudly and stretched out her arms. "So you fucked him and got pregnant and now he never has to be a teacher again because he can spend the next two years behind bars."

"I thought we had to let people speak?" Jane asked Marc.

"That's quite true," Marc agreed. "Please Helen, let Alice speak."

"Sorry, carry on." Helen's eyes rolled.

Alice continued. "Well that's just it, I didn't *just* fuck him. When he started at the school I fancied him straight away, I mean he's very good looking; totally not like a teacher; he's got lovely green eyes and a really nice smile. I've been having some terrible problems at home, my mum and dad just don't understand that I'm not their little girl anymore and I should be allowed to have a life. They want me to get home at like ten o'clock every night and they don't want me to sleep over anyone's house or go to parties, I mean I'm not eleven.

I was really upset and moody for a bit and then Mr Brown, Kieran, asked me to stay after class and I spoke to him and he was really kind. He listened to me about my parents and he would let me sit and talk to him for ages when I should have been at lunch or break. We started to talk every day, about anything, he was so kind to me; is kind to me. We became friends, but I started to get feelings for him which were more than just friends; I would listen to loads of songs at home and every one of them reminded me of Kieran, he became an obsession to me; it was like he was a pop star or something, I just couldn't stop thinking about him.

One day I got the courage to tell him how much I liked him, he told me that that wasn't allowed; teachers and pupils were not allowed to ever become more than friends and he said that he didn't think of me like that, I was just one of his students. He asked me to try and stop feeling the way that I did and I tried, I really did try but I just couldn't get my mind off of him. We carried on speaking because I kind of got depressed after that, it was like there was a bus waiting to take me to a whole new life but I just couldn't get on it. Kieran was brilliant, he didn't push me away, he kept talking to me every day and making me feel better about things, he helped me and then he said that he couldn't help it either, he had fallen in love with me." Alice looked around with a beaming smile on her face.

"He loved me, he told me he loved me; it was amazing. The trouble was we couldn't be together. Kieran told me that if he ever got caught dating or seeing a pupil then he would be sacked and could even go to court. He was dead against us doing anything together, but I kept on and on at him, telling him I wasn't a baby, when I'm sixteen, I can get married. I begged him and begged him to meet me outside of school, for us to go somewhere where we could be together, alone. Eventually he said that I was right, he couldn't pretend anymore, he loved me and he had to be with me. He agreed to take me out in his car so we could go somewhere and talk.

One day after school we arranged to meet behind the Big Value store, there's a car park there and it's so big, the bit behind the store is always empty. I walked there after school and Kieran was waiting for me in his car. It was amazing." Alice looked around her. "Oh we didn't sleep together, it was just cuddling and kissing, but it was so warm and it felt so right. Kieran said that he had been dreaming about holding me in his arms for like, ages. We sat there forever just telling each other how much we loved each other and how we wanted to be together. Kieran told me that he had a girlfriend, Sharon, someone he'd been with since University, but that she was nothing like me, he didn't want to be with her; he wanted to be with me. We started to meet up quite a lot after school, but obviously because he had *Sharon,* we could never go to his house and he couldn't see me at weekends because he had to pretend to want to be with her.

Sometimes we would go to the hotel and get a room for the night, although we would only stay for an hour or two." Alice giggled. "It was so funny because I would have to sneak in; we obviously couldn't turn up together."

"Hilarious," said Helen.

Alice shot her a dirty look, but continued. "Well eventually we were always going to have sex; I knew what it was all about, what fifteen year old doesn't nowadays? We had spoken about having sex before, but Kieran said that he wanted to wait until I was sixteen. He said he couldn't help how he felt about me and was already risking everything to be with me, but that having sex with a fifteen year old was a line he wasn't willing to cross. We had to wait; it had to be right, legal; that way he could live with himself. I thought that was such a nice thing, it showed he really cared about me. But I wouldn't stop asking him; every time we kissed I tried to take it a little bit further. I wanted to have sex with him, I love him.

Eventually we did it; it wasn't even in the hotel room, it was in the back of his car in the Big Value car park and it only lasted about thirty seconds. It was completely my fault again; I kind of sat on him and, well, one thing led to another and before we both knew what had happened, we did it. Kieran was so shocked that he was almost sick; he said he was really sorry and that we shouldn't have done that. I said, 'Don't be silly Kieran, we love each other.' But he kept saying that we should have waited.

Well after that it was easy. We'd already been bad so we might as well carry on. We still couldn't see each other more than we wanted to because obviously he was still a teacher and I was his student and he had *Sharon*. But now I'm pregnant." Alice looked down at her stomach. "There's a little baby in there and it's mine and Kieran's. I would love to have the baby, it would be everything for us, but Kieran says no. He says that if I let anyone know I'm pregnant then he is going to be arrested; everything will change. He will lose his job and I will never be allowed to see him again. If the baby is around then both our lives will be over, forever. I said we should run away together, elope to another country, I've got a passport, but he showed me stories on the internet about young girls who had ran away with their older partners. They always get caught and then the man has to go to prison. I don't want that to happen to Kieran, I love him too much. Kieran says that if I abort this baby, then when I am older, we can be together properly and start a family. That's when I can have a baby, that's when we can get married. I have to wait until then.

I haven't told anyone about Kieran, not even my best friend Sarah. Kieran says it's so important that we keep everything a secret because he would be in so much trouble. But I'm going to be sixteen in six months; then we're going to be able to tell people, I think. Oh no wait," she shook her head and laughed. "No we can't do that because he will still be my teacher. It's going to have to be once I've left school, after my GCSE'S; *then* we can start to tell people about us, I'm not sure if he would still get in trouble; I will have to ask him about that. Anyway, we will eventually be able to let people know about our relationship, I don't know what my parents are going to say, but by then I'll probably be about eighteen, so there's nothing they'll be able to say anyway, right?"

"How do you feel about the baby?" Jane asked.

"I don't know, I mean I love it, it's something that me and Kieran made, it's like, our love isn't it? But I know we can't have it. It's like Kieran says; who do I love more? Him or a baby that hasn't even been born yet. I mean if I hadn't have got pregnant then there would never have been a baby. Kieran exists now, is alive on the planet, breathing and loving me. I can't let him go to prison, we want to be together. There will be time for a baby when we are older. Kieran says I can't miss something I've never had. It will be all over by Thursday, I might have a little cry but then we can get back on track. Kieran's good at explaining things; he makes it all sound so right."

"He's a real hero," said Helen.

"He really is," agreed Alice, who then noticed the look on Helen's face. "You can think what you like," she said, "I know Kieran, I know he loves me and I know we're going to be together; one day."

"Is there anything else you'd like to say?" asked Marc.

"No I don't think so; I'm going to have the abortion. I'm only here because they said I was so young and don't have the support of my parents so they felt that I should come to this session. But I do have support; not of my parents, but Kieran is supporting me, he talks to me all the time about it. It's *all* we've spoken about for the last three days; I've never spoken to him so much." She laughed. "I think he's panicking. But he doesn't have to; I'll do the right thing."

"I think we'll end there for about ten minutes," said Marc. "If everyone would like to have a drink and have a think about what Alice has been saying, I would ask that we refrain from discussing it with each other until we come back as a group. I will see you back in this room in fifteen minutes.

"Just time for a fag then," Helen reached for her handbag; "Anyone coming?"

"You're pregnant." Jane said in disgust.

"That hardly matters does it?" Helen guffawed. "We're here to get rid, you daft mare, what difference does it make if I'm smoking or not?"

"It's just, wrong," a perturbed Jane answered.

"Wrong? I think you're fucking wrong," Helen countered; "Wrong in the head." She grabbed her bag and left the room, Jane and the other women walked over to a tea urn which sat on a solitary table by the window. A plate of biscuits lay invitingly on the white cloth and Alice reached for an iced ring. "My favourite," she uttered, biting down on the crunchy snack.

Discuss . . .

Marc returned to the room and sat in his chair, quietly waiting for the women to re-take their seats. Jane, Verity, Lorraine and Amelia stood with cups in hand, but Alice and Helen were no longer in the room. On seeing Marc's arrival, the four women put down their cups and returned to their chairs. Marc looked at the empty seats and then questioningly at the four.

"Helen went out for a cigarette and I think Alice is being sick." Amelia offered; "too many biscuits."

"Oh dear, well we will wait for them to return." Marc looked at his clipboard and made some notes on the paper in front of him. "Was the tea ok?"

"Yes fine."

All five sat in quiet reverie whilst awaiting the return of the absent women. Jane continued her incessant staring at the floor; Amelia looked around the room and Lorraine bit and picked alternately at hangnails on her finger and thumb, whilst Verity watched, silently taking in all those around her. Eventually Helen returned and Alice came in her wake. Helen sat in her chair and Alice, looking a bit grey sat in hers.

"Are you ok Alice?" Marc enquired.

"Yes, I think its morning sickness."

"Should have had the ginger nuts instead of the iced ones," Lorraine smiled at her, "I think they help."

"Nothing helps." Alice smiled back. "But thanks."

"You're a nice girl Alice," Verity smiled, "I hope the sickness doesn't last for too long."

"Well that's a stupid thing to say," Helen observed.

"Oh god, so sorry," Verity looked horrified, "I don't know what I'm saying."

"It's fine, really." Alice reassured her, "This isn't normal for any of us."

"So mature," Verity smiled again, "thank you Alice."

Marc cleared his throat to draw their attention back to him. "Thanks for all returning. I would like to thank Alice for starting off our session, it's not an easy thing to do and it took bravery. Thank you as well for being so succinct in your story."

"I don't know what that means, but you're welcome." Alice smiled.

"Right, as I said before, I am a facilitator only so I will not be giving any input into this part of the session, what I would like to do is open up the session to you other ladies. Is there anything you would like to say to Alice about her story or any advice you can give her? Who would like to go first?" Marc scanned the room, "Lorraine, what about you?"

Lorraine tensed her relaxed frame and sat up straight in her chair. "I suppose I could try."

"Thank you Lorraine, go ahead."

"Alice, I don't think you really want to get rid of this baby," Lorraine began. "From what you are saying, you love it already; you see it as symbol of yours and

Kieran's love. Are you sure you want to go ahead with a termination?"

Alice's colour returned to her face as she blushed. "Well, it's like I said; I do kind of love it, but I think it's only because it's a part of Kieran. I mean I don't really know it to love it properly. Not like I love Kieran, not like I love my parents."

"That just doesn't sound like the voice of someone who wants to abort their baby." Lorraine said. "I mean if you love something, why would you do that?"

"Oh don't be ridiculous, she doesn't know what love is." Amelia interrupted. "Listen Alice, love is a very strong word and can mean all sorts of different things; it's just a way to describe an emotion. I think it's true to say that you probably don't even love Kieran, it's a flash in the pan; you're too young to know what real love is."

"I do know what love is." Alice protested, "Just because you're young, doesn't mean you don't know your own emotions, I know what love is, I love Kieran. You may be right that I don't love the baby. I love what the baby is, it's Kieran's, but ok, I don't love a bunch of cells, I just need to get rid so that we can move on together."

"Such a lovely girl," Verity said again.

"Oh my god, is that all you can say, you toffee nosed prat. He's a *paedophile*." Helen spat.

"What?"

"He's a paedophile, a man who preys on young girls; a monster for god's sake. He has groomed you and entrapped you and then had sex with you. You're underage, he should be arrested and he *should* go to prison."

"That's exactly what Kieran said everybody would be saying about him." Alice's eyes began to fill with tears, she blinked them away; "But it's *not* like that at all. Didn't you listen to what I said? He didn't want to have sex with me until I turned sixteen. He said that was a line he wasn't prepared to cross."

"But whoops, he did."

"Helen, look at me." Alice stood up, her long hair swishing around her shoulders. She stuck out her chest, "Look at these," she said pointing to her breasts. "They're not exactly small; I don't *look* like a child do I?"

Helen looked Alice up and down. "No," she grudgingly agreed, "You don't, I'll give you that."

"Exactly, I look like a woman. I think like a woman. In six months, by law, I'll be a woman. You can hardly call him a paedophile can you?"

"She's got you there," Amelia said, "When you put it like that Alice, no, you're right, I wouldn't say he was a paedophile, but he has acted inappropriately."

"How?"

"He's your teacher; it's against all their codes of conduct. He should never have allowed a relationship to begin between the two of you. Teachers should always be aware that young girls get crushes, they should keep themselves distant; having little tete-a-tete's in the classroom with girls like you, alone, is never going to end well."

"He didn't know it was going to happen."

"He's not fifteen Alice," Amelia shrugged. "He's twenty six, he should be worldly wise enough by now to realise that if you get intimate with somebody emotionally then a physical attraction can occur. It's like you say yourself, you don't look like a child. You are actually a stunning looking girl; all the boys are after you. He should have realised that to spend time alone with you was asking for the wrong thing to happen."

"You can't help who you fall in love with," said Alice. "I don't think he even thought about that, he just wanted to help me, he was just being a concerned teacher."

"A concerned teacher that got in your knickers," said Helen. "I wonder what he was really concerned about when he decided to speak to you. I think it's sick, someone should report him to the board of education."

"Oh no please," Alice pleaded, "Please don't do that." She looked at Marc. "These sessions are supposed to be confidential; she can't do that can she?"

Marc made a note on his clipboard, "Well, these are confidential . . ."

"But I can do whatever I like." Said Helen, "I'm not under any contract, I don't work here, and I am a normal woman, a member of the public. If I think it's wrong then I have every right to make a report, isn't that right Marc?"

"We need to speak about that later on; for now I'd like to see if we can resolve this here and now in this session. Maybe you can tell Alice why you think he should be reported?"

"It's not rocket science, I've already said he's a paedo, it doesn't matter what you look like Alice; you are still a child by law. Still a baby, you have the rest of your life ahead of you and should not be getting into relationships with grown men. It is babies having babies. It's not right."

Alice began to tremble and tears formed in her eyes. "Helen, you don't understand, if you report it, not only is his life ruined but mine will be as well."

"Your life wouldn't be ruined Alice," Helen took on a milder tone. "You really do have a whole lifetime to live through and you would get over this blip and carry on. That said; you could always keep the baby."

"How could I possibly do that?"

"Well I've lived by myself since I was sixteen, yeah it's hard, but it's not undoable. You would easily get a house and could go onto benefits; in fact a baby is quite an advantage nowadays. It's the only way to get housing at least."

"That's ridiculous." Amelia said, "Housing, pah."

"I'm just giving her all the options."

"She's a young girl, doing her GCSE'S, she should be finishing them, going to University, getting her degree and becoming a teacher. A career is the most precious thing any person can have - it makes you. Babies are just a cause of nature; it's not essential that we all procreate; there are plenty of others doing that for us in bucket loads. I may not agree with the whole teacher, pupil thing, but I know that Alice should go ahead with the termination and get her life back."

"He will probably leave you now anyway." Lorraine offered. "Men are like that, they get themselves into situations, following their penis rather than any logic and when it all goes tits up they leave. Men are actually pathetic; little boys who never grow up. The

25

reason they have an extra bit on their body is because God knew men would need something to play with."

Light laughter broke the mood in the room.

"I won't tell." Helen said to Alice. "I'm not here to hurt anyone; I was just playing Devil's Advocate. If you want my real opinion, it's completely your choice; if *you* don't feel ready to have a baby and if *you* want to terminate the pregnancy then that's what *you* should do. But, if it's Kieran who is making you abort because he is more worried about his life than yours, then I think you should consider how you are going to feel once the operation is over. Can you live with yourself knowing that you have killed a baby?"

"Please, it's not a baby." Amelia protested. "I know you are in a very different situation Helen and I'm sorry for that, but Alice and I are just four weeks, it's *not* a baby. It's a gathering of cells that may one day become a baby if allowed to progress. All we are doing is stopping that. There is no murder, no breath leaving a body, no consciousness being killed. It's purely a stopping of the process *before* it becomes any of that."

"That's a good way of putting it." Alice opined.

"What do you think will happen afterwards?" Jane spoke quietly.

"Oh I forgot you were here." Helen shouted over to where Jane sat. Jane lifted her face and stared directly into Helen's eyes.

"I've always been here, just because I'm quiet, doesn't make me an idiot."

"Ooh, sorry." Helen rolled her eyes.

"Alice, what do you think will happen afterwards? What will Kieran do?" Jane repeated.

"Well he says we have to leave each other alone. This has been a huge mistake, getting pregnant, and it's made him see that we have to be even more careful than we have been. I mean it's been fine, nobody knows, but look what nearly happened here; you threatened to report him. No, Kieran says that after this we have to keep away from each other until I leave school; then we're going to meet up again and start afresh. He's going to leave Sharon and make sure that he is single by the time I finish my GCSE'S. It's going to be great, he said that I can move in with him and we might even get married."

"That will be nice," Jane smiled.

"Yeah, it's going to be massive." Alice's eyes shone.

"All's well that ends well." Verity added.

"So he's going to leave you completely alone for the next two years?" Helen asked.

"Yeah, it's the way it has to be." Alice nodded sadly.

"Darling, believe me when I say that I truly hope it goes your way; that in two years' time you will still want to be with him and he will still want to be with you."

"Oh we will."

"I'm sure you will."

"We will." Alice insisted.

"Well that's alright then."

"Ok, leave her alone now Helen; we all know what will probably happen. She has to find that out for herself." Amelia interjected.

"Oh and find out she will," said Helen.

"I think that's enough for now - Alice how do you feel about your part of the session?" Marc asked.

Alice sat quietly for a moment and reflected on how the morning had gone. "Well I suppose I am still in the same mind; I'm going to terminate the pregnancy. But I think Amelia is right, I'm doing it for me, so that I can get ahead in my teaching career. I did think at first that it was murder and was starting to feel a bit bad about it, but she's right as well when she says that it hasn't developed into a child yet. I don't know how I feel about Kieran, I guess time will tell."

"Thank you Alice, and thank you everyone else. We will break for lunch and then return in an hour; I would ask that you do not discuss these sessions with each other outside of the meeting room area."

"Thank god for that," Helen said, "I needed a fag."

Session Two

"Thank you everyone for coming back, I hope you all had a nice lunch?"

"Fabulous."

"That's great Helen. Does anyone wish to offer any reflections from our morning session? Alice?" Marc looked at a flustered Alice, the grey skin from her morning's sickness now a bright red; tears rimmed her eyes, threatening to spill over.

"I've spoken to Kieran."

"Would you like to share with us?"

"Well, yeah, ok. He rang me. I told you he's been ringing me a lot since I got pregnant. I told him I was at these counselling sessions and that I'd been speaking about our relationship." Alice's face crumpled and tears exploded forth. Jane left her chair to console the young girl and put her arm around Alice's body, holding her gently and rocking her back and forth.

"Let it out Alice," Jane soothed, "It's been a long hard morning for you darling."

Amelia produced a tissue from the depths of her handbag. "We're going to need a lot more of these," she said to Marc.

"Just give me a few minutes," said Marc, excusing himself; he left the room and returned with an armful of hand towels. "Best I could do," he apologised, setting them on the same table which housed the tea urn and biscuits. "Help yourself," he offered.

"Great now I can get sore cheeks as well as eyes," Helen whined, "That paper is rough as fuck."

"Sorry."

Jane let go of Alice and returned to her chair. Alice's sobs had subsided and she composed herself once again.

"Are you ok Alice?" asked Marc.

She nodded, "Yes, sorry."

"You don't need to apologise, do you want to speak further?"

"Yeah, I guess. Well, I spoke to Kieran. When I told him I had mentioned our relationship he went mental. He said I had betrayed him and that he probably could never trust me again. I promised that it was all confidential and that no one is going to say anything but he's really frightened now." Alice wiped her eyes with the tissue Amelia had given her. "He says he's going to resign from the school now and move to Cumbria. He has to get away before it all gets too much for him. He thinks he may be getting depression; I can't believe I've done this to him."

"How have you done it?" an incredulous Helen asked. "It's not your fault Alice; it takes two people to make a baby and two people to have a relationship. He's eleven years older than you for Christ's sake; he knew exactly what he was doing."

"What if I never see him again?" cried Alice. "I don't know if I can live without him."

"He was never going to stay with you, you silly girl. Can't you see, all you've done is given him the excuse he's been looking for to put a stop to all of this."

"You don't know that Helen," said Amelia. "Leave her alone, she's already upset; she doesn't need to hear that kind of information."

"Someone has to tell her how it is."

"Sometimes we need to just find things out for ourselves." Lorraine interjected. "Alice, don't worry; he will think a bit more about things and when he sees that no one has said anything, he won't be as angry with you. He's just scared, anyone would be."

"I hope you're right."

"Of course she is, she knows *all* about men," said Helen. "Don't you Lorraine?"

Lorraine chose not to entertain Helen's comment. "I'm sure everything will be fine Alice, do you think you could speak to your parents?"

"Don't even go there," Alice sniffed back her tears. "I'm ok, I'm sure everything *will* be fine. Once I've had the operation I can go back to normal and we can talk about the future. If he goes to Cumbria I'll find a University up there and we can start fresh."

"I'm sure everything will be fine darling," Verity said, "We all had crushes on the teachers at boarding school, I'm pretty sure some of the girls even went into the cupboard if you know what I mean. No harm done, don't tell your mum, you know?"

"Uh yeah, I think," Alice's face blatantly said the opposite. "Anyway we will definitely get married."

"And all live happily ever after; how nice."

"I can't wait to hear *your* story Helen," Amelia said loudly.

"Maybe it is time to move on," agreed Marc, "Helen would you like to begin?"

"No I fucking wouldn't. I'm only here because they won't give me the termination unless I come here. My life is none of your business."

"If that's how you feel, we will respect your wishes. Jane?"

Jane shrank back in her chair and shook her head. "I'm not ready," she mumbled.

"I will go next," Amelia said.

"Thank you Amelia. Start when you're ready."

Hi, my name is Amelia . . .

"Hi my name is Amelia and I am going to have a termination on Thursday. I don't see it as killing a baby; as I said before I am just stopping a biological process that if allowed to continue will possibly become a human being."

"Swallowed a medical dictionary?"

"Please Helen," Marc interjected. "We all agreed to show each other respect."

"You might have," Helen sniped back, but kept quiet nevertheless.

Amelia shook her head, allowing her curls to settle, took a breath and then began again. "To understand my reasons, I suppose I need to take you right back to my childhood. Believe it or not I am number eleven of thirteen children. My mum and dad met in the seventies and are sort of old age hippies. My dad's black, he came over from Trinidad and my mum is white. They had all sorts of trouble when they got together; it wasn't exactly racially tolerant back then.

I had a lot of problems with growing up because of it as well; not in the way you would think though. Yeah I mean *society* found me socially intolerable. I had name calling, finger pointing and out and out racism as an everyday experience in my life, eventually I became immune to it, unconsciously accepting of it I suppose you might say. I would just smile along and be self-deprecating; my humour finally allowed my milky white peers to accept me and rather than being the dirty shit kicking nigger, I was the person that they referred to as 'Not you, you're alright. You're my friend.' Lucky me," Amelia smiled and was amused to find the other women in the group all looked uncomfortable and apologetic, apart from Alice who looked shocked and bemused; Amelia was pleased that times had changed and the younger generation seemed to be growing with a more diverse outlook on life.

"Sorry if I've offended anyone by using the 'N' word," she appeased, "But I had to hear that nearly every day of my younger life; I quite miss it now that it's illegal. Anyway if that was the worst I had to deal with, it would have been fine, but my family? Well that was a whole different ball game let me tell you. Not the Grandmas and Grandpas; they were fine. I could have been green with three heads and they would have loved me; but the aunties and uncles? The wider family; they were the worst. I was white chocolate or a coconut; black on the outside but white on the inside. I would never fit into the black community, my colour was diluted and so was my heritage. Dad had sold out in their opinion and whilst they would always embrace their son and brother, I was the outcast; not black, not rooted, no soul. My mum's family were the same; I wasn't white, I had been stained, I needed to go back on the banana boat with my plantain loving father and leave Britain clean once again.

Not only was I racially outcast, but I was one of thirteen. I couldn't be outstanding or *different*. Not the biggest or the smallest, there were ten other people before me who covered every stereotypical trait which could be had. There was the tallest, shortest, fattest, thinnest, prettiest, ugliest, plainest, most intelligent; thickest and yes, there was even a *special* one before I was born. There didn't seem to be anything left for me to be."

"Annoying?" asked Helen.

Laughing, Amelia answered, "Believe it or not, my brother Emelyn is the most annoying person on the planet. No I had to be something else. I had to climb over the parapet, break through all the barriers and surpass the socially acceptable skills that black people could have. I had to bypass *all* of those. I needed to be the best. Do you know what being one of thirteen makes you good at? Manipulation, lying, mentally beating at all the walls around you. Getting what you want when no one else wants it for you. I learnt all those skills and I became the best saleswoman this side of West London.

I started right at the proverbial bottom and wormed my way into a cold calling position selling hard drives to the public and companies. Because I barely had a social life and being at home with the family was *so* claustrophobic; it was much easier being at work. I didn't have set hours as it was a commission based job at first and if I sold I earned. I spent countless hours on that phone. I reckon I've dialled every number in the Business *and* Local pages. If I said I spoke to a thousand people a week I would probably be underestimating.

Well I sold my little arse off and made my way up the ladder; supervisor, then area supervisor, then off to the Head Office up town. I drove everywhere, up and down the country, hundreds, if not thousands of miles every single day, week, month of the year."

"Brrm, brrm," Helen motioned driving a car.

"I know right?" Amelia grinned. "Anyway, I became top saleswoman of the year and then I spotted an opportunity to get on the Board of the Company. Now you would think that all of the things that I had achieved and the *millions* of computers I had sold would be qualification enough for them to come to me and *beg* me to head the company? But don't forget, not only am I black but I'm also a *woman*. There's a certain code in the penis party that women do not get to the top.

But I did find a way; there was this guy, Gary. He was young, fit, and as successful as me, if not more successful. He was made one of the Company Directors and I knew he would be my ticket to the top. Oh he was my biggest challenge yet. I had to use every trick in my repertoire; instead of selling hard drives, I was selling me. I was relentless in my pursuit of him and he was a tough nut to crack. The biggest challenge was getting him to see past my skin colour and to just see the me underneath, you know?" heads nodded in understanding.

"Well it worked and we got together about two years ago. It works. We are top of the company; both workaholics and we are totally in love with the job and with each other. We got married about six months ago; a hundred thousand pounds wedding and then a honeymoon like you could only ever dream of in Mauritius. I'm a Regional Manager now, it's all worked out as I planned it; until I started feeling sick." Amelia's eyes glistened with unshed tears. "I couldn't believe it when I saw the positive line on that pregnancy test. The doctor said that I had probably cancelled out the effects of the Pill by taking some antibiotics for an abscess which I was suffering from." Amelia breathed out a long hard breath. "A baby; a living breathing baby, made out of me; warm and loving, burping and farting. Oh how I would love to begin a little family of my own. I started to imagine the three of us in our house and then I realised there is just no way it's ever going to happen.

Gary is so much more ambitious than me. He wants to conquer the world; the computerised world first and then who knows? And I'm his wing woman; he says together we will do it. He's got it all planned out for the next twenty years and babies do *not* turn up for at least another ten. I just know that if I tell him I'm pregnant then it will be all over for me and the little one. He will probably demand a termination anyway or accuse me of trying to trap him. Then he will make sure he destroys me in the business world. Before I know it I will be back out in the cold calling centre; that's if I can get back to work whilst having a new born baby. I can't do it to Gary, I can't do it to myself and most of all I can't do it to the baby.

The way I see it, stop it before it starts. Don't put Gary in the position where he had to demand the termination, just do it. Don't say anything, carry on as normal. In ten years, after we've made five million, then we will try properly for a family. It's very sad, I'm upset about it, but I know it's for the best." Amelia looked around her, "That's it, that's my reason."

"Thank you Amelia." Marc made a note on his clipboard, "Shall we discuss?"

Discuss . . .

"Yes let's discuss the murder of another innocent child." Helen spat.

"How dare you say that?" Jane's voice was loud and angry.

"Hit a nerve have I?"

"It's not your life; you're not living in her situation. You have no right to judge her." Jane continued loudly, "I'm sure she would keep the baby if things were different."

"Oh of course I would," Amelia agreed, "If I thought for one minute that Gary would want the baby, I would be so happy. But I know he hasn't figured for this and his ambition is the most important thing in his life. If he had to make a list, career would be at number one, money at number two and me at three. I'm not stupid; I knew what I was letting myself in for. Hell I chose this life."

"People do change though," said Lorraine. "Things change and so do people. You may find if you go home to Gary tonight and speak to him about the baby, he may surprise you."

"I doubt it."

"Sometimes people don't know they want something until it's offered to them, you know?"

"No, I don't know what you mean."

"It's like we're all sitting here now, a person could come in and give us all a cake. We weren't thinking about having cake, none of us need cake, but it's been introduced and some of us will say 'yes'."

"Only if it was chocolate fudge cake," Alice smiled.

"Lemon drizzle for me," Amelia smiled back at Alice.

"You're missing the point," Lorraine tutted, "It's not about the cake."

"What *is* your point, come on."

"Ok Helen, we can't all be as quick as you," Lorraine shifted her position, bringing herself forward in her chair. "My point is, the people who take the cake changed their minds when something new was offered. They hadn't wanted the cake, hadn't thought about cake, but when it was offered, they changed their minds and took the cake. After they ate the cake one or two of them probably even said, 'I'm glad I had the cake, I really enjoyed it.'"

"Yeah and some said 'I wish I never had that cake, I feel sick now,'" said Helen.

Lorraine sat back in her chair again and began inspecting the silver rings on her fingers. "I was just trying to show Amelia that people can change their minds very easily."

"When it's cake."

"No, it's not about the sodding cake; it's about ideas. If you put a new idea or concept to someone, even when they weren't originally considering it, they *can* change their minds. I think you owe it to Gary to at least consider the idea it's his baby too."

"It's *not* a baby," Amelia objected, "Please stop saying 'baby' like it's a living breathing person, because right now it just isn't. It's a bundle of cells no bigger than the tip of my little finger. It doesn't have a brain, or feelings or a beating heart. I am not killing a child. I am preventing one from being grown. Surely any person who uses contraception does exactly that every time they prevent an egg from being fertilized? That's why churches are even against contraception. All this is, is a very late contraceptive measure."

"You can talk yourself through the text a million times but you are still killing a baby, *contra*ceptive; stopping conception. You have already conceived, you are with child and you are going to get rid of it without even offering him the opportunity to say 'No we'll keep the baby'. For all you know he may think that it's you who doesn't want one so he just plays along with his five year plan. Have you thought about that?" Helen asked.

"Trust me babies are not on his horizon."

"Kieran didn't take the cake." Alice's little face blushed red as she spoke. "I told Kieran didn't I; gave him a chance to say 'No let's have the baby' but he didn't. He said straight away that it would ruin his career. He made *me* get rid of it."

"Your situation is a little different darling," Jane spoke gently to Alice. "Don't forget your age difference. Not only would Kieran lose his job, but he'd probably lose his freedom as well."

"Yeah, but I'm just saying; Gary might not say everything is wonderful and then, like Amelia said; he might hate her for getting pregnant. I've lost everything now. Kieran's leaving and I'm not stupid, I know I will probably never see him again. Amelia likes her life. She's worked hard to get there and she doesn't want to lose what she's already got."

"You really are a mature young lady." Amelia smiled warmly at Alice. "What do you think Jane?" She asked.

"I can't tell you what to do," Jane shrank back to her position of staring at the floor.

"No, I'm not asking that, I'd just like to know what you think. I mean Helen thinks I'm a murderer, Lorraine thinks I should tell Gary and give him the chance to keep it and Alice, I think agrees with me?"

Alice nodded her agreement.

"So it's one vote each way, I could really do with an extra opinion."

"My opinion counts for nothing."

"No honestly, it does. I'd really like to hear it."

"Well alright, I probably agree with Lorraine. I mean it's true that there is no baby at the moment and if you have a termination and say nothing then it would be like it never existed. But how would you feel? I mean you will always know what you did. It will be an unspoken secret that you will carry with you for years; if you have the termination you may regret it. Suddenly the small bundle of cells may become the baby you never had; the *life* you never had. It's the part of the puzzle which could have made your life whole and you never gave it a chance. Years from now you may get drunk and tell Gary about it, and then it could tear your relationship apart. I think the only way you can hope to terminate with a clear conscience is if it really is a decision you both made. You should speak to Gary and get him to confirm what you believe. If he loves you then he will believe you that it's not a trap and a trap for what anyway? I mean you're married, he couldn't get any more trapped than that." Jane grinned, "You are just as ambitious as him by all accounts; I think you will be stronger as a couple if you go through it together. Surely he has proven he loves you; you are married and stable. I honestly believe you need to make him part of the decision if you want to live the rest of your live with a clear conscience."

"I hadn't thought about it like that."

"I could be wrong; I mean I don't expect you to do what I say."

"No, no but you make a lot of sense. I know he's going to want a termination, but you're right, it should be a decision that he's allowed to voice. I don't want to keep secrets from him, that would just eat me up inside. Thank you Jane."

"Yay for Jane," Helen clapped slowly.

"Oh I can't *wait* to hear your story." Jane shot Helen a dirty look.

"You ain't hearing nothing about me." Helen shot back, "I'm just here to make up the numbers. I don't need any counselling. I *know* I'm killing this little parasite inside me. Tick tock, tick tock, three days and I'm free of the thing." Helen coughed, a loud hacking cough; the sound so loud in the room it alarmed those sitting in there. "God I need a fag." She gasped once the coughing had subsided.

"You are disgusting," Jane cried.

"No, I'm just honest," said Helen. "We're all here for the same reason. I don't think anyone here really thinks any different to me. Just get it over with and move on, no time for tears. Tell your husband you selfish cow. It's not all about *you*. Right, is that it?" she said looking at her watch, "Can I go now?"

Marc checked his own watch. "Yes, the session time is coming to an end. Does anyone else have something they would like to add?"

No one replied.

"Ok, well thank you once again for being here today and thank you Alice and Amelia for telling us about your situation. It's given all of us a lot to think about I'm sure."

"Not me."

"Well some may find these sessions more helpful than others Helen, but who knows what tomorrow might bring."

"More bleeding hearts."

"Thank you everyone, I will see you tomorrow." Marc got up from his chair and left the room.

"You are such a bitch," Jane said to Helen, "I don't know how you live with yourself."

"Oh fuck off, you know nothing about me."

"How do you sleep at night?"

"Hanging upside down from the rafters," Helen retorted, "I sleep just fine thank you. Have a great evening." She smiled as she walked out of the room, "I'm going for a fag."

"She's a very angry woman," Alice said to Jane as she put her coat on.

"Some people are like that," Jane agreed, "Sometimes it's to hide the hurt though. They put on a front. It's like offense is the best defence."

"Do you think that's what it is with Helen?"

"No I think she's just a bitch." Both women laughed. "Come on let's get out of here. Oh Amelia?" she stopped as she got to the exit.

"Yes?"

"Whatever you decide, good luck."

"Thanks."

"See you tomorrow?"

"Yeah, see you tomorrow, bye." Amelia turned on her phone and dialled her office number; she pulled her coat around her as she waited for the phone to be answered.

"Hello?"

"Hi Dave, I'm calling for today's figures." She continued to walk out of the door as her colleague relayed the day's happenings to her over the phone."

Home

Marc pulled up to his pretty nineteenth century cottage. He and Eleanor had bought the premises ten years ago when they had decided to spend their lives together. Both were very much in love after a chance meeting; literally falling into each other's arms at the local ice rink.

Being in their early twenties and both fresh out of University, embarking on new careers; Marc as a social worker and Eleanor a solicitor, they had limited funds and the cottage was bought as a fixer upper. Countless hours had been spent by Marc and Eleanor alike, using all their precious time off to repair, renew and create a wonderfully cosy home for the couple; with room for one more should that ever happen.

Marc sighed as he considered the possibility of a family, looked up at the newly varnished sash window which dominated the top level of his home, he thought back to Helen's comment about his freshly painted home. Why had he never seen her before? They lived on the same street, put the rubbish out on the same day, she was right about that. What she wasn't right about, was the perfect couple. What she didn't know was that Marc was so caught up in his own world, that he sometimes found it hard to look around him. What she didn't know was that every day was a struggle for him and no amount of freshly painted house fronts was going to give him, or his wife, the life they craved for. He put Helen to the back of his mind, and then fixed a smile on his face before walking through the front door.

"How was it?" an inquisitive Eleanor came rushing out from the back kitchen on hearing her husband. "Was it just awful?"

"Can I please just get a coffee and a sit down before we talk honey, I'm shattered."

"Oh of course, of course, sorry." Eleanor backed off and walked through to the kitchen, switching on the kettle as she arrived and searching for cups and coffee.

"I had a busy day." She offered.

"What happened?" Marc was glad of the opportunity to change the subject.

"Oh some idiot decided he wanted to do the plank on the ten foot diving board down at the swimming pool."

"What's so wrong with that?"

"Well he was naked at the time."

Marc started laughing, Eleanor grinned. "Wouldn't have been so bad but unfortunately he got the urge to urinate whilst up there. You can guess the rest."

"Oh, golden showers all around." Marc laughed again.

"Yeah needless to say it made for quite an amusing interview. I lost count of the amount of times he asked the officer interviewing him if he was taking the piss."

"What happened to him in the end?"

"Antisocial Behaviour Order and a £80 fine."

"Ouch."

"He was lucky. If I had been the copper I would have gone down the Common Assault angle; urinating on people, it's disgusting."

"It's lucky you're on the defence side or everyone would be in prison."

"Damn right." She nodded her head in agreement and fist pumped the air in righteousness.

"I still think it's kind of weird that you are a defence solicitor when you have such an 'everybody is guilty' attitude." Marc commented, not for the first time.

Eleanor gave her usual reply, "It's what my dad wanted."

"Well he's not around anymore Ellie, maybe you could do what *you* want to do for a change."

"Marc, we've been here before, I promised him on his deathbed, I'm never going to change that."

Marc knew he should change the subject, but was reluctant as the other subject was much more painful for him. He decided to drink his coffee silently and enjoy the few moments of peace left to him. Eleanor watched the coffee cup rise and fall as Marc quietly supped the beverage. She tried to wait, but the question just burned inside her brain. Eventually she could wait no longer.

"How was it Marc?"

Marc took a deep breath, set down his coffee and began. "It was kind of how I expected it to go. There are only six women because they terminate on a Thursday and we can only really fit in two a day. It's not that they take long to say their piece, or even for us to discuss it, but it would be just too emotionally draining to do more than that I think."

"Must be hard for them."

"Yeah, some more than others. There's one girl there, she is so rude about the whole deal. She's calling everyone baby killers, including herself."

"Well technically they are."

"Come on Ellie, you're not stupid, people have different reasons for doing it."

"Yeah, yeah I know, carry on."

"I don't know what her problem is and if she is to be believed then I won't know either. She seems determined that she is only here to fulfil the terms of the termination and won't be participating actively in the sessions; other than to bitch and moan."

"Nice."

"My thoughts also."

"What about the others?"

"Well I only really got to know about the two who spoke today."

"And?"

"The first girl, she's only fifteen."

"Oh my god."

"Yeah, that's not the worst of it, but I can't really tell you too much about that."

"Why is she terminating?"

"I can't discuss that either really but trust me when I say that it *has* to go ahead."

"Ok," Eleanor dismissed the topic easily. "And the other woman?"

"Ambitious, driven, successful career woman."

"And baby gets in the way?"

"That's the long and short of it. Although she *is* married and very well off, I think the other women have managed to convince her to speak to her husband at least and discuss it with him before she takes that final step."

"Oh, I hope she does. It would be such a shame for both of them to lose something so precious."

Marc's breath caught in his throat, "I know, I'm sure she will speak to him tonight and find her reasons for terminating have gone."

"I hope so for the baby's sake; life is so hard isn't it?"

"I love you Eleanor."

"And I love you Marc," She reached for Marc's outstretched hand. Both sat silently for some time, holding each other and contemplating their own loss.

Marc thought back to the earlier time when Eleanor had miscarried four children previously. Each pregnancy had been a real blessing as they had been unable to conceive naturally for the first five years of trying. Eleanor's profession made fertility treatment a possibility, so they stepped out into the whirlwind of torment and grief of attempting to artificially create a baby.

First Eleanor was given tablets to promote egg release with each cycle, hoping that Marc's little swimmers would be able to hit home when there were many more targets to choose from. It became clear after six tries that this wasn't going to happen; it didn't seem to matter how compatible Marc and Eleanor were in their lives, something was stopping that compatibility reaching the womb.

The next thing to try was to remove the eggs from the womb and to enforce fertilisation in the science lab. "Our own little test tube baby," they would say to each other. The eggs were replaced into Eleanor's womb in the hope that at least one would be able to settle, take hold, root itself into the fleshy wall and life would begin. Marc and Eleanor joked they would never eat eggs again and after each cycle would pray for the blue line to appear on the endless pregnancy tests that they would take 'together'.

Finally when all hope seemed to have gone, money reserves had been exhausted and hearts and minds had been taken to the very brink of breakdown; there appeared a strong blue line, telling them they would be parents. An early scan predicted quadruplets, it seemed that this time every blessed egg which had been introduced to Eleanor's womb, had taken residency quite nicely and life was beginning in earnest.

"Four pregnancies at once," they would tell excited family and friends. When four became three, Marc consoled Eleanor with the doctor's prediction that they may not keep all four and may even have to consider terminating two so two could survive.

"It's taken that decision away, which is a blessing." Marc had said. "Besides three will be a real handful."

Three became two, ten weeks into the pregnancy. "Some people can only carry girls, a lot of people will lose a boy at ten weeks," A gem of consolation from Marc's boss, Shirley. Eleanor was put on major bed rest. "Feet up, don't move, keep those legs crossed." The pain of losing her treasured cargo was replaced by joy at the twelve week scan when two little souls were seen on the screen; scrabbling about in their own fluid beds, hearts beating and fingers and toes clearly visible on the black and white screen."

Both marvelled at how much the little people moved around, "They're doing the jive in there and I can't feel a thing," Eleanor would joke. Both Eleanor and Marc would talk to and kiss the scan photos which had been placed on the noticeboard in their kitchen. A flutter of movement at sixteen weeks brought tears of joy to both their eyes and Marc longed to feel those same movements so he could share in the joy rather than feeling the butterflies of fear which hovered over them.

Each day was a triumph and each week which passed became a miracle. Both Marc and Eleanor relaxed into the pregnancy and had even discussed decorating the spare room ready for their new arrivals. Bed rest seemed to have worked, Eleanor finally getting up and venturing out into the real world, happily patting her growing bump and discussing the hoped for arrival of the twins, who were *obviously* girls. Marc had been desperate to know the sex of the babies and the twenty week scan would have brought that information had Eleanor not woken covered in blood on Sunday morning.

Marc woke to agonized screams and on seeing the tell-tale trail of blood clots heading towards the bathroom, Marc followed it, already crying and lamenting the loss of his never-born children.

"There could still be one." Eleanor pleaded from the floor of the bathroom. "One Marc, we only need one."

"Come on, we'll go to the hospital, they can scan the babies and see what's going on." He helped his wife off the bathroom floor and gently led her to the back of his car, holding her head to his chest, his tears falling and mingling with her own.

"One baby, one baby," Eleanor repeated and continued to silently repeat; through an examination, a scan and finally during the pre-op checks as she was taken for her womb to be cleared of the tissue which was all that remained of her no longer viable twins. Marc waited anxiously for Eleanor to return from her operation, ready to hug her and tell her that everything was going to be ok and they could try again. Sadly when the babies were removed from their fleshy cell, the only part of Eleanor to return to Marc was her physical body. The pressure of failure and the devastation of the loss was just too much for Eleanor to bear and her mind closed down, shut itself off from the world, checked out of being, leaving Eleanor's body behind, living, breathing, but not thinking or feeling. It was hard for Marc to even get her to look into his face; she just stared vacantly into space, curling herself into a foetal position and rocking herself backwards and forwards. Eleanor was lost in a world of torment, the pain in her physical body reminding her of the loss she had suffered.

"It will get better," Marc had been reassured by the nurses who tended to Eleanor, "She will come around; we will get the Psych Team to speak to her."

But Eleanor never came around, days turned into weeks and eventually the hospital announced they were unable to cater to her needs. Physically she was perfectly healthy and did not need the care of a hospital; it was suggested that Eleanor be put into a Mental Health Unit where she could have the space to heal and recover. Marc fought vehemently against his beloved wife being committed to a Mental Health unit; he could not bear the pain of that. Eleanor had always been such a forthright woman, intelligent and humorous; she wasn't the kind of person who would end up in a mental institute, he just would not put her through that. So Marc searched the country and finally found a rehabilitation centre on the Norfolk Broads. The centre focused on convalescing after all manner of illness and although ordinarily they would not accept mental health patients, Marc convinced them that Eleanor was different and they accepted her into their fold.

The home was situated on the Broads itself, with a sloping garden that led down to the beautiful green banks of the river. Each morning Eleanor would sit herself on the jetty at the bottom of the garden, watching the morning mist rise from the calm waters. Fish jumped out into the air, catching the flies which hung above the water, ducks and Canadian geese would drift silently by, some offering a dull quack as they saw her perched on her chair. The bobbing of the grebe's heads would momentarily hold her attention as the bird came up for air and then disappeared back into the water, on its constant quest for the little fish which populated the Broads. As the sun came up to its fullest, the river would be host to many happy holiday makers who would go by in their river cruisers, little heads poking out of life jackets which threatened to suffocate the wearer by its very size; everyone passing waving happily at her, none aware of the cacophony of rage which twisted and pounded inside her mind, the force which urged her to jump into the tranquil river, to put her head under and to breath in the water, fill her lungs, calm her pain, join her little ones.

Each day Marc would arrive, the two and a half hour journey from London not preventing him from coming or offering him the easy excuse why he should only visit 'sometimes'. Eleanor was his life; she drew him to her like a magnet, the force of which he could not resist. Life was on hold until they could be together again as a unit, as a whole. Eventually the many months spent sitting on the jetty allowed Eleanor's rage to calm, the pain subsided just enough so that she was able to see a light at the end of her own personal dark tunnel and to finally gather the strength to face the world she had removed herself from both physically and mentally.

"Hi Marc," were the first words she had spoken in seven months. When she turned and looked him in the eyes, for the first time acknowledging his quiet presence on the jetty beside her, he cried; big fat tears. Tears which he had refused to allow to consume him as he fought the battle to be at Eleanor's side, to be the rock she had needed through such a terrible time. Those two words gave Marc permission to start his own grieving process now that they were able to do it together.

Eleanor relied heavily on Marc at first, to nurture and protect her, but gradually with his help, she was able to accept her grief, box it up and shelve it into the far recesses of her brain and allow her life, their life, to begin again.

Eleanor threw herself into the workplace, using each case as a plaster for her grief. Every so often they would allow the box to open and they would grieve together, mourning the loss of the babies that never were and they believed never would be. Eleanor just wasn't strong enough to suffer the loss of another child and her walls were built so high against another pregnancy that Marc had to come to terms with the fact it was unlikely they would ever try again.

Marc shook the memory from his mind and brought his attention back to Eleanor, stroking her hand, his eyes followed the lines of her arm up to her shoulder, so delicate yet so strong. He looked on passed her neck which he liked to nuzzle and came to rest on her face, the dimple always there waiting to deepen with her smile. Her hazel eyes which had always been alive with positivity, love and ambition were now faintly lined with grief, the pain etched upon the once smooth skin. Eleanor looked quietly at Marc then gave him the dimple he so loved when she smiled at him.

"You know I think you're very brave for taking on the role don't you?"

"Yes, I just," Marc reached over and kissed the dimple. "I just don't know if I'm doing it for the right reasons."

"Saving a life?" Eleanor pulled away from Marc's embrace.

"We don't know that will actually happen Ellie,"

"It will, I know it will," she was adamant.

"Just don't get your hopes up."

"Look what happened today," Eleanor persisted, "It seems you may have convinced the career driven woman to take a step back and reconsider her position. That's one life potentially saved."

"True and I hope she does the right thing for her, but the *group* helped her with that decision. I'm not sure I can do it on my own."

"You can," Eleanor grabbed Marc's face between her hands and moved onto his lap. "I know you can do it Marc, I know you can save the baby. You just have to find the right person."

"What if that person isn't there? What if I fail?" he pulled her hands from his face. "I don't know if I can carry on Ellie, I really don't."

"Please Marc, for the women," she kissed him tenderly on the lips. "For the babies," she kissed him again and pushed her body into his familiar embrace. "For us Marc," she whispered, nibbling his earlobe, "for me."

Marc responded to her touch and began to kiss back. "I will go back tomorrow," he told her before picking her up in his strong arms and taking her to their bedroom. "Tomorrow." He said again as they began to kiss once more.

Home . . .

"You are a snivelling pathetic cunt." Freddie looked at his wife who was cowered before him on the floor. "Get off the floor for fucks sake and go to my wardrobe; my shoes need rearranging."

As she got up from the polished wood, holding her face where he had slapped her, he sneered, "God you are so unbelievably weak, why did I ever marry you?"

Jane walked away from Freddie, head bent low, ensuring she didn't make eye contact with him.

"I asked you a question."

Jane stopped and turned back to where Freddie stood, hands clenching and unclenching, face red with anger and a fleck of spittle on his chin. "I asked you why I married you," Freddie repeated. Jane kept her eyes pointed at the floor, unsure which response would cause the least harm.

"Don't bother replying, we both know why. You are my slave Janie, you are here to serve me aren't you?" he reached out to pull at Jane's bedraggled hair. She flinched as he tugged at her locks, but kept her eyes down and said nothing.

"Yeah you know not to talk, there's a good slave." He pushed her face with the tips of his fingers. Jane quietly turned, walking away from him, praying that

Freddie had had enough of tormenting her for one night.

"Janie," he walked towards her, pulling her hair once again and bringing her back towards him. Jane bit her lip to stop herself crying out in pain; Freddie hated it when she cried in pain.

"Daddy's bringing some girls home later; we're going to have some fun. I want you to get the bedroom ready; clean sheets, champagne. You know the drill, if you're a lucky dog daddy might let you suck his knob."

He pushed her once more. "Now fuck off," he smirked as Jane scuttled away, and then went into his large study, his man cave as he liked to call it. There was just enough time for a couple of lines before he headed up town to his favourite night club and the panoply of whores who were waiting for Freddie and his enormous wallet.

Jane sat inside the wardrobe Freddie had directed her to; she picked up shoes and rearranged them into colour order before straightening the belts which hung along a rail of the walk-in wardrobe. As she put them into a proper line, she prayed that one of those belts wasn't going to be around her throat one day.

Morning . . .

"Morning," she smiled as Marc opened his eyes reluctantly when he heard the incessant alarm. He had a brief shock when he saw Eleanor staring intently at him.

"Good morning my Ellie, how did you sleep?"

"I've been just lying here thinking for most of the night," she admitted to him, moving over to nuzzle into him. Marc put his arm around her slender frame and pulled her close, inhaling deeply the smell of sex still faintly on her.

"What are you thinking about? How much of a stud I am and how lucky you are to have married such a vision of dark loveliness."

"Eleanor slapped Marc's chest playfully, then rested her arm across his chest, her milky white skin a striking contrast to Marc's deep chocolate tones.

"You are beautiful," she admitted, "But seriously Marc, today could be the day."

"That I get a blow job?"

"Marc, please," Eleanor pulled away, sitting up in the bed.

"Hey come on," Marc got up to sit beside her. "Ellie we had a lovely night, why break the mood?"

"Marc," she turned and stared him in the eye. "I love you so much; we have had the *most* wonderful relationship, which has even managed to survive *the* most terrible situation. When I lost our babies my world fell apart. The very fabric of my brain just unravelled and I was lost in a world of darkness; rocking back and forth in a chair, surrounded by crazy people. I thought that is where I would be for the rest of my life and, oh, how I wanted that life to be cut short. I just wanted it all to stop. I wanted to go to sleep and never wake up again. All I could see was those scan pictures in my mind and bit by bit they fell to pieces *just* like my babies, *our* babies. Their flesh just falling apart inside me while I was happily patting my bump and putting names to their faces.

"Ellie don't."

"I have to."

"You really don't."

"Yes, yes I do," she stopped him, grabbing both his hands in hers. She smiled tenderly at the man she loved. "You saved me Marc. Every day that I prayed I wouldn't see daylight; you would be there to show me it was worth waking up. You must have been going through your own personal torture because not only did you lose your babies, but you thought you might be losing me." Marc nodded silently in agreement. "And you stayed Marc, you came every day to see me, you never asked me for anything and you waited until I was ready. I have never even come close to giving you that level of support and you have never asked it of me. You are the most wonderful, amazing husband a woman can have." She reached over and kissed him on the forehead. Marc took his hands out of Eleanor's and wrapped his arms around her.

"I would wait forever for you Ellie."

"I know Marc, I don't deserve you."

"Of course you do, we are soul mates, we're meant to be together."

"Piano keys?"

"Yeah baby," Marc grinned. "You know it takes the black and white keys to make the sweetest sounds."

"Everton mints."

"The sweetest ones."

"Zebra?"

"Without the stripes it's just a horse." They both giggled.

"I want a baby Marc."

"Please Eleanor." Marc released himself from Eleanor's embrace. "Please don't do this." He got up and began to collect his clothes, ready to have a shower.

"Today could be the day," she insisted, "Couldn't it? Could today be the day Marc? Tell me it could be today."

Marc sighed and turned to his beloved wife. "Yes Eleanor, today could be the day." He walked into the shower room, closing the door behind him and leaning momentarily on the door, biting his lip to prevent the tears which hammered at his eye sockets. He couldn't let even one tear escape or he knew there would be an endless deluge of pain which he may never be able to shore up again.

"I'm sorry for what I'm going to do to you. I would never do this if things were different, but I can't keep you baby. I want to, I really do, but life just won't allow it.

If there is a heaven I will meet you there. I can be your mummy in heaven.

Just wait for me there.

Please."

Tuesday . . .

Tuesday - 10am

Marc sipped his coffee and waited for the arrival of the women. Once again he wondered why he had agreed to take the session; it was so out of his comfort zone; he was used to dealing with people coming to terms with drug use or alcoholism, not abortion. He decided that his report would recommend that this kind of group session should not be run in the future. Nothing would have pleased him more than to stop the sessions and walk away, but he realised that the women were now invested in it, their lives were about to change drastically either by terminating a child or choosing to keep one, he made a pact with himself to stick it out to the end. He hoped also that today would be the day Eleanor was waiting for, he would not like to take bad news back to her at the end of the week; he just wondered which of the women were going to give him what he wanted.

Verity walked into the room and smiled briefly at Marc before helping herself to coffee from the urn which sat on the table in the corner of the stark room.

"Good morning."

"Hi Marc, how are you?"

"Just fine thank you Verity. How was your evening?"

"Oh had some trouble in the paddock with one of the mares, but other than that all was fine, just had a hot bath and an early night. It's quite exhausting being amongst so many hormonal women." She laughed. Jane walked silently into the room, straight to the chair she had been sitting on the previous day and sat down.

"Good morning Jane," Marc smiled, Jane nodded her head in his direction, but would not look him in the eye, choosing instead to take her normal position of floor staring. Marc noticed a slight redness around Jane's neck and bruising to her lower jaw; he would have loved to ask her how she had come by her injuries, but knew to keep his questions inside. Lorraine, Alice and Amelia walked into the room together in silent camaraderie, it seemed as though they had arrived together and been chatting elsewhere. Amelia carried a large brightly coloured bag which weighed her down as she walked. She put the bag under the table where the tea urn was, dismissing the offered help from the other women. Marc was pleased to see that relations were being built between the women; he knew things were always easier to deal with when there was a shoulder to lean on.

"Good morning ladies."

"Morning," they said in unison, then headed to the tea and coffee, Alice grabbing a handful of biscuits with hers. Helen walked in a few minutes later.

"Morning," she grinned at everyone around her. Muffled grunts of recognisance met her, the women apparently reluctant to converse.

"Good morning Helen, how are you today?" Marc obliged.

"Just fine and dandy thank you; ready for another day of death talk, I just love it." She looked around, waiting for a response, the other women refused to meet her eye line and Jane continued to stare at the floor, apparently oblivious to Helen's entrance. Helen didn't bother with a drink; she took her own place between Lorraine and Amelia who had taken their own seats. Alice and Verity sat also and all waited in silent anticipation.

"Good morning everyone," Marc smiled at the women. "Thank you all for returning, I am glad that you are all here."

"No place *I'd* rather be," Helen grimaced, "Tuesday is a perfect day to discuss murder."

"Does she really need to be here?" Jane came to life, looking at Marc. "I mean she's not actually interested in any of our reasons for being here. She has no intention of sharing anything with us. Why on earth is she allowed in the room?" Jane shook her head in bewilderment, and then looked directly at Helen. "Why don't you just leave Helen? Don't you have *any* idea what we all might be going through? I mean surely somewhere inside that hateful body of yours there is just a glimmer of compassion for people who have to make such a terrible decision." Tears flowed freely from Jane's eyes, her anger and frustration at Helen's indifferent behaviour was becoming too much to bear.

Helen looked over at Verity, "She obviously didn't get any last night." Helen said loud enough so the whole room could hear it.

"Oh come on now, poor show Helen. She does have a point Marc," Verity indicated to Jane. "Helen just doesn't seem to want to join in, in any way which is helpful. I really don't believe this is the place where Devil's advocate has any standing. This is such an emotive subject; *this* poor woman," indicating Jane again, "is obviously suffering and Helen is just adding to it. I vote we have her removed from the group."

"That is not going to happen," Marc spoke calmly. "We have to all understand that everyone in this room has been identified as a person who would benefit from this group. Any of you may choose to leave, but no one will be asked to leave."

"In your face."

"I would ask of you though Helen, to please refrain from any negative behaviour in this room. We are all adults and it would be nice if we could all respect each other."

"Not all adults," Helen spat back. Alice tried to shrink into her chair. Helen made a show of zipping up her mouth and throwing away an invisible key. Jane breathed a sigh of relief and the tension which had been building in the room began to dissipate. Marc felt like he had already sat through a full morning's session. He was really feeling the strain of the women's emotion; it was so thick in the air that he could almost touch it; he hoped he could get through the rest of the day without walking away. Eleanor's face in his mind reminded him why he was at the session and gave him the strength to continue.

"Ok," he smiled his practised, calm, counsellor's smile. "Who is ready to speak this morning?"

"I think I am ready." Lorraine spoke for the first time that day. She sat directly opposite Marc and he noted she had added a few piercings to her face overnight. He wondered if she had actually visited a parlour or if the holes had been there previously.

"Thank you Lorraine, it would be nice to hear from you,"

"Ok, here goes."

Hi, I'm Lorraine . . .

Lorraine Cheveaux to be precise; lesbian extraordinaire.

Alice giggled, "Why extraordinaire?" she asked.

Lorraine smiled, "I just like to call myself that; I'm not just an ordinary lesbian, I'm *extra* ordinary. I think I probably fit every stereotype you would associate with a lesbian."

"How so?" Verity asked.

"Well my lovely ones, I will begin at the bottom and work my way up." Lorraine stood and put her body on full display; opening her arms and turning from side to side as she spoke.

"Firstly," she said, pointing to her feet, "sensible shoes."

Amelia joined in with Alice's giggles, making Lorraine smile again. She stuck her foot out into the middle of the circle to show off her black beetle creepers with a very sensible one inch sole along the bottom of the whole shoe. "Secondly," she continued, "Tight trousers on chubby legs, sagging at the back to show men's boxer shorts." She turned around, "For modesty and comfort reasons of course. Now onto my considerable stomach; bigger for obvious reasons, but generally on the larger side anyway. Up to the strapped down boobs; minimiser used; hurts like a bitch at the moment." Lorrain unconsciously adjusted her bra as she spoke. "All wrapped up in chequered shirt with heavy silver jewellery, including my manly rings." She flashed the bulky silver rings on her fingers.

"Tattoos, naturally," she said, giving a quick flash of her colourful arms, "Then up to the face; hairy lip, pierced brow, ears and tongue; all topped off with a sharp, short back and sides, spiky on the top and don't forget the hair gel. Bob is your uncle, or maybe your aunt in the circles I mix with. There you have it; I am an extra ordinary lesbian; from lesbian town on the island of Lesbos. David Attenborough could set up his cameras and do his little speech." Lorraine switched her voice to mimic the dulcet tones of the TV presenter. "And here we have a classic example of lesbian virginosa; watch as she struts like a man, dressed like a man, looks like a man but doesn't want to be actually be one. It's the biggest conundrum of our modern world; how women say they like women, but will only mate with a woman who looks like a man."

The room burst into laughter at Lorraine's show. She grinned and took her seat once again.

"I always wondered about that," said Helen.

"What?" asked Lorraine.

"The whole woman and man thing, it's bloody daft, why do you do it?"

"Well if you let her speak then maybe we'll find out." Said Jane.

"What the fuck is your problem Jane?"

"I don't like bullies," Jane retorted.

"The fact that I speak my mind does *not* make me a bully, just shut your mouth."

"Your mouth is bullish Helen, therefore you are a bully."

"Come on girls," Verity interrupted, "I want to hear from Lorraine. If you can't be nice to each other, just leave each other alone. Good lord, if you were horses I'd be putting you in separate paddocks."

"Well we aren't horses, cheeky cow."

"And I'm not a cow Helen."

"Maybe we should be getting back to Lorraine," Marc quietly asked. All the women looked embarrassed and sat back, allowing Lorraine to continue.

"Yes, thank you. Well as I was saying, I am a lesbian. I have been since the moment I began to have sexual feelings towards the woman at the bakery shop who would sell me sausage rolls on a Friday after school. They were so delicious that I literally fell in love. I was about twelve or thirteen I think, so very young. I told my mum straight away; she was always very liberal and right on. A vegetarian feminist type, you know?" heads nodded. "When I told her, you would have thought she had just won the lottery. My sexuality ticked all her feminist boxes. She could parade her clit licking daughter to the world and her notoriety would increase tenfold in her circles. So it wasn't a problem at all for me.

Obviously I received some comments from the stalwart heterosexuals who had not yet come to terms with same-sex relationships. I've had priests try to lure me and cure me and plenty of fellows who would want to turn me back, but I have fought these people and stayed firmly on the side of the pussy massive."

Lorraine's delivery and twinkle in her eye caused light laughter again around the room. Marc glanced at his watch and made some notes on his clipboard.

"Sorry," said Lorraine, "I know I'm kind of skirting around the real issue. I will tell you now that I met a girl called Barbara about five years ago. Before I met her I was very promiscuous; I just couldn't get enough of women and there were far too many available to stick with just one. To say I had fun is a real understatement; I am totally serious when I say one girl a night was the normal thing for me. I would spend most nights in bars up town and you could almost guarantee there would be someone to meet. The amount of women who wanted to *find* themselves would shock you. They probably come looking for someone like me, get what they want and then go back to their three bedroomed semi-detached house, with Gary and the two kids, a Labrador and a family car."

"I don't believe that," said Amelia, shaking her head in denial.

"Oh I don't know," said Verity, "Try being in boarding school, or prison," she snorted. "Most of them are gay for the stay."

"Have you been to prison?" asked Alice aghast.

"Well no, but I've a friend who ended up there when her husband embezzled a few million; she got convicted of money laundering and ended up in the clink for six months. She got felt up within six minutes and it was a whole new world; if you know what I mean."

"I would never be tempted," Amelia insisted. "I'd probably enjoy the rest."

"Trust me," said Lorraine, "There are a lot of loose women out there. Anyway, back to the point again; after a few years of doing the circuit, I either became older or just bored of the same old thing. It became more important to me to have a partner than a one night stand. Suddenly being at home with a wife, pipe and slippers, was the most appealing thing to me. Barbara came along through a work contact; I own a car rental company. High class cars, real top dollar. Barbara was an events coordinator and she would rent the cars for any events she was organising; you know the kind of thing, picking up guests, transferring clients from one venue to the other.

We would see each other and always have a bit of banter; very slightly flirtatious, but I always thought she may be straight. It obviously didn't stop me from wanting to hit on her, but she actually left me a bit nervous. I had the fluttering, shakes and nerve sweats at the thought of rejection and possibly losing her as a customer, so I had always steered clear from asking her anything remotely close to 'can we have a drink together'. Eventually she asked *me* for a drink.

That began the most amazing relationship I had ever had. It was actually perfect; we just clicked and we travelled to the *best* places together. We went to the Mardi Gras at New Orleans, carnival at Rio and so many Pride marches; it was brilliant, until . . ." Lorraine paused, "Babies. All of a sudden after two years of bliss, she comes at me with 'Lorraine, wouldn't it be fantastic if we had a baby?' I was like, hell no, in my head, but I was so in love with her, I said, 'Hell yeah.'

We got married because she wanted to do everything the right way, that was nice. Then we began looking for a sperm donor. God that was so weird; going to the sperm bank and reading a catalogue of men. Age, skin colour, hair colour, eye colour; you don't get pictures or names, just numbers. I didn't know if I was ordering a baby or egg fried rice."

Giggles again sounded from around the room.

"Stupid ain't it? Well we ordered number three hundred and Barbara went off to have all the necessary done. Of course she would be the one to have the baby; I'm the manly one, she was the woman, you know? Oh she was absolutely beautiful; such dark long hair and boobs like zeppelins, I mean honestly," Lorraine held her hands out in front of her chest indicating a large bosom.

"So we waited on that cycle and nothing happened. It didn't matter, it's very rare that you would get pregnant first go. We tried again and again and again; nothing was working. Every month the same shit, pick a number, open legs, talk about the baby; what it would look like, how we would be as parents. Then two weeks later the test; the anticipation, the disappointment, the argument and then the tears. Our whole life became about Barbara and her baby; it done my fucking head in, but I loved her and I wanted whatever Barbara wanted.

We stopped using sperm donations and went onto Barbara actually having sex with one of her friends."

Alice, Amelia and Jane gasped in unison.

"Sounds shocking doesn't it?" Lorraine agreed, "But it seemed to be the only way. Barbara was convinced she needed fresh sperm which hadn't been exposed to the air. I didn't feel like it was cheating; they never kissed each other and I was actually in the room when it happened. It was very clinical."

"Yeah right. Did you hold her tits while she was humped like a dog?" asked Helen.

"It wasn't like that."

"Sick."

"You're entitled to your opinion. Can I carry on?"

"Please, I am *so* interested in your sordid life."

"Why thank you; you can go off people you know." Lorraine winked at Helen. "Nothing worked, Barbara just wouldn't fall pregnant. I was secretly pleased; children weren't really on my agenda, but she was so unhappy. I took her for tests at the clinic and it turned out she had polycystic ovaries and blocked tubes. They flushed them tubes out and we tried again but, no. I was ready to call it a day when Barbara pointed out the fact that I was a woman also. I was like, 'no shit Sherlock,' but what's your point? She asked me to have the baby.

At first I was completely against it; the very notion of me using my body as a vessel was just so out of my mind set. It felt alien to use my sex organs for childbearing; they were for sexual pleasure only in my world. Barbara went on and on about it; about how the baby would make our lives better, our relationship stronger. I suggested adoption, but she said the Social Services would never give a pair of dykes a child. She also said she wouldn't be able to love someone else's child, but if I had the baby it would feel like her own.

She said she would do all the work, the maternity leave, the night feeds and all that shit. All I had to do was carry the child; kind of like a surrogate I suppose. I loved her so much that I agreed. Back down the sperm bank we went, out comes the catalogue and we pick number three hundred again."

"He must have been a busy boy." Said Verity.

"You're not wrong," Lorraine agreed. "Would you believe that I got pregnant on the third try? Fuck me, I was shocked, but she was delighted. We went out and celebrated with some friends and I spent the next few weeks eating chocolate oranges and then throwing them back up again."

"What went wrong?" asked Verity.

Lorraine laughed, "You wouldn't believe me."

"Go on."

"Well I was trying to work my normal hours, but having real problems with morning sickness. One day it just got too much for me so I decided to go home early. I felt so ill that I didn't take the car like I usually would; I thought I might crash it if I started heaving at the wheel. I walked home, losing my guts behind a few trees on the way; got there, let myself in and stumbled up to my bedroom hoping for a lie down. I opened my bedroom door and there is Barbara with the same sperm donor friend, humping away like the dirty camel that she is."

"Oh dear."

"Oh dear indeed Verity. The dirty bitch had enjoyed her experience with the warm fleshy sausage and decided that my finger and expert tongue was no longer enough for her. She confessed that she had fallen in love with the guy and announced that she was leaving me. I was like, 'But you still want the baby right?' 'Oh no,' she says, 'that's the other thing; I'm pregnant'.

Pregnant. I mean for fucks sake, could it get any worse. She's gone and I'm left with this thing inside me. I have spent the last four weeks battling with myself. I was so devastated about what Barbara had done that I thought about ending my life. I know I appear to be a happy go lucky girl, but really I'm dying over here. I'm either a coward or just not ready to die, because I couldn't go through with it.

I have really tried to come to terms with being a parent, but I just can't see that I will ever be any good at it. I really don't want to be tied down with a child. I don't want to be a mother, but at the same time I'm not sure I can just abort. I think that's why they asked me to come here. I am probably the most undecided I have ever been, but I'm nineteen weeks. I don't have that long left to make my decision; I can feel it moving around inside me and it scares the life out of me. I just don't know what to do and I can't think of anything else to do other than to abort."

"Adoption?" Amelia challenged.

"But that means finishing the pregnancy; going through the whole birthing process and then just giving the baby into the hands of the unknown. I've read so many stories of babies in care and foster care; I've even been there myself. I'm not convinced that I would be doing the right thing. I could be sending an innocent thing into a lifetime of sheer hell, just because I'm too selfish to look after it myself. I don't know if I could live every day of my own life with that on my conscience. If the baby is never born then that will never happen.

I feel like it's not meant to be here. Barbara tricked me into getting pregnant. She should have ended our relationship when she realised she had fallen out of love with me, but selfishly, she pushed me into this. If she had never got pregnant I think she would have waited until the baby was born and then left me, taking the baby with her. But she's having her own baby now. She doesn't need this little one. Its collateral damage as far as she is concerned."

"What a complete bitch."

"I know Helen, she really hurt me."

"I'm talking about you."

"Me, why?"

"God, you really can't see it can you? You're really that selfish."

"I don't understand, I didn't want this to happen."

"You didn't want her to leave you, obviously not, but you wanted the baby."

"No, no I only got pregnant for Barbara."

"You *never* get pregnant for somebody else. If you allow yourself to get knocked up then you take responsibility for it. It's not the baby's fault that Barbara went off. It deserves a chance at life. You owe it that at least."

"I couldn't be a mother."

"You *are* a mother. There is a little baby kicking around inside you, but you're not going to look after it.

You're going to murder it so you can carry on with your disgusting life. People like you make me sick."

"Who are you to judge her Helen?" asked Jane, "You have no right; you're here for just the same reason."

"You know nothing about me shrew."

"I know you are here to kill a baby. They're your own words 'Hi, I'm Helen and I'm here to kill my baby.'"

"That's different."

"Different? How is that different?"

"Wouldn't you like to know?"

"Yes Helen, yes I would. I'm sure we'd *all* love to know." Jane indicated the rest of the group who watched quietly as the two women fought.

Helen opened her mouth to speak, but no words came out. She sat forward in her chair and leant over to grab her bag from under it. "Can we have a break now?" she asked Marc.

"Lorraine, would you like a break or do you have more to say?" Marc asked.

"No, a break is good," Lorraine agreed, standing up. "I'm feeling a bit sick." Tears filled her eyes and she rubbed at them frantically, "I'll just go to the loo."

"I'm going for a fag," said Helen, stomping off out of the room.

Discuss . . .

Marc and Helen left the room; the rest of the group heaved a sigh of relief and visibly relaxed as she went.

"She is just intolerable," Jane said.

"She may be going through her own type of suffering," Verity offered, "We just don't know why she is here. For all we know she could be going through a whole heap of pain."

"She is just one big pain," giggled Alice. "I don't like her very much."

"You and me both Alice. Let's go and have a cup of tea, I am feeling really thirsty."

They walked over to the urn which was bubbling away in the corner; Alice poured two cups of hot water over the cheap tea bags which were piled on a plate next to some equally cheap coffee sachets. Thin milk turned the tea a pale biscuit colour and both women sipped gingerly at the liquid.

"I feel a bit sick," Alice admitted. "Still, it won't be for much longer."

"How are you feeling now Alice?"

"I don't know, I mean I know I still have to go through with it. There is just no way that I can have this baby. My mum and dad are getting very suspicious that something is going on, they keep asking me if I am ok and if there is something I want to tell them."

"And do you want to tell them?"

Alice looked around the room, searching for an answer in her mind. "I don't think so," she concluded, "Sometimes what the heart doesn't know won't hurt it; that's what my mother says, so I think I will listen to her . . . for a change."

Verity smiled at that. "Well it's a good time to start listening to your parents."

"Yeah." Both supped their tea again and then opened their group to allow Jane and Amelia access as they had come across the room to also get a drink. All the women smiled at each other.

"Where did Lorraine go?" Verity said, looking around her as she realised Lorraine had disappeared.

"Probably to the toilet," said Amelia, I find I spend *so* much time going for a wee nowadays."

"Won't be for much longer," observed Alice again. Amelia blushed at the comment and self-consciously rubbed her stomach. "Oh gosh Amelia, I'm so sorry for saying that," Alice apologised, "I am an idiot."

"No, its fine," said Amelia, "You're probably right."

"Didn't you talk to your husband last night?"

"Yes, we had a long conversation about things."

"Did you tell him you were pregnant?"

"Yes."

"Oh that was brave. What are you going to do?" Alice asked.

"I will talk about it when everyone is back in the room, I think it's only fair and it means I don't have to repeat myself." Amelia grimaced, "This tea is disgusting, ah here is Lorraine." She turned towards the door where Lorraine was striding in. "Do you want tea Lorraine?"

"No thank you, I don't want to go to the toilet any more today, I swear I can smell my own fanny from here, which is a bonus as I can't actually see it anymore." She tried to look over the small swelling of her stomach.

"That is disgusting," laughed Verity.

"I know," grinned Lorraine, "But it made you laugh though didn't it? We're all so miserable in here, it's depressing."

"It's a depressing subject," Verity agreed. "Not much to laugh about, but you're right; *you* made me laugh. Oh and by the way; your fanny *does* smell." She winked at Lorraine who laughed out loud.

"Having fun are we?" Helen said as she re-entered the room. The women stopped laughing and turned to look hostilely at Helen as she took her usual seat in the room.

"Don't stop on my account, murder is a wonderful thing to laugh about." Helen continued. "What were you joking about anyway? The sucking of the abortion pipe, or the amount of blood that might come out with lumps of baby in it."

"You are sick." Amelia stood in front of the other woman. "Just sick Helen."

"Yeah well pregnancy does that to you."

"Just shut up."

"Well I would, but we are all here to talk. It's good to talk, didn't you know?"

"Fuck off." Lorraine interjected.

"Touchy." A light cough alerted them to Marc's return to the room. Tea cups were replaced on the table and everyone took their seats, all giving dirty looks in Helen's direction, whilst she made a swimming action with her arms and appeared to bathe herself in their stares.

"Ok, that was a short break, but I hope you felt it was long enough?"

Heads nodded.

"Good, well, thank you Lorraine for letting us into your story, it was certainly interesting. Does anyone have anything they would like to say to Lorraine?"

Helen opened her mouth and took a breath.

"Anything constructive?" Marc added and Helen sat back with a sour look on her face.

"I think your girlfriend was very mean to you." Alice said. "I mean to make you go against everything you believed in about yourself; to allow you to go through with a pregnancy and then to just leave you. That was very nasty."

"I know," agreed Lorraine, "It did come as a bit of a shock. Although in some ways I think it's a kind of justice being meted out on me by the big guy up there," she said pointing at the sky. "I mean when I was single, I broke a lot of hearts. This is just divine justice; I have to pay my dues."

"You can't really believe that?" questioned Verity.

Lorraine shrugged her shoulders, "Have to make sense of it somehow. I feel really evil, I mean it's not the baby's fault, but I really do believe that I will be consigning it to a life of absolute hell if I allow it to be born. I mean it's the same kind of argument for if you know your child is going to be severely disabled, don't you think?"

"How?" asked Alice.

"Well ok, maybe not quite the same, but let's say you go to your twenty week scan and they tell you that the baby is very sick. It has a condition which just can't be cured and if you allow the pregnancy to continue and the baby is born, then it will live a very short life and that life will be in agony. Would you carry on? Would you let that baby, who you know is going to suffer, be born?"

"Of course not." Amelia said, "That would just be cruel."

"People do it though," said Verity. "I have read in the papers how some women go ahead with conjoined twins, even though there is probably no chance that they can lead a normal life and one of the twins is so badly deformed that it will probably die; which then causes the other twin to die. I saw one woman who said that God had given her those babies and she was supposed to allow them into the world so that God's will be done."

"Really?" Alice asked, aghast.

"Yes, really, she also said that she just wanted to look at the babies, see what they were like; after all, she made them. They were a product of her and she wanted to see what she had made. I couldn't make head nor tale of the story, but she seemed very confident in her decision."

"What happened to the babies?"

"They died as soon as they were born, but she got them christened and had them buried. I suppose it gave her closure. It must be so difficult to come to terms with a baby who is supposed to be perfect, being so badly deformed. Not even one, but two babies. I just can't imagine what I would have done in that situation."

"We all know what you would have done," Helen snapped. "Just what you are doing now, instead you are killing a perfectly healthy baby. No extra limbs, no conjoined twin business, no little horns and devil's tale. A brand new *perfect* baby and you are killing it."

Lorraine looked uncomfortable; she shifted in her chair and looked around her, waiting for someone to step in. All the other women looked away; it became clear to Lorraine that not one of them believed she should be terminating her pregnancy.

"I know this may make me seem like a bad person," Lorraine said. "But I have already explained, I know I cannot look after this baby. I can't put it any other way. I can't make it sound better; it's just how I feel." Tears filled Lorraine's eyes, "I'm such a bad person."

"Yes you are, evil cow." Helen agreed.

"But we are all here to terminate." Lorraine objected. "You are here Alice, for all we know there's nothing wrong with your baby. It's a lifestyle choice for you to abort. You are here Amelia, again we don't know what's wrong, but it's a lifestyle choice for you to abort. Mine is a lifestyle choice also; just because the baby is a little further along, I'm not doing anything different to what you two are doing."

Amelia nodded, "You're right," she agreed. "I suppose it just seems worse because you are further along. I mean I just have cells inside me, you would have a fully formed baby wouldn't you?"

"The government are happy for me to do it, they say its fine. They don't recognise the foetus as a baby and neither do I." Lorraine shrugged. "I have to think like that. I can't dwell on it too much."

"In one week there is a good chance that if your baby was born, it would survive outside the womb," said Helen. "Could actually live and become a human being, another lesbian roaming our planet."

"How far along are you Helen?" Lorraine asked.

"None of your fucking business." Helen retorted.

"You have quite a bump there," Lorraine persisted. "I would say you are even further along than me, could you be more than twenty weeks? Why are you terminating?"

"None of your business again," Said Helen.

"You have to tell us sometime."

"No I fucking don't. I am only here . . ."

"Yeah blah, blah, only here because you have to be," Lorraine rolled her eyes. "Believe me Helen; your burden will be lessened if you share. I didn't want to say anything when I first came here, but it's really helping me."

"And me," Alice said.

"And it helped me," agreed Amelia. "I spoke to Gary."

"Really," Verity focused on Amelia, glad for the change in subject.

"Yes I told him about the baby."

"What did he say?" Alice asked, "Was he very cross?"

"No, no; not cross." Amelia shrugged, "He actually seemed quite pleased."

"Really?" Verity smiled, "That's fantastic, tell us everything."

"Well I got home; before him for a change, but of course I hadn't been in the office so I couldn't work late. I actually cooked him a dinner, a Thai green curry; it's his favourite. I set a lovely romantic scene, opened a bottle of wine which he liked, dressed the table with candles. It was just how we like to spend evenings together so I knew that I would get him in the best mood possible. He came home, very pleased to find me waiting for him and with his dinner ready, so we sat down and started to have a lovely meal; made small talk, spoke about the office. It was all so normal, it didn't seem like it was the right time to spoil it with a conversation about a baby, I mean I thought it was going to turn my world upside down you know? So we had the dinner, we finished the bottle of wine; like Helen said, not much point in abstaining when I'm going to get rid is there. We went to bed together and we made love; it was so tender and he told me he loved me." Amelia looked at her hands and twisted her wedding ring around her wedding finger. "I cried." She said, "Cried like a baby, big fat tears; they came and they just wouldn't stop coming. You know when you start to hyperventilate and you just can't speak, and ... you ... talk ... like ... this? That was me; snot pouring from the nose, *so* attractive."

"I'm sure you could never look ugly," said Verity.

"Believe me, I looked like a monster. Well Gary was so shocked that I was crying, he obviously knew that something was wrong and he insisted that I tell him. I said it was nothing, just feeling emotional because I loved him so much; he was like 'No I know it's more than that, there's no way you would cry because you love me.' I asked him if I could trust him not to get angry, he was like, 'Yes of course, come on Amelia tell me; I love you.' So I told him. Just like that, 'We're having a baby. I am sorry Gary, I didn't get pregnant on purpose, it was an accident.' He got off the bed and left the room; didn't say a word. I sat there for about half an hour just waiting for him to say something, *anything*; just to let me know how he was feeling, I mean was it over, did he hate me? I was so scared sitting there."

"What happened?" urged Alice.

"He came back, walked up to me and sat on the bed; took my hands in his and said, 'Amelia I love you, that's why I married you. I am gonna love anything that you make, especially if I have helped you to make it.' I said to him, 'What about taking over the business world?' He told me he could do that on his own, he was going to work harder than ever so I could stay at home and look after our little baby."

"That is wonderful," Verity smiled, "Just wonderful, so different to what you thought would happen. How lovely that you can be a little family together."

"Yeah, it's just . . . great," Amelia grimaced.

"You don't seem too happy about it," Lorraine observed.

"That's because she isn't." Helen jumped up, "She fucking isn't is she? Oh my god, it was all an act, 'He's so driven, so ambitious, he wants us to take over the world.' What *bullshit*, it's you isn't it? You are the one with the ambition, the greed?"

"Don't shout at her," Jane said, "Please make her stop." She looked to Marc.

"Helen sit down and please lower your tone," Marc agreed.

"Yeah I'll fucking sit down alright," Helen sat on her chair and then pointed at Amelia. "Little Miss Business here doesn't want a baby because it gets in the way of *her* world domination."

Amelia shifted uncomfortably in her chair.

"Go on, admit it, I'm right aren't I?"

"It's not like that."

"Yes it fucking is, you know it is. Tell them; tell them just what you're thinking." She looked around at the women in the room, all looking slightly pale and worried. "Look at them, you're about to burst their little bubbles. Come on Amelia, tell us the truth."

"Leave her alone," said Jane.

"No, stop." Amelia quietened Jane, "She's right."

"You don't have to humour her," Jane insisted, "You don't owe any of us an explanation, that's not why we're here."

"I want to explain," Amelia continued, "I feel we owe it to each other now to give the full truth. I mean it started off as me being here on my own, but the more we're here and the more we're sharing with each other, I'm starting to feel like we're all in this together, don't you agree?"

Alice, Verity, Lorraine and Jane all nodded their heads in solidarity; Helen rolled her eyes again.

"Whatever Amelia, let's have it, come on."

"Ok, ok, I don't want the baby. Is that what you want to hear? *I* don't want it. I don't *want* it. I don't want *it*."

"You see?" Helen said in triumph.

"Shut *up* Helen, for God's sake, let her speak."

"Alright *Jane*, boss woman."

"Just, shut up." Jane mumbled, going back to her floor staring.

"I don't want a baby," Amelia admitted. "I want a career. I want to be more than just a mother; I don't want to be stuck at home looking after a child, changing nappies and babbling on in baby speak. I had enough of that when I was at home with all those brothers and sisters. I saw my mum and dad do nothing but be parents; their whole life was about them being parents, they weren't people in their own right. Once we had all grown up and moved on they just became husks of humans, now sitting around waiting for death. It's like they're useless now, nothings. I don't want to be that person; I want to be a somebody."

"What are you going to do about Gary though?" Alice asked.

"Well that's another thing; Gary isn't who I thought he was at all. I mean I always thought that he was as driven as me; I believed that he wanted to run the world with me at his side, the two of us together, strong and powerful. I couldn't believe how easily he put me in the pigeon hole of mother and wife. It took him half an hour to completely change his outlook on our relationship and to decide that I was only good enough to be the mother to his baby whilst he went out and did his own thing. I was disgusted by him; I won't lie, it shook me to the core. I have gone from believing that we were the epitome of success to knowing that we are just another normal couple where the man believes that he can look after the little woman whilst she sits at home, breasts out with babies hanging off them."

"Not what you wanted?" asked Verity.

"Not at all," Amelia confirmed. "I am now of the thinking that I don't want the baby and I don't want Gary either. That was the biggest revelation to me; I thought I loved him, but what I really loved was what he stood for. I wanted to succeed and he was my stepping stone to get there, I didn't love him, I loved what he could do for me. I am a bad person."

"No you're not," Alice said.

"Yes I am Alice, I am going to terminate the baby and I am going to leave Gary. Now that I've told him that he is going to have a baby, I am about to tell him that he is not only losing the baby, but he's losing me as well. I am going to destroy his world and do you know what? I don't care. It doesn't matter to me, I just want to be up there," she pointed to the ceiling. "I am going to be at the very top of my tree and I am not going to let anyone stop me. I *am* bad."

"You don't have to do it," said Lorraine."

"*You* don't have to do it," said Amelia, "None of us *have* to do it, do we? But here we all are, ready to sacrifice a life to make our own lives better; that's basically what we're doing."

"You may be," said Helen.

"We all are aren't we?"

"Oh we all are, yes we are all here to do something, but some of us have completely different reasons, in fact we all have completely different reasons to do the same thing. I just think it's sad, so very sad that we are here at all," said Verity.

No one said anything; all lost in their own thoughts and reasons for being at the session. It seemed like the perfect time for reflection, Marc noted that the silence was comfortable, he could see that the women were working towards resolutions for their own dilemmas and was pleased that the session seemed to be having the desired effect. He made a note on his clipboard to add the change in atmosphere to his report and how long it had taken them to get to that point. Marc took some time to look at Lorraine. He thought about Eleanor and the promise he had made to her; his stomach churned with nerves at what he was going to do later on in the day, he just hoped that Lorraine was the right one and that he would have good news for Eleanor.

"How are you feeling Lorraine?" asked Amelia, "I'm sorry, this was supposed to be your session, but I have taken it over; that's me, a selfish cow."

"Don't be silly," Lorraine smiled, "This whole session is about all of us. I needed the breather anyway," she chuckled. "You kind of took the heat off me."

"Yeah well not for long, it's back to you now, what do you think the answer is?" Amelia urged.

"I really don't know. I've got till Thursday, maybe something will happen before then, but I don't have the time to think for any longer than that; it's not fair on this little thing to keep it alive for any longer just to end its life."

"But keeping it alive for twenty weeks is ok?" Helen asked.

"Make all the snide remarks you like Helen, you are not me. Did you listen to my little story? I had a wife; we were going to be bringing up the baby, *her* baby together. Sorry that my life is not perfect and I am not the best person in the world, but sometimes people have to do what's right for them. They have to be selfish," Lorraine looked at Amelia, who nodded. "Sometimes it is actually about me. I don't care what anybody else thinks, I am not fit to be a mother and I am not going to have this child."

"Fair enough." Helen shrugged, "Can we go now?"

"I'm dying for a fag." Jane mimicked Helen.

"Come with me if you like, Shrew, you could probably do with something to chill you out. There's plenty of floor for you to stare at."

"Thanks, I'll stay here."

"With your friends?" Jane looked around at the other women and then back at the floor.

"We are her friends," Alice said.

"After one and a half days?"

"People fall in love in a heartbeat, it's easy to become friends if you are open enough," Alice opened her arms. "I feel like I have made friends here, I am only fifteen, but it's like, I don't know, it's like age doesn't matter here, because we are all in the same boat, you know?"

The other women nodded. "Absolutely Alice," Verity smiled, "We are all friends here and are all helping each other."

"Helping each other feel sick," Helen said as she began to walk out of the room.

"Don't want to stay for lunch then?" Amelia asked.
"Fuck off."

"You're welcome." Legs were stretched and mouths yawned as the bodies were released from their seated positions.

"Did you say lunch?" asked an expectant Alice.

"Yes, I thought we could all sit and have lunch together today instead of going off somewhere on our own. I brought a salad and some sandwiches, that's what that big bag is in the corner."

"Wow, where did you find the time to do that?" Verity asked, "With everything you were going through last night, I would have thought the last thing you would be doing is making sandwiches."

"It's amazing what someone can achieve at three in the morning," grimaced Amelia. "I couldn't sleep and I always find that doing something practical helps me take my mind of my worries. It's just one of those things."

"Works for me," Lorraine said, patting her tum. "Hope there's no peanut butter."

"Are you allergic?"

"No, the baby." Lorraine reminded. "Oh for God's sake, look at me, I have spent so long looking after it, it just comes naturally." Tears formed in her eyes again. The women moved around her to offer her comfort.

"Could I have a word Lorraine?" Marc asked quietly from his chair.

"Yes Marc, what is it?"

"Not here, if you would come outside with me for a chat, I would be grateful."

"Yes sure." Lorraine moved away from the women, "Save me some sandwiches," she mouthed as she followed Marc out of the room.

Don't Kill The Baby . . .

"Thanks for coming outside with me," Marc said to Lorraine.

"No problem Marc, what's the matter?" Lorraine could see that Marc was itching to say something to her.

"I am going to ask you something; it may offend you or it may be what you have been waiting to hear. I may get sacked for saying it and if you feel that you want to report me for it, then you have every right to do so. I have just got to ask." Eleanor's face flashed into Marc's brain. "So please understand that there is a very good reason why I am going to say this."

"I'm not being funny Marc, but you haven't actually said anything yet and I'm getting kind of tetchy waiting." Lorraine tapped Marc on the arm. "Come on please, just say what you have to say, I've probably already had the same from someone else by now anyway."

"Oh I don't think you've been asked this before."

"Asked?"

"Yes." Marc stopped, eyes looking around him, searching for the right words to say to Lorraine.

"Please Marc, just say it."

"Ok," Marc took in a deep breath and then his words tumbled out with the air that left his lungs. "Don't kill the baby." He said.

"Ok well thank you for your input, I have just heard that from some of them in there. Not particularly helpful when I am trying to get on with the rest of my life."

"No, no wait," Marc stopped Lorraine from walking away. "I am asking you not to terminate because I have a plan for you which will stop you from having to do it."

"Go on."

"I listened to everything you said in there, I can see that you don't actually want to terminate, but that you also don't want the baby yourself."

"No shit? You got all that from what I said?" Lorraine tried to walk away again, fed up of hearing the same lines about her pregnancy.

"Let me finish, please Lorraine just stop and hear me out."

"Ok, but I really need to pee at some point and I am getting hungry so please make your point and let's just move on."

"I want your baby."

Lorraine looked very hard at Marc, she wasn't sure that she had just heard him correctly. "*You* want my baby?" she asked incredulously.

"Yes, I do, well we do; my wife and I."

"Can't you have your own babies?"

"No, it's a very complicated story and it would really be better if Eleanor and I could speak to you together. It's such a major thing for all of us that I don't think we could stand here in this corridor and discuss it in such a short period of time. I know there's two days left before you are due to terminate and I am obviously never going to see you away from this environment, so this really is the only chance I had to ask you." Marc took out a piece of paper with his address written on it and handed it to Lorraine.

"If you want to come and see Eleanor and I at home tonight, we will be waiting for you; it's completely up to you if you come, but what I am suggesting is that we adopt your baby. I can promise you that we are so willing to look after the baby just as if it was our own and that no harm would ever come to it. Eleanor is a wonderful woman, just wonderful; she is so loving and kind, she would make the perfect mother. We both have good jobs so money wouldn't be an issue and we would love that child with every bone in our body. God it seems so wrong to be having a quick chat in a corridor about the life of a little one, but it's the only way I can think of to get through to you."

"Nothing about this week is normal," Lorraine agreed. "I don't know what to say to you Marc, it's a real shock to hear that someone wants to buy my baby."

"I didn't say 'buy' Lorraine," Marc looked offended. "I'm talking about an arrangement where we are all helping each other. You have a child inside you that is nearly fully developed, nearly able to breathe and to see; can already hear and feel. You don't want that baby and I completely understand that; your lifestyle and situation doesn't have room for that type of commitment. I could see as you were talking that you don't want to terminate, but you also feel responsible for the child and you don't want to consign it to a life of misery."

"That is true; we have just said all that in there." Lorraine agreed.

"Yes and I listened. I realised as you were talking that you are in the perfect scenario for Eleanor and myself. You have inside you what we desire more than anything in the whole world, you don't want it and we do. In a blink of an eye you can get rid of that little baby, but it would take us an eternity to ever be able to have our own child." Marc looked imploringly at Lorraine, "Please come tonight and meet Eleanor. We can talk more about it, you can see our home and how we live. There is no pressure to commit to anything, we can't force you to make any decisions; all I'm asking is that you have all the facts and really think about it before you decide to go ahead and terminate. That baby could have a life, a good life, a loved life and you could even be part of it."

Lorraine laughed, "How can I be part of that? I barely know you."

"We can get to know each other." Said Marc, "You still have twenty weeks left of the pregnancy; we can get to know each other really well in that time."

"Yeah and I could get to hate the pair of you in that time and it will be too late for me to do anything about it. Then I am left with a baby that I don't want and that I am too scared to give away in case it becomes me."

"What do you mean?"

"I was the baby left on the doorstep," Lorraine sat on one of the cheap plastic chairs that lined the corridor of the building they were in; Marc sat beside her.

"But you mentioned your mother earlier."

"Yes I know that, but she's not my real mother. She was the right on Mother Earth foster parent type person you know? I went to her when I was about ten, but before that I had *many* parents and not all of them were the best parents in the world." She chewed on her finger, suddenly very interested in the little pieces of hard skin which were peeling off around the nail, Marc noticed that all her fingernails were chewed and the skin around them was red and sore. "I was abused," Lorraine admitted.

"I am sorry,"

"Sorry for what? Sorry that I was left on a doorstep, or sorry that a dirty old man who fostered kids just so he could feel them up, got hold of me?"

"You don't have to say anymore Lorraine, I understand."

"No you really don't understand Marc. There's a reason why I don't want my child to go into care. There's a reason why I'm a lesbian also; some people say that it's genetic, that people are born gay, but I say some of us have it fucked into us."

Marc grimaced, finding it hard to hear the words coming from Lorraine's mouth.

"Sorry if that offends you, but that's what happened, I was abused, fucked by a disgusting pig of a man who thought that orphans were his to do with as he wished. Once I had been touched by his flesh I was never going to go near another man again"

"How old were you?"

"Well what difference does that make?" Lorraine asked angrily. "Does it make it any better if I was twenty or if I was two; he raped me. He came into my bedroom at night in a place where I should have been safe and he raped me, once, twice, three times; more times than I could ever count and there was nothing I could do about it. No one to tell, no one to help me; he *was* the help."

"Sorry."

"Again with the *sorry*. So many people have apologised to me, why do people do that? My cat has died, 'Oh I'm sorry.' I fell over, 'Sorry', I got butt fucked by my foster parent, 'Sorry.' It means nothing to me that you're sorry."

"Sor . . ." Marc didn't know what to say, he took Lorraine's hand. "Well I am sorry, sorry for you, sorry for your situation and sorry for your baby. But not every person is bad, not every person is going to do that to children."

"Yeah, priests are good people aren't they? Doctors are good people, foster parents are *great* people; all these great people and yet all you hear is about another child hurt, another child raped, another child killed and thrown away like it's nothing but rubbish. I don't want my baby to be one of those children. I just can't do it Marc, I'm sorry." Lorraine burst out laughing. "Now I'm fucking *sorry*."

Both sat in silence for a short time, Marc contemplating his next move and Lorraine waiting for his response. Finally Marc stood up, "Lorraine, I can never hope to understand even a small amount of what you have been through in your life and I know it must be one of the hardest decisions you've ever made to terminate the life of your child. I am not going to force this onto you; I just want you to know that the option is there. You have my address, if you change your mind and you want to meet us then please come around to see us tonight at eight o'clock. Just meet Eleanor, have a chat with her, find out about *our* story; we may change your mind and I promise you, you could be involved. Every child needs an aunty right? You could come and visit, you could even live with us."

"Yeah because that would work."

"Stranger things have happened."

"You're deluded."

"No, I'm desperate," admitted Marc. "I'm going to have my lunch now, I would ask please that you don't talk about this with the other women, it's very personal and private. If we see you at eight tonight; that would be a great thing."

"Yeah thanks for the chat." Lorraine said sarcastically, "I feel so much better now."

"Sorry."

The look from Lorraine caused Marc to quickly walk away; he didn't want to alienate her any more than he already had. He thought about Eleanor again and wondered whether to tell her about Lorraine or just wait and see if the doorbell rang later on that evening. He decided to keep his mouth shut, there was no point getting Ellie's hopes up for them to just come crashing down again; she wasn't ready for more heartache in her life and what she didn't know wouldn't hurt her.

Session Four . . .

Lorraine walked back into the room and placed herself amongst the women who were standing around the back table, eating silently. She picked up a sandwich and started to eat it, waiting to feel sick but actually enjoying the fresh lettuce and juicy tomatoes as they squished together in her mouth.

"Everything ok?" Alice asked.

"Yeah," Lorraine forced the food down in one swallow. "He just wanted to ask me something."

"Oh," Alice picked up a pink iced biscuit from a plate on the table and began nibbling at it.

"You'll get fat," said Verity with a wink. Alice put the biscuit down.

"Oh I was only joking Alice," Verity instantly worried, "I'm sorry, I didn't mean to make you feel bad."

"No it's fine; my mother always tells me I'll get fat," said Alice, "I'm only young and I need to be careful what I eat; that's another thing she tells me."

"Well it doesn't do any harm to control your weight, but a biscuit every now and then won't hurt you." Verity picked the biscuit up and offered it in Alice's direction, "Go on Alice, it really won't matter if you have just one biscuit, here, enjoy it."

Alice took the biscuit from Verity and bit into it again, "I do like these biscuits."

"Me too," Verity said as she took one for herself.

"Who do you think is going to speak next?" said Alice looking around her. "Will you Verity?"

"I may," agreed Verity, "It all depends, I'm not in any rush to talk, I think my story is really rather pathetic after hearing all of yours."

"Oh I'm sure it isn't," Alice disagreed. "All our stories are important because they are unique to us. It doesn't really matter what the reason is; I mean it matters to us, but not to anyone else. It's a personal reason and very important to us isn't it?"

Verity nodded, "Yes Alice, you're right. The reason is special to the person doing it and although one may not agree, it's how *we* feel that is important. I still wonder why Helen is here."

"Just to be a thorn in everyone's side," Jane took a step over to Alice and Verity so she could include herself in their conversation. Amelia and Lorraine also turned to listen. "I don't think she is even going to terminate," Jane continued.

"Really?" asked Amelia, "Why do you think she is here then?"

"I reckon she's one of those pro-life people who has infiltrated the session and is just here to make everyone feel bad about their decision so that they don't terminate their pregnancies."

"No, that can't be it." Amelia shook her head. "She is pregnant herself; even has a bump so must be in her second trimester. She is so full of hatred and anger; I think she's having real problems."

"Yes," Jane said, "Problems with people aborting. It's not unusual for pro-life campaigners to be very aggressive and active against people who are hoping to have an abortion. They are so strong in their beliefs. I know that they have stood outside abortion clinics and screamed at women who they see going inside. They've even sabotaged doctors' cars and houses in an attempt to stop them from going to work. She seems to be one of these people. I mean her actions and words are all *so* aggressive, and she seems so against any of us having an abortion. Why would she be here to terminate if she's so against it?"

"What lies beneath is always much muddier than what you see on top." Verity offered. "We see an angry Helen, bitchy, intolerant, hateful, but underneath she could be screaming in pain. You just don't know."

"I can't imagine what she must be going through," said Alice, "To be so angry, she must be having a really hard time."

"Yes, or she might *just* be a complete bitch," said Jane. "All I know is I'm sick of her being here. We're all getting along so well, I feel like we're helping each other come to terms with a really important decision in our lives. We're not just saying, 'Oh poor you', we're offering advice and support to each other. Amelia, look at the change you've had."

"What do you mean? I'm still aborting the baby," Amelia shrugged.

"Yes, but now you know your real reasons for doing it," Jane continued, "You're not sitting at home feeling guilty that you are depriving Gary of a baby or a future. You know that you should never have been with

Gary in the first place, that really you want to be a success in your own right and you didn't need a man to get there. Yes you are terminating, but it's for the right reasons now."

"Doesn't make me feel any better,"

"Maybe not, but later on; remember we spoke about later on? A few years down the line when you look back at things you've done in your life, you won't have that awful feeling of 'What have I done to Gary'. You will probably think, 'I did the right thing'.

"I hope so."

"I think I am doing the right thing," said Alice.

"Oh you absolutely are," said Amelia and Lorraine together.

"Yes Alice," Lorraine continued, "You most certainly are. You are a very young girl with your whole life ahead of you and you must focus on the future. This is just a little glitch, very easily put right; I am in no doubt at all that in your situation, you must terminate." All the women around them nodded in agreement.

"Sometimes there are no choices but the right choice," said Jane. "If I was your age then I would definitely do the same thing, you have so much time in the future for babies."

"Yeah and there's the whole Kieran thing," said Alice. "I can't get him into trouble; I love him too much."

Jane put her arms around Alice, "I know you do Alice, but you understand that you can't be together? It's just not the right thing to do; Kieran is finally doing the right thing by moving away."

"I will move with him when I'm older," said Alice. "He said I had to finish my exams and leave school so that I am no longer a pupil, then I can move to Cumbria to be with him."

"Yes and I am sure that everything will turn out ok in the end," soothed Jane.

"Cumbria my arse," Lorraine whispered to Amelia, "She's never going to see him again."

"I know, poor thing, well that's what life constantly teaches us isn't it?"

"What?"

"That men are either fucking you or fucking off."

"Not just men honey," Lorraine patted her stomach, "My wife did exactly the same thing to me; I think people in general are just selfish. If they're not getting what they want, then they're off; it's that simple."

"It has to be better these babies *don't* come into this world, it's so shit," Amelia grimaced. "The more I think about it, the more I think we're doing them a real good favour by stopping their agony before it starts."

"Do you think the world is really that bad?" Lorraine asked, "I mean do you think *all* babies are doomed to an awful life? Is the world that bad that someone can't come into it and just have a nice, safe life?"

"I really don't know the answer to that question," Amelia shrugged, "Its way bigger than me to answer that. All I can say is that my life is pretty darn shitty at the moment."

"Yeah but it's going to get better isn't it? You will go back to work and have the world at your feet, live in expensive houses, drive expensive cars and eat expensive meals. You will be successful and that surely is a good life to have."

"Yes but at what price? I am sacrificing everything to get there."

"Sacrificing it to be happy though, isn't that right? This will make you happy?"

Amelia stood for a while looking up at the ceiling, searching for an answer to Lorraine's question. Lorraine hoped for the answer to be 'yes'; she needed to know that happiness was a reality.

"Yes," Amelia finally said. "Yes, I will be happy. I will be doing exactly what I want to do and I will have left behind me all the things that are bad in my life. Other people might think that I am a bitch or a heartless cow, but I *will* be happy."

"So happiness is possible?"

"Yes, do you know what Lorraine? I think it actually might be."

Marc entered the room and silently walked over to his usual chair, picked up his clipboard and started to make notes on it. He glanced up at Lorraine who turned her head away from him. Jane walked over to the chairs and took her seat once again, Amelia, Verity, Alice and Lorraine followed suit.

"Helen?" Marc asked. Everyone shrugged their shoulders and sat back in silence waiting for Helen to return. Jane took up her usual stance of staring at the floor, Lorraine chewed on a finger and Alice picked at a piece of thread which stuck out from her top. Amelia sat in quiet contemplation and Verity tapped her foot on the floor in a tarantella, nodding her head in time to the rhythm she played out. Just as Marc was about to suggest going ahead without her, Helen walked into the room and slammed herself into her chair; her face dared anyone to ask where she had been, there were no takers on that offer.

"Hello Helen," said Marc.

"Hello mine Fuhrer," Helen smiled sweetly back at him.

"Refreshed?"

"Yes thanks, had a lovely fag and a glass of wine from the pub down the road." Helen grinned.

"Disgusting." Jane whispered.

"Oh fuck off," Helen spat at her.

"Helen."

"Sorry Marc."

"Right we have three more people left to speak, who would like to begin? Verity?"

"Yes I can." Verity agreed.

"I would like to go next," Jane's quiet voice offered.

"Ok Jane," said Verity, "You go next, I can wait."

"Sorry Verity, I didn't mean to butt in."

"No, it's fine, honestly, you go ahead, I think you're more ready than me anyway."

"Yes I actually think it's now or never for me." Jane grimaced.

"Thank you Jane, when you're ready."

Hi, My name's Jane . . .

"Well we all know by now that my name is Jane."

"Shrew."

Jane threw Helen a withering look, but didn't bite. "I'm here because I have to be, I really can't see any other choice but to be here. Just like Amelia, I would have to tell you my story from the very beginning or it won't make any sense, so bear with me and I will start." She took a sip from the cup of water she had brought with her from the table and spent a few seconds looking at the floor. The air was thick with anticipation and Alice fidgeted in her seat whilst waiting for Jane to begin.

"When you're ready." Helen's eyes rolled.

"Come on now Helen, poor show," said Verity. "Let her take her time; we will give you as much time as you need when you're ready."

"Won't be needing that."

"Yes, quite, you have already told us that."

Helen repeated what Verity said in a mumble and sat back in her chair, eyes rolling again. Marc gave a quiet cough, which quietened Helen.

"Ok," Jane began. "My father is the head of Max Incorporated."

A loud gasp filled the room, "Max incorporated?" Alice said excitedly, "The computer company?"

"I work for them," Amelia enthused. "Wow, that's amazing. So your dad is Brian Knox?"

Jane nodded.

"They are a huge company," Lorraine agreed, "You must be minted Jane, what on earth are you doing here?"

"Money isn't everything," interrupted Verity, "This is real life Lorraine, money doesn't solve *everything*."

"No it certainly doesn't." said Jane. "Ok now we've all got that out of our system I will carry on," she gave a wry smile. "Yes I am Brian Knox's daughter, have been all my life. When I was a young girl I looked a little bit like Alice. I had lovely long hair, the best of everything, clothes, make up, shoes, jewellery like you wouldn't believe. I had just about anything that a girl could desire. Every weekend was filled with trips to the different shops and to beauty parlours, it was an amazing life."

"Was?" Lorraine asked.

"Yes, was; still should be, but my life just isn't working out like that."

"What happened?"

"Freddie Farnham." Another gasp, this time from Amelia.

"He's on the board of directors of Max Incorporated."

"The very one," Jane nodded, "He's my husband."

"Oh . . . dear."

"Why do you say that?" asked Jane. Amelia blushed and then suddenly also found the floor a very interesting place to look at.

"I can easily guess," said Jane, "From what you were saying earlier about sleeping your way to the top, I can pretty much guarantee that you had some sort of fling with Freddie."

"Oh no, *I* haven't," insisted Amelia, "I would never sleep with a married man and of course I had Gary, but I'm afraid I know a few people who have."

"Just a few? Believe me there have been many. It's not like I don't know about them."

"Why do you stay with him?" asked Lorraine.

"Well let me tell you the rest of the story and you will understand. So as I said, I was a young, beautiful girl with the whole world at my feet and pots of money to spend. Nothing was too much or too expensive, I had a limitless credit card and my daddy loved me so much that he would buy me the world. I went through boyfriends like quicksand, used them, cheated on them and toyed with them. It didn't matter to me if I hurt anyone as I had the cushion of home and my dad would be the one to keep my company, he was my world. I went on like that for years after finishing school, travelling the world and doing the party scene; it was great." Jane stopped, reminiscing about the days gone by. She could see herself in her mind's eye, happily laughing without a care in the world. Freddie's handsome face flashed into her memory, bringing her out of it quickly.

"One night my father hosted a dinner party at his home. I'm sure you've been to one or two of them Amelia?"

"Yes, they are glorious."

"Of course they are, he spares no expense. Well I would ordinarily never have attended one of those bashes, they are so tedious and boring; I was far too busy to waste my time at one of daddy's work things. One night though he asked if I would stay as he wanted me to meet his new CEO. He seemed to just be in awe of Freddie, was talking about him like he was some kind of superstar and said that he really thought I should make an effort with him. I knew he wanted me to date him, I couldn't think why, but he seemed so keen and it was no skin off my nose; just another one to chalk up on the board, so I said yes. Freddie came to our house that night and I sat beside him. We spoke and I just fell in love with this guy. I could understand why my dad was so keen on him; he was so charismatic, attentive. He could look into your eyes and in a room full with people; make you think that you were the only one there. Something in him just takes your breath away. Have you ever found that Amelia?"

"To be honest, I have always found him to be a little bit creepy, but then I suppose he hasn't been interested in working his charm on me."

"That could be true, he's definitely a racist."

"Really? I just meant that he hasn't been interested in me sexually."

"Oh, sorry, but no he's a racist, amongst other things. There aren't really any nice bits about Freddie Farnham."

"He keeps it well hidden."

Jane laughed, "He keeps a *lot* of things well hidden. Anyway, that night Freddie blew my socks off. We talked until way past when everyone else had gone home, hell I think I would have jumped into bed with him on that very night if my father hadn't been at home. Freddie seemed to know just what I liked and disliked, he knew a whole heap about my father and just seemed to fit in you know? He asked me on a date and I said yes immediately; he came and picked me up the next day and do you know what we did?"

Heads shook. "Helicopter to Paris?" asked Lorraine.

"No," laughed Jane, "Although that wouldn't have been a big surprise, I had other boyfriends who did that for me. No, we went fishing."

"Fishing?" Alice was incredulous.

"Yes, fishing. Freddie said that he wanted to be with me away from the world, somewhere we could talk and get to know each other. He wanted me to see that he wasn't interested in money or status; he was just interested in me. Well I was the fish on the line, hooked right by the gills and reeled in. We sat and spoke and once again I felt like I was the only important person in Freddie's life and that he was really starting to like me. We went on a lot of other dates and at first they were always at the most obscure locations, for someone like me anyway. McDonalds, the cinema, ice skating, rowing a boat on the river. There was no Monaco, skiing, The Ritz. It was a whole new world for me and I kind of loved the simplicity of it. Of course it also meant that I wasn't mixing in my normal circles. I hadn't seen my friends for months and hadn't met anyone else who knew Freddie. At the time it didn't matter to me, Freddie was my world and I was enjoying the fact that he wanted to get me to himself. What I didn't realise at the time was it was also his way of ensuring that I didn't get to hear any gossip about him, or meet any of his previous conquests. It was a very clever move on his part, he managed to date me and ostracize me from all my friends at the same time. I was in a Freddie bubble and I was loving it. Days turned into weeks, weeks turned into months and before I knew it, we had been dating for two years. Freddie had literally become my life. The strange thing when I look back on it, is how he managed to also get me to stop my beauty regime. Before, I would visit the hairdressers at least three times a week, just for a blow dry; my nails would be manicured and I would have make up ladies. Freddie convinced me that I was a natural beauty and that I shouldn't be wasting my time on added extras. He loved me eau naturel; he said that I wasn't one of the most beautiful women he knew; I was *the* most beautiful woman he knew. I stopped going to the parlour and just put my hair up in a ponytail; Daddy nearly had a conniption the first time I walked down the stairs without make up on, he didn't recognise me at all and thought I was a burglar."

Alice giggled.

"It *was* funny; he only knew it was me when I started talking. Of course he still thought I was beautiful also, so it wasn't such a big deal. Daddy was thrilled that I was going out with Freddie, he thought a lot of him and it was just fine by Daddy that we were together. He even hinted that he hoped the wedding bells would be sounding soon and I was hoping for just the same thing. I had found my perfect man; one who loved me just for being me, had no time for anyone else *but* me, honestly I don't think we spent any time apart from each other. Freddie would go out to work and then come straight home to me, spend the nights with me either at my house or at his flat. Weekends were taken up at these places that he would find, each one so plain and yet so enriched with our love."

Helen made heaving noises.

"Yes it sickens me now as well, but everything was so different then, he just captured me. I was brainwashed by Freddie. He was like the head of a cult and I was his follower. I would have died for Freddie in those moments, given everything to him so that he could live. Then he asked me to marry him." A tear fell from Jane's eye. "That was one of the best moments of my life. This man who had stolen my heart, asked me to marry him. I obviously said yes and when we told Daddy, he was so excited.

"What about your mum?" asked Alice.

"She passed away when I was very young.

"Sorry."

"Oh don't be, it was so long ago now that I don't even think about it; I can't really remember what she looked like other than what I see in photos. I was only eleven, she seems like just a dream to me now."

"Still, I'm sorry."

"Thank you. Well yes, you would think that I am going to tell you we had the most amazing wedding ever, no expense spared right? Wrong. Freddie just wanted something intimate; he said that our love was about us and not about everybody else. Daddy was actually quite happy about that, he liked the fact that Freddie didn't want to spend millions of pounds, 'I like a man who doesn't throw money away," Daddy had said, 'That's why he's such a good CEO, must think about making him up to the board of directors.' Freddie had smiled and said that he was happy as CEO and happy just being part of the family. So again I didn't invite my friends or the usual social crowd, I hadn't actually seen any of my friends for the whole two years; God alone knows what they thought had happened to me. It made me realise that none of them were actually *best* friends; I mean who allows their friend to just disappear? That's the problem with being in the social circles I mixed with; it was all very superficial; no real friendship bonds were made. I mean if one person had sex with another, everybody would know about it before the day was out; there was no loyalty amongst the crowd. It was all about how much you had, who you were and who you knew. Freddie knew this also, that's why he said he didn't want to mix with them, then after a while and when nobody had bothered to even ring to see how I was, I agreed.

The wedding was small, just Freddie, his parents and his sister; Daddy, his latest trophy girlfriend and me. I did wear a beautiful dress and had my hair and nails done, perfect makeup and gorgeous shoes. I had to splash out a little on those things; after all I *was* getting married. When I walked up the aisle, at home, Freddie gave me a wonderful smile but as he kissed me, he whispered that he hated the makeup. I was a little taken aback. I mean Freddie had never been openly negative towards me, every time he had suggested that I didn't wear makeup, that's all it had been, a suggestion. He had never been mean or said that I wasn't to wear it, but here he was, on our wedding day, whispering in my ear, 'what have you got on your face? You look like a clown.' I didn't know what to do; I looked around and there was Daddy beaming, his smile lighting up the room. Freddie's family were the same, everything looked so happy, I didn't want to start an argument, so I just mouthed 'sorry' and then turned to the registrar. It was all over in fifteen minutes, Freddie had said his vows to me so sincerely and had been so wonderfully gentle, holding my hand and brushing the hair from my face; it was almost as if his comment had never happened. I put it out of my mind and as soon as the service was over, I ran upstairs and cleaned my face, changed into something more comfortable and then came back down.

Like an idiot I had completely forgotten about photographs and when I came down. Freddie and Daddy were standing with the photographer, waiting for me. I had to go back up the stairs and change into my wedding dress again, but I had no time to put on any make up so the photos of me are a little shabby to say the least. Freddie was happy though, he was the perfect gentleman once again and we all had a ball for the rest of the day. Dinner and dancing in the ballroom at my house; a little empty but fun nevertheless. I hadn't invited any friends to the wedding, as I said, Freddie had wanted it intimate and as he had pointed out to me, if they were really my friends I would have seen them at some point in the last two years, but I had happily dropped them and it seemed like they had dropped me.

We went off on honeymoon together which was one night in a hotel near Windsor. Daddy loved the frugality of it all; he found it very amusing that Freddie refused to spend the company's money on lavishness. 'Should have married him earlier,' Daddy would wink at me. 'My bank balance has never been so healthy,' he would say. I know he wouldn't have minded either way, I mean he had always given me whatever I wanted; I just think he found it funny. The night we spent together was much the same as all the nights we spent together, we cuddled and made love then went to sleep, nothing different to all the other times we had shared a bed. We went home and Freddie moved into the house with Daddy and I, he went to work and I stayed at home, riding my horse or walking in the grounds."

"Sounds delightful," Verity smiled.

"Does, doesn't it?" agreed Jane. "Was, actually, but then things started to change."

"Oh here we go, he hit you." Helen guffawed. "He knocks her about, same old story."

"That really isn't very helpful Helen," Marc interjected. "I would ask that you don't jump in when Jane is trying to tell her story. Please have some sensitivity."

"Oh for fucks sake, I've heard it all before, girl loves boy, boy makes girl thinks he loves her, gets her home then bam; he bashes the fuck out of her. What is he? Controlling? Jealous? Come on Jane, let's see the bruises."

"It's not like that," Jane picked up her usual pose of looking at the floor.

"No?"

"No, actually, it's worse."

"Come on then let's hear it." Helen swung her arms around in exasperation, "I haven't got all day."

"Helen, please." Marc stopped her again.

"Sorry, please carry on Jane," she said sarcastically. Jane lifted her eyes off the floor and stared directly at Helen for a period of time, long enough to make Helen break the stare and look away. Once Helen had sat back and didn't appear like she wanted to butt in anymore, Jane continued.

"Yes it was much worse than just being hit. I think I could have handled that; my whole life in boarding schools etc. you had to have your wits about you and be prepared to defend yourself. Girls can be such bitches and if you pissed someone off, God help you in the middle of the night when there weren't any teachers about. I've had to break a few noses in my time."

"Hear, hear." Verity agreed.

"I can't really tell you how it started, it just seemed to happen. One day I was this rich, confident girl with the world ahead of me, then I met Freddie, became devoted and a married woman and suddenly I'm a slave. It didn't take long for Freddie to suggest that we needed our own place away from daddy; daddy was absolutely smitten with him, it was as if Freddie was now his son and I was the in-law." Jane laughed, "Daddy barely spoke to me; he would just give me funny looks all the time, you know when someone looks at you as if they don't know you anymore? I think Freddie had been saying things about me, telling daddy that I had lost my mind or that I was doing something wrong, I really don't know what happened there, but he turned against me anyway. No, turned against me isn't fair, it's like he switched off from me. Anyway, Freddie said we had to move out and that daddy was going to buy us a house. I expected something small, Freddie had been so frugal up to now, always saying how life wasn't about the money but about the living; maybe a four bedroom house, somewhere for kids, you know; a normal family house." Jane shrugged. "I couldn't have been more wrong, this is where Freddie became *the* most lavish person. We moved into a six bedroomed mansion, with a swimming pool, sauna, gym. Two kitchens and four bathrooms, room for a pony - nothing that daddy couldn't afford, I mean our house was already twice that size, it was just the first time I noticed that Freddie wasn't so reluctant to spend you know?"

Nods came from around the room, but Jane could tell that people were getting a bit bored of her, Alice was looking at the split ends at the bottom of her hair, Helen was looking anywhere but at Jane, Amelia studied her nails and Marc continued to look at his clipboard.

"We moved into the house and at the exact moment that Freddie closed the front door to my daddy leaving, he switched. Someone, somewhere pressed a button in his head and his whole face changed, he turned to me and he said, 'Get to work,' I laughed and said, 'Don't be silly Freddie, come on, let's go watch TV, I will make you some dinner,' something like that, but he walked up to me and grabbed my hair and told me that I was his now, I belonged to him and I had to do everything he wanted. I still thought it was a joke, you know, some sick game that Freddie was playing, but he didn't stop. He pushed me into the kitchen and down onto the floor, told me to lick the tiles clean until the whole kitchen was done.

I must have sat on that kitchen floor for about thirty minutes just looking at the tiles, I didn't know what to do; if I got up, I believed he was going to hit me, if I started licking the floor was he just going to laugh and say, 'you silly cow, get up,' or would he really let me lick the floor? I was waiting for him to tell me to get up, but he just stood there, waiting for something to happen. I can't explain exactly how I knew I had to do it; there was the smell of menace in the air you know? An electric danger very present, something in the air that just made me instinctively know that I was in danger."

"What did you do?" Alice asked, attention now drawn completely to Jane.

"I started to lick the floor," Jane's eyes glistened with tears.

"Oh my god." Amelia said.

"Yes, I licked the floor. He clapped his hands with delight and said, 'Good dog,' then walked away to sit in the lounge. It was so bizarre, I don't know why I was so scared of him, am still scared of him. I licked the floor for about ten minutes; I mean who the hell does that? I just kneeled there, head to the floor and licked at it. It's not like it was cleaning it, the floor was shining, brand new - daddy had had the whole house cleaned and furnished ready for us to just move in there, but there I was like a little dog, lapping away at the floor.

Freddie came back and he said, 'what are you doing on the floor you silly cow, get up and make me some dinner, there's a love.' So up I get and make him dinner, take it through to him, put it on the table in front of him where he was sitting waiting and then set my own plate down at the other end. 'What are you doing?' he asks me. 'Having dinner,' I reply. 'Dogs eat on the floor,' he says. Again I am in a state of *what do I do now*, I just stand there like an idiot staring at him, waiting for him to laugh or become violent, something to give me a clue what's going on. Nothing happens, he just sits and waits, but the electric danger is there again, the warnings are tangible, I know I have to do it or something really bad is going to happen. So I put my plate on the floor and kneel down once again. 'Dogs don't use plates,' he says."

"Oh you poor thing," Lorraine was shaking her head, "He shouldn't have done that to you."

"That's nothing," Jane shook her own head, "I mean, it was something at the time, but compared to the rest of the stuff he's done to me? That's nothing. It went on like that all through the first day, every point where he or I would do something new in the house; sit on the sofa, 'dogs don't sit on sofas.' Watch television, 'dogs don't watch TV,' and then the worst one was going to the toilet."

"Oh come on," Amelia said very loudly.

"Yes, this was when it became a little worse, 'dogs go in the garden.' He walked out to the back garden with me following behind and he pointed to a fenced off area at the back of the lawn; he must have arranged to have it put in there when the plans were being made for the house you know? It was fenced off and had sand inside it, something you would make for a dog. 'That's where the dogs go,' he announced to me and once again just waited. He didn't smile, or frown, didn't even push me out there, just stood and waited for me to do what he wanted. I was just too scared to question him, it was so bizarre, so completely out of my world of experience; I didn't know if it was some sort of game to him, like a first day initiation into the home, some old school boys' club thing you know? I just couldn't work it out. I am ashamed to say that I went outside and squatted in the sand like a dog, I didn't seem to have any other choice."

"Disgusting." Lorraine was still shaking her head in disbelief.

"It's nothing." Jane continued. "So that night, the first night in my brand new home with my *fabulous* husband, I slept on the floor of the bedroom, at the end of the bed like any faithful dog does. Only after I'd licked his feet and given him a good blow job though, dogs are obviously useful for other things as well." Jane laughed. "At least he didn't rape me that time."

Verity moved her chair closer to Jane and rested her hand on top of Jane's shoulder; Jane smiled thankfully at Verity, and then continued.

"So the next morning, Freddie woke up, let the dog out for a wee," she pointed at herself, "And then announced that he was going to work and what job was I going to do that day? I replied, 'Dogs don't work.' And he hit me; oh he hit me *so* hard. It came completely out of the blue and so fast, I didn't even see his hand moving. He was so calm and so still when he did it. I went flying across the room and slamming into a cupboard. I lay there dazed for a while, again not knowing what to do or say. He walks up to me and, still calmly, said something like, 'You have to earn your keep around here; don't think I am going to pay for your living. You've had it so easy all your life little rich girl, now it's time to graft. Go out and get a fucking job and don't come back until you've got one.' He came right up into my face and was like, 'I mean it Jane, you won't be getting another penny from me.' Then off he went, whistling away as he got in his Jaguar, left me alone to get a job."

"Did you leave?" Alice asked. "Tell me you left the house."

"Yes I left the house, but only to go and get a job."

"Why didn't you go back to your father? Tell him what had been happening?" Alice was incredulous, "You can't have just let this go on."

"I really don't know." Said Jane. "I mean like I said, my dad had been getting further and further away from me, he was looking at me already like I was some kind of freak, mental patient, I don't know, but he had a look in his eye. I knew his loyalties were with Freddie. I thought that if I went and said anything to daddy then he would just dismiss it, tell Freddie and then I would *really* be in trouble. Oh I just don't know why I never said anything; it seemed easier just to do what Freddie wanted. So I went out and I got a job. I walked into a few shops and offices, asking around; I hadn't actually ever needed a job before so didn't really know what I was doing, but this guy that I spoke to in a little shoe shop said that he needed somebody and he took me on. I suppose I was lucky because god knows what would have happened if I had gone home that day without a job. I could have gone to daddy and asked for a job, or used the qualifications that I had got in all those damn fine schools daddy had paid for, but I obviously didn't want to work with Freddie now after everything that had happened and to be quite honest, I'm not the brightest spark in the box, office work just wouldn't be my thing at all."

"So you just went to work?" Alice asked. "You didn't tell anyone what he had done to you?"

"Life isn't always that cut and dried Alice," said Amelia. "You haven't told your parents about your pregnancy have you?"

"Well no, but this is wrong, I mean it's just wrong, you can't let someone do that to you. If you had told someone Jane then they could have helped you."

"Told them what?" Jane asked, "Told them that I was a dog? That I was sleeping on the floor and weeing in the garden? Do you really think you could tell somebody that, a stranger? I wanted to keep the job not get myself laughed out of the shop. I need a break." Jane looked at Marc. "Please Marc, I need a break, there's so much more to tell but I don't think I can do it just now."

Marc looked at his watch. "Shall we have a comfort break? Everyone can use the loo."

"Or garden," Helen said.

"Bitch." Lorraine spat at her. "Why don't you fuck off out of here?"

"I'm having so much fun, I just can't leave." Helen smiled. "I'm going for a fag."

"I hope it chokes you." Lorraine called after Helen as she sauntered out of the room. "God, how can anyone be so hateful?" she looked around her for an answer, but none was forthcoming. Jane left the room and the others stood up, either stretching out their arms, or shaking their legs to get the stiffness out of them.

"Any more biscuits over here?" Alice asked as she went back to the table.

"My dear lord, what she has gone through is just awful," Verity said to Amelia.

"It's what she's going to tell us that is worrying me," said Amelia, looking towards the door that Jane had walked out of. "I just can't imagine what words are going to come out of that girl's mouth, but they aren't going to be pretty."

"Better have another cup of tea then." Said Verity.

Ten minutes later and everyone reconvened on the chairs, Helen had only briefly left the room, but came back smelling of cigarettes nevertheless. She shunned the tea and biscuits on offer at the table, preferring to sip from a water bottle which she carried with her.

"Everyone refreshed?" Marc asked, adjusting himself on the chair. He looked at Lorraine, searching her face for any clue as to what her decision would be. Lorraine remained steadfast in her refusal to look at Marc, but didn't seem to be upset or angry with him. Marc hoped he would see her at his house later that day, Eleanor would be anxiously waiting for him to return with good news and he hoped that for once in their life, he would be able to give it to her.

Jane coughed and shook her hair away from her eyes. "I'm ready." She said.

"Thank you Jane, we are ready to listen," said Marc. "Please continue."

"Ok, well life continued on with Freddie for a few months. I became his faithful hound; working through the day and paying into the home. He let me keep my wages as I was expected to provide cleaning products and stuff like that. Obviously I didn't earn enough to give him the champagne lifestyle he wanted so he bought all of that on his work's business card. I don't know why he doesn't use the money daddy gives me, or even his wages; I think he's saving for something, but God alone knows what that is. The blessed relief when I got home from work was that he was never there. I actually don't see Freddie that often; I suppose that's why I've been able to carry on living like it for so long. He works long hours at the company and in the evening he loves to go out. He is definitely a different man to the one I met - we never went out on the club circuit for the whole two years I was with him, now he goes out almost every night to all the places I used to go with my friends. I know he goes to the Marmot Club in Westminster; that used to be *my* favourite haunt. It's almost like he's pushed me out of my old life and is taking it over. I started to get messages from my old friends telling me that Freddie was at the club, or at the hotel, or at the country club and I should come down. Can you imagine if I ever went there? The messages stopped soon enough, Freddie was obviously feeding them some spiel about me being a nut job and lost to society.

Anyway, when Freddie wasn't there my life was just fine. I would go to work at the shoe shop which I loved because it was the only time that I would be able to have conversations with people. It would all feel so normal, speaking, smiling and laughing with others; something which just wasn't happening to me anywhere else in my life. When I got home, if Freddie wasn't there, then I could be, once again, 'normal'. I would make sure the house was spotless, although that doesn't actually matter because if he decides he wants me to clean, I have to do it all again anyway; at least by cleaning it first I know I'm not licking any shit off the floor." Jane laughed, but no one seemed to find her joke funny. She shrugged her shoulders. "Tough crowd." Which did draw some smiles.

"Yes, so I would clean, make myself a dinner, enjoy a poo on a real toilet, have a bath, watch a bit of television, lie on the sofa, *my* sofa and pretend that my life was just fantastic. Then the click of the door. I would have to jump up from whatever I was doing, turn off the TV, get on the floor and crawl to his feet; he would wait for me by the front door sometimes until I appeared and then I would have to take off his shoes, lick his feet and wag my tail."

"Wag your tail?" Amelia asked.

"Yes, actually wave my arse about in the air like a dog pleased to see its owner."

"Sick."

"I agree, but that's what he wanted. It was ritualistic, every time he came in that's what I had to do. Then he would speak to me 'Good dog' 'has doggy been a good girl?' 'Now *sit*'. Then I would have to sit at the door whilst he inspected the house. White gloves, the works. Around he went rubbing shelves and wiping fireplaces with his white fingers, tutting and shaking his head in disgust. Eventually he would find a place which wasn't up to his standards and then he would just point and say 'Lick'. Off I would go to start licking and always the same, five minutes later he would say, 'what on earth are you doing you stupid cow, go and get me some dinner please.'"

"This just isn't right, I mean we can't allow this to go on," Amelia shouted, "How on earth can anyone live like this? Marc I know we're not supposed to get involved in people's lives here, but why are you just sitting there staring, write this down, make a case for her with the police, she needs saving from this guy."

Marc put his clipboard down and took his glasses off; wiping them slowly with a yellow cloth which he had removed from his trousers. This wasn't the first time he had heard a story like Janes and he knew it wouldn't be the last. What seemed too alien and awful to people who had never suffered domestic abuse, was just another story to people who had.

"We have to respect Jane's wishes and only get involved when she asks for help." He said. "Please allow Jane to tell her story, we are here to support each other and to listen."

"I know, but it's so hard to listen to."

"I'm sorry," said Jane.

"Oh no, I am so sorry Jane," Amelia said quickly. "That is so selfish of me, I'm not thinking straight. Of course it's harder for you to tell than for me to listen. I will try and keep my gob shut."

"It's fine."

"No it's not fine, I am just making things worse. Please, carry on."

"Ok well you'll be pleased to hear I wasn't his dog for much longer. He got bored of doing that to me and I became so good at it that he never had reason to hit me, unless it was just for the hell of it. I actually settled in quite nicely to being a dog, I like to think I was a Pomeranian; I've always liked those dogs. Like I said, Freddie was hardly there so most of my life was quiet and peaceful. Well maybe Freddie wasn't happy with me getting comfortable so the next thing I became was his horse. That room for a pony I mentioned? There was a stable yard out the back with a school and paddock. I had assumed when I moved in that Freddie intended to buy a horse, but no, why buy a horse when you already have one? I was the new pony, sent to live in the stable. I had to make my own bed out of straw and lie on blankets and when Freddie was home he would come out to the stable and put a halter on my head, lead me into the kitchen or bedroom, or whatever room he fancied and then ride me like a horse. Now I'm not a big person and Freddie is definitely bigger than me but he would make sure that he kept his feet off the ground and even made some little jumps for me out of cushions on the floor. Oh how he would scream with anger if I ever dropped him or fell to the side, he would kick me and hit me with the whip screaming 'bad horse' or 'you fucking donkey'. Never on my face though because obviously I had to go to work the next day. When he got bored of doing that, if I was lucky, I would be allowed to go back out to my stable, but sometimes he got a bit frisky with all the horse riding and then would ride me in the other way. Horsey style, but up the arse so he could really hurt me, pulling my pony tail and shouting 'yee ha cowboy' as he came. Such fun." Jane started to cry.

"This just can't be true," said Helen.

"Oh I'm sorry Helen," Jane sneered sarcastically. "Sorry that my story isn't good enough for you to believe."

"It's just wrong," said Helen quietly.

"Yeah well life is wrong and that's not even the worst of it. I have been every animal under the sun in that house. Next it was a mouse, locked in a dog cage in the front room, eating corn out of a tray and my cage being shaken every time he walked past me. Sometimes he would forget to unlock the cage door and I wouldn't be able to go to work. I would have to piss on myself and lie in my own shit until he came home and finally let me out. Then I would get a beating for being a dirty mouse and have my food taken away from me, threatened that I better not lose my job or I would be in even more trouble. Oh the lies I had to come out with at work to keep that job. I think my boss knew there was something going on; he always looks at me with such sadness in his eyes. There's no way he would have kept me on if he didn't understand. He's let me come here this week and has promised I will still have a job at the end of it. After the mouse, I was a cat; that was actually quite a luxury because I got to use a litter tray and was even allowed to sit on the sofa as long as I purred. Then things changed again. Suddenly I was no longer an animal to Freddie, I was his wife again. He started to be really kind to me; oh he never apologised for what he had done or even made any mention of the months of torment that had gone before him, but he was nice. When he came home and I scampered out to him like any good rabbit would, he said, "What are you doing on the floor Janie darling, come on, let's go and have some dinner together." That was the first time he had used my name in about six months. I had just been dog or cat or whatever animal I was at the time. I jumped to his attention because I have learnt not to hesitate, he doesn't like that; I must always go along with whatever he wants. We made dinner together, he was chatting away like we were a happily married couple. Then he looked at me and told me that I should go and change into some nice clothes as people were coming over. *People were coming over.* I couldn't believe it; people were actually going to be coming to my house. Freddie was being so nice and it was like the past had never happened. I honestly thought that maybe he realised what he had been doing was wrong or maybe my father had found out about it and warned him away from me, but whatever it was, it made me so happy. I thought my life was about to change and it was."

"Nothing can be that easy." Verity grimaced.

"No it can't." agreed Jane. "It got much worse. We had dinner and he spoke to me, I must confess I didn't really say anything back to him. He doesn't like me speaking to him and if I am ever allowed to speak, it usually results in a slap. I just ate my dinner in silence and hoped I was smiling in the correct places when he told me what his day had been like. Then the doorbell rang; I hadn't ever heard it before, it sounded so normal 'ding dong' like that. Freddie jumped up and said 'Our guests are here', I must admit I got a little excited, butterflies in the stomach, anticipating visitors and conversation, but I didn't know what to do. How did Freddie want me to behave? Who was I supposed to be? What was I supposed to be? A host, a wife, a friend? It was very confusing and made me really nervous, so I just followed him to the door and stood behind him. Three men came into the room and behind the three men were three women, all wearing diamond studded collars and all being led on leads which were attached to the men's hands. I knew then that my visitors weren't the relief I had hoped they would be, they were there to make my life so much harder.

I won't bore you with *all* the details of what happened that night but basically the men were dominators and the women were their slaves, but these slaves wore diamond collars and were whipped with velvet; they were purring with delight and obviously happy to play along; that's all they were doing, playing. It was a sexual game to them, one which they all participated in willingly and there was no real violence going on. That was reserved for me. We all went straight up to the bedroom, Freddie talking excitedly with them all but no one really making any eye contact with me or any attempt to speak to me. It's like they knew; what am I talking about, of *course* they knew.

I was taken upstairs, stripped and redressed in leather, with a mask over my head that just had a hole for the mouth, no need to see or to breathe though a nose apparently, even when your mouth is full of cock. Then I can't tell you exactly what happened to me because I couldn't see any more, but suffice to say I was the target for everyone's anger. I could hear people having sex around me, Freddie sounded like he was having a fabulous time. I was just sort of pinioned in the middle of the room and was hit, whipped, poked, fucked, sodomised, face fucked, blah, blah, blah, you name it and it was done. I knew the women were doing it too because I could smell their perfume when they came near me and feel their nails when they ripped into me. And yes, I just took it. Took it all. I realised that the months I had been Freddie's animals was all training for his real agenda. This was what he wanted, I was to be his sex slave, but there were no safe words for me, no tapping on the shoulder when I wanted out, I was to take it like a good dog and I am ashamed to say that I did. That I do. The only thing I know for certain is Freddie is the only person who ever uses my vagina. He is determined to get me pregnant. He needs an heir to his throne and says he's always wondered what it's like to fuck a pregnant woman; 'can the baby feel it' he even said aloud once." Jane gagged heavily. "I'm sorry." She gagged again. "I need to go to the toilet." She ran from the room gagging loudly.

Silence enveloped the room where the foul words had been spoken. Young Alice looked dazedly at the other women around her; she felt so out of her depth in a room surrounded by people so much older than her. Where had her life gone so wrong? Just a few months ago she had been in class laughing with her friends and worrying about what shoes she should be buying next, listening to her music through her headphones and planning what her life was going to be like with Kieran. Now she was sitting in a room pregnant, about to undergo an operation, listening to women talking about things she never knew existed in the world. Sex had always been an enigma to her, something mums and dads did behind closed doors, making babies. Not something which could be enjoyed, and definitely not something that could defile you. People didn't hurt each other in Alice's world, parents argued, but made up and everyone's life was lovely. Was her life going to end up like that, did people really hurt each other so badly? Alice started to weep with fear. Lorraine jumped up from her chair and ran to Alice's side enshrouding her small frame in strong arms.

"It's ok Alice," she soothed. "She's going to be ok; we're going to help her."

"How can we do that?" asked Alice.

"Just wait until she comes back, we will talk with her, we can help her." Said Lorraine. Amelia and Verity nodded in agreement.

"He needs to be shot." Helen said in disgust.

"Not very helpful," said Verity.

"But true," Amelia smiled at Helen who grimaced back at her.

Marc cleared his throat to draw the ladies' attention to him. "I know that what we have just heard may be very hard for all of you, but please remember why you are all here. Jane needs to tell someone her story and she is here to get help and support with her decision to terminate her pregnancy. I would like it if you could all spend the next few minutes in silence and considering what words you can use to offer Jane some support."

"I'll offer her support; I'll go and kill the bastard." Said Helen.

"Productive support would be more helpful please Helen." Said Marc although he was silently pleased that for once Helen appeared to be in support of one of his subjects, rather than against them.

"I'm back." Jane said, walking into the room. She sat in the hard plastic chair and used a tissue to wipe tears from her eyes, which were red from the strain of just being sick. "I'm sorry, again," she said. "It just makes me feel so ill when I think of the things he has said to me about being pregnant. I can't even go there with you all I'm afraid, it's really just too much to bear."

"We understand Jane. You only have to tell us what you feel comfortable with." Said Marc. "Are you happy to carry on?"

"Yes, I need to get this out and finished with so I can go back to just staring at the floor," smiled Jane. Marc smiled kindly back at her.

"Then when you're ready Jane, so are we," he said.

"Thanks. Well that's probably just about all you need to know, I would be here for hours if I had to relay all the things that go on, but I suppose that's the main part of my life. Freddie pretty much leaves me alone in the house now, he doesn't treat me like an animal any more, he allows me to move freely around the house and sit on the sofa. He still isn't home much and when he's out I know he's with other women, he doesn't hide anything from me. Sometimes he will make me watch him from the wardrobe whilst he has sex with women in our bed - I say our bed, I am still not allowed to sleep with him; my place is on the floor. Ninety percent of the time my life is like that but the other ten percent is when we are having people over. That's the worst part of my life; I am ashamed of it, ashamed of myself; that I let it happen."

"Is it always the same people?" asked Verity, "Do you know them?"

"Actually no, it's not always the same people. I think Freddie is part of a club, some sort of S&M sex club and that's where he finds them, but they just seem oblivious to me. It's like they have already agreed before they get there that I am the slave, the gimp as I have heard them call me. I don't know if they are aware that I am not complicit in it; why would they be? I have never complained, or screamed or said 'no'. They probably think I am enjoying it just as much as they are. I can't blame them for what goes on. It's Freddie that invites them there."

"Can't you whisper in one of their ears?" Alice asked, "Ask them for help I mean."

"Oh God no, can you imagine what he would do if he ever found out I had spoken to one of them? I would be dead." Jane wiped another tear. "Although that's not such a bad idea, I've thought about it more than once, dying I mean."

"Oh no, please don't do that." Alice cried out. "Please Jane, don't ever do that."

"Relax Alice; I'm too much of a coward to do it. That's all I am in this life, a coward."

"I don't think you're a coward," said Amelia. "It takes a strong woman to go to work every day and pick herself up the way you do. To be able to pretend that everything is ok. I would be shouting and screaming it from the roof tops, telling anyone who would listen because I would be that scared. I think it's incredibly brave of you to keep it all in and yet behave so normally."

"I'm a coward," said Jane, "Come on Amelia, how is it brave to stand in front of someone at work and say nothing. Inside you are screaming 'help me' and there is someone standing directly in front of you who can help. A word to the police or a word to my father, that's all it would take and he could be gone. But I just stand there and say nothing. I haven't got the guts to see what would happen if I put a stop to it. I haven't got the guts to face my father and admit that I've allowed myself to be used like that and done nothing about it for all this time and lastly, but most probably more importantly; I'm ashamed to say that I haven't got the guts to live without Freddie. I need him in my life and he needs me."

"Are you actually serious?" Amelia almost shouted from her chair. "How in the hell can you need someone in your life who does that to you? I have heard of people in domestic violence constantly going back to their abusive partners because when they're not being abusive, they are lovely towards them. I've heard the stories, 'he loves me' and all that shit, but when does Freddie ever do that to *you?* From what you've told me there are no good bits, no 'I'm sorry', no flowers and chocolates after a massive beating. There is just hell, hell and more hell."

"No, I told you, for the most part, ninety percent of it, he leaves me alone."

"*Leaves you alone?* Amelia was incredulous. "How can you call what he does to you leaving you alone, you have become so desensitised to the torture that he puts you under, that anything which isn't the sex part is seen as being kind to you; Jane, you have to get away from him. You have to get away from him now before you even see the sex as being normal, before you start to enjoy it for fucks sake."

"Please don't say that, I could never enjoy it."

"No? Well you seem pretty happy sleeping at the bottom of someone's bed, that's him being kind to you apparently."

"Don't judge me Amelia; you don't know what it's like."

"No you're right; I don't know what it's like, because I would never allow something like that to happen to me. I am a strong woman; I believe in myself, I would never allow a man to treat me like that. It's just not right."

"I was strong once," said Jane.

"And you can be strong again," Lorraine now spoke. "You can beat this Jane, you can leave him and live your life once again; you could even have your baby."

"Ha, don't be ridiculous. I will never have this baby. Never."

"Why? Don't you want a baby?" asked Alice.

"No, it's not that," said Jane. "I can't have this baby because Freddie wants it. I can't trust that I would be safe throughout the pregnancy and I can't trust that Freddie won't harm the baby when it's born. My worst fear is that Freddie loves the baby. What if that child becomes a massively loved part of Freddie's life and grows up with the influence of his father? What if that sweet innocent little child grows up to become Freddie? I can't unleash that on the world. I can't have a baby for Freddie. I need to stop this before it starts and go back to normal." Jane framed the word normal with her fingers. A burst of feeling sprang free from Jane's mouth, screaming into the air. "I can't do it, I just can't do it." She wailed and fresh tears freed themselves from her eyes.

Helen got up from her chair and walked towards Jane. Jane shrank back as she saw Helen move towards her, scared as to what Helen was going to say or do to her now that she had shown what a weak person she was. Helen grabbed Jane by the arms and pulled her up into an embrace, then stood and held her, allowing Jane to crumple into her arms and release her pain in waves of tears and anger. Helen gently soothed her with words of comfort and the rest of the room sat silently watching the two women in their embrace. When Janes lament subsided and she began to compose herself again, Helen let her go, helping her back into her chair.

"I'm going now." She said into the air and turned to collect her bag, walking away from the five women who watched every step as she left the room.

Verity shuffled over to Jane and continued to comfort her.

"Shall we end there?" asked Marc. All heads nodded in agreement.

"Ok, I will see you all here tomorrow morning please, nine o'clock start once again." He gather his stuff and began to leave the room. "Lorraine if I may see you outside?"

"I will see you later on," Lorraine said to him. "At eight."

Marc's heart jumped when he heard Lorraine's words. For all the pain and suffering he had heard in the room over the last couple of days, there was maybe a light at the end of the tunnel and he may have something good to tell Eleanor at long last.

Helen, home . . .

Helen threw her car keys down on the little wooden stool Brian had brought her back from one of his charity walks in Africa. She thought back to the time he had brought the stool home.

"Carried that for two hundred miles," he had grinned at her when he handed it over.

"What is it?" Helen had asked, face crinkled at the foul smell which emanated from both the stool and her husband.

"It's a fertility stool," Brian grinned again, "Carved by a witch doctor from the Matabele tribe; look at the legs." He thrust the black ebony wood towards her with the legs pointing towards Helen's chest. She took it off him, turned the stool over in her hands so the legs were pointing upwards and saw four black phalluses standing proudly in the air.

"Not sure which side of the stool you're supposed to sit on," he laughed.

"Prick." Helen said, giving it back to Brian.

"Four of them," he agreed.

"And where the hell am I supposed to put the damn thing?"

"In the bedroom?" Brian offered.

"How about no. It's going as near to the front door as I can get it without actually throwing it out," said

Helen, dumping the stool legs down in the gap behind the door.

The stool had sat there for the last five years. It had become a place to dump stuff as you entered or left the house; home to keys, coins and the odd discarded sweet, sticky and fluffy from where it had been found in an old coat pocket.

"I'm home," Helen shouted into the cold house. Emptiness sucked her in and enshrouded her, the sound of silence almost too loud to bear. Helen hummed a tune to keep that sound at bay, walking into her front room and turning on the television before going into the kitchen and filling the air with noise from the radio.

"Hi Brian," she spoke to his photo which sat near the kettle. "Another shit day, full of muppets." Brian smiled back at her from the moment in time captured in the glossy paper. Helen stroked his face then turned on the kettle, pulled a coffee cup from the cupboard and searched for a teaspoon in a crowded drawer before deciding to just use a dessert spoon to make a very strong coffee. As she turned with her coffee to sit at the kitchen table, she felt a sharp pain in her side. She sucked in a gasp of air and grabbed the area which had caused her so much pain. Helen sat at the table and took a few deep breaths, waiting to see if she could feel anything more.

"Just a twinge," she assured herself loudly. The radio played on, its music loud but not reaching into Helen's thoughts. She wondered at how Jane had allowed herself to get into such a shit situation. There was no way she should be killing her baby. It was so obvious that what she really needed was to get rid of that piece of shit husband of hers. Helen knew if Brian had been so cruel to her, she would have fought tooth and nail to get away; stamped all over the bastard's head until he couldn't get up again and kicked him the fuck out of her life. There was just no way Helen, would ever be a victim if she had actual control over her situation.

Another sharp pain broke Helen out of her thoughts, this time close to her abdomen.

"What are you doing to me baby?" she asked, looking down at herself. She felt some wetness in her knickers and immediately jumped up to run to the bathroom. As she jumped Helen felt a gush of liquid leave her vagina and looked down at her jeans to see a spreading stain of crimson emanating from her groin.

"Oh for fucks sake," she grimaced, heading for the stool in order to retrieve her keys; remembering to grab some black bags on the way out of the house. Helen spread the bags over the seat of her car and then sat on them and turned on the engine.

"Looks like you're taking the chore out of my hands you little git," she said to the foetus in her stomach. "I suppose I should thank you really."

Jane, home . . .

"Are you alright Jane?" asked Lorraine, "Is he home?" she held her breath as she waited for the answer, Lorraine silently hoped the answer would be an emphatic no.

"No he's still at work," Jane told a relieved Lorraine. "He would never be home before six o'clock and even then I wouldn't know if he was going out to a club or not. He likes to keep me guessing.

"Right, come on then let's get your stuff. Let's be as quick as we can, I don't want to take any chances. I want to get in and out before he comes back. I mean I'm quite handy when I want to be but I don't really fancy a fight, especially in my condition." Lorraine patted her bump.

"He would never fight you; he's too clever for that."

"What? Are you telling me that he comes home to find wifey leaving him and he will do nothing?"

"That's not the way he operates." Jane grimaced. "Why do you think my father has no idea what is going on? He just thinks I have lost my mind, I told you that."

Lorraine thought back to Jane's earlier story and felt the hairs on the back of her neck prickling her. "No more Jane," she said sternly. "This isn't going to happen to you anymore. Come on, you're leaving this evil piece of scum behind. You're going to have your baby and you, my little princess, are going to live happily ever after."

"This is no fairy tale Lorraine."

"Well you said yourself, it used to be. Once you get away from here and I speak to your father, let him know just what's been going on and get him to see Freddie just for what he is; Daddy will sack the bad guy, take back your house and one restraining order later, the princess is back in her castle." Lorraine clapped her hands and rubbed them together, "Ready?" she asked.

Jane's hands began to tremble as she put the key in the lock of her front door. She had felt so confident back at the counselling session; opening up and sharing her life story had seemed like the best thing that had ever happened to her. Each word that had left Jane's mouth had made the heaviness in her heart one gram lighter. As she told her tale she could feel the stress leave her body until a euphoric state had overtaken her. Helen's embrace had allowed Jane to release all the pain from her body until she was so light she felt she could float away. The cuddle had kept her feet on the ground that prevented the take-off that she had felt so sure must happen her load was now so light.

When Helen had left, the other women had joined hands around Jane and embraced her in a show of solidarity. Amelia had begun to whisper a plan of salvation. Each and every woman gently spoke words of emancipation, promising a new life for her and her unborn baby. So soothed and empowered by their words, Jane had allowed Lorraine to bring her home in order to start the first stage of her quest for freedom.

The key clicked in the door and the familiar warning beep from the house alarm sounded in Jane's ear. She rushed to the white metal box under the stairs and as she began to type in the digits of Freddie's birthday, the weight of her true existence pressed heavily onto her shoulders.

"Jane?" Lorraine called into the house. She walked in and closed the enormous front door behind her and let out a whistle as décor screamed opulence at her.

"Some gaff," she said approvingly, "Jane? Jane, where are you?"

Lorraine walked further into the house, looking left and right to see where Jane had gone. She walked in the direction she had seen Jane going and came across her standing, statue like, at an alarm box, hand held frozen in the air.

"Jane?"

"I can't," Jane dropped her hand and turned to face Lorraine.

"I can't, oh my God, what am I doing? I can't do this."

"Of course you can do it." Lorraine protested. "It's just a few minutes away. All you have to do is pack your stuff and walk out of that door."

"No, no I can't leave. I can't just *go*. Freddie will kill me."

"When your dad finds out what's been going on, everything will change. I promise you honey. Everything will be ok. If you just take that leap of faith," Lorraine took Jane by the hand and led her back to the front door.

"Look out there," she indicated outside the door, pushing Jane to face the outside. "That's your future. That's your freedom. Hell Jane, that's your baby's freedom. If you can't do it for you then do it for the baby inside of you."

"You just don't get it do you?" Jane turned sharply. "It's not *my* baby. It's his baby. Freddie's baby. Even if I leave today I will still carry his child. If I have this baby then I am tied to Freddie for life. He will never leave me alone. He will pursue me to the ends of the earth, bring me back and then probably abuse us both; me *and* his child. We would be his possessions; me his slave and the baby his key to my father's fortune. He doesn't really want to be a father, the same as he didn't really want to get married. They're just a means to an end. He's a psychopath, an absolutely one hundred percent psychotic control freak. He will never let me go."

"But your dad . . ."

"My dad is a power hungry, big headed, misogynistic and greedy bastard. He loved me when I was his little princess, but now I'm just his sad pathetic daughter; ready to be committed to the looney bin. Freddie is the blue eyed boy, bringing new money into the company with his ideas. Boosting dad's profits and ego. He has my dad's ear now; I am no one to him. There's no way he'll listen to me."

"That's not true, he's your dad. We will all be with you. We can go to the police first."

"Police?" Jane snorted, "You are out of your mind." Tears cascaded from her cheeks. "I will never

ever be free of this man and my child will never survive in this environment. He or she will either be persecuted and mercilessly bullied by Freddie, or yes, he may love the baby once it's born and then what? *Two* Freddies? Another person to hate me and hurt me? No, I can't have that. I can't bring a new life into this, this mess." She wiped snot from her face." The only way I can ever hope to be free and to bring this baby into the world is if Freddie is dead."

Silence invaded their conversation. Lorraine let go of Jane's hand and both stood for a few moments, looking out of the front door. Finally Lorraine broke the silence.

"So what now?"

"Now I go back to being Freddie's bitch. I'm going to have the termination and save his baby from a fate worse than death. He will never know about it, I can carry on licking the house and being the good gimp that I am."

"I can't just walk away and leave you here," Lorraine protested. "I don't even want to think about what your evening is going to be like. It's like leaving a little duckling to a pack of magpies."

"He's more like a vulture." Jane smiled. "Listen Lorraine, this is my life and I'm used to it. If I hadn't got pregnant you and I would never had met. You would still be doing what you do every day and I would still be here and at the shoe shop. In a few weeks we won't even be thinking about each other. I will be just a distant memory to you."

"No, I will *never* stop worrying about you."

"Well you never know, maybe once I've had the abortion I will get the guts to leave him," said Jane.

"Really?"

"Yes, I mean this is the first day since I got into this mess that I've even thought it possible to escape. Maybe once the baby has gone I'll give you a call and we can try again." Jane began to cry once more. "But I just can't do it now. Oh why can't he just get hit by a bus? Bang, all over, dead. My baby would be saved and I could bring him up to be the complete opposite to that pig. "

"Anyone know a hitman?" Lorraine asked around her to which Jane giggled.

"Don't tempt me," she smiled. "Look Lorraine, I really appreciate what all of you have done for me in the last few days, but in two days I'm going ahead with the termination. My mind is set, I'm staying with Freddie." Reaching out her hands, Jane pulled Lorraine into an embrace. "I thank you so much for trying to help me. It's been so nice to have just an ounce of kindness shown towards me, but I need to be real. I need you to go now."

"Are you going to come to tomorrow's session?" asked Lorraine.

"Well hell yeah, it's Helen's turn tomorrow; I can't wait to see what the spawn of Satan has got to say."

Lorraine grinned, "She won't talk."

"We can live in hope."

"You sure you want this?"

"It's the only way. I will see you tomorrow." Jane gently pushed Lorraine out into the gravelled driveway. Lorraine walked over to her car and looked back at the palatial prison. "It's not the only way," she murmured to herself before she got in the car. "Not the only way at all."

Helen . . .

"How many weeks along are you dear?" the kindly looking midwife asked Helen.

"What difference does that make?" Helen snapped back.

"Well if you are less than thirty four weeks we can give you a steroid injection to help baby's lungs develop quicker and give him or her a better chance of survival."

"No need for that."

"Honestly dear, it makes a huge difference. Now, how many weeks along are you exactly?"

"It doesn't make any fucking difference." Helen insisted. "I was due to have a termination this Thursday, I'm not keeping it."

"Do you still feel that way? Things can sometimes change your mind."

Helen walked up to the midwife who stood behind the marbled top of the reception of Olinsbury labour ward. She put her face very close to the midwife's and said, "Maybe you should think about reading my notes before you ask me any more stupid questions?"

"Is there a problem?" the midwife took a step back out of Helen's space.

"Oh I don't know, there might be," came the sarcastic reply. "I'll tell you what. I'm going to go and sit over there," Helen pointed to the black plastic chairs which lined the walls of the reception area. "I may bleed onto your floor or pop a baby out, or, I don't know *die* over there, but you take your time. Go and find my notes and come back to me when you've got a fucking clue what you're doing ok?" Helen grinned sardonically.

"Please don't speak to the staff in that way," a chubby face popped up from behind the counter. An equally chubby hand pointed to a poster bearing the proclamation 'Anybody acting in an aggressive manner will be asked to leave the building.'

"It's ok Jenny," the midwife said. "The young lady is right; I should go and read her notes. Take a seat please dear, I will be right back."

"At last, some sense." Helen said and walked over to the black chairs. Carefully taking a seat, she could feel the wetness squelching in her vagina and still felt the insistent heavy pain in the very bottom of her abdomen. She pulled her bag into her lap and checked the contents; pyjamas in case she had to stay. Wash bag, disinfectant spray so she could clean the showers before she used them. Clean knickers, her purse and Brian's photo in a waterproof frame. Another one of her favourites, him sitting on a steel gate, the bars not really wide enough to support a human torso. Stroking the picture Helen remembered how Brian had lost his balance and fallen off the gate just moments after the photograph had been taken.

"Sorry Helen," the midwife returned, holding medical notes under her arm. "I'm Patricia by the way," she said holding out her hand for Helen to shake, which she did. "I apologise, you are quite right, I should have read your notes. I have now."

"Oh good, so you know?"

Patricia patted Helen on the shoulder, "Yes dear, I know. Do you want to come with me? I will get you settled into a room and then we can speak about what is going to happen."

"I already know."

"I'm sure you do dear, but just so my mind is at rest I'd like to go through things with you. It could be a bumpy ride and we may be together for a few hours so let's get to know each other a bit better." Patricia led Helen to a room, almost bare except for a hospital bed, cupboard and sink. The bed looked more like a massage table; no sheets, black PVC covered mattress which was split into two. Metal stirrups were propped either side of the end of the bed. Helen gave a silent prayer that her feet wouldn't end up in those cold loops. Patricia went to the cupboard and removed a thick paper sheet, placed it on the top half of the split mattress and gestured for Helen to join her at the bed.

"If you want to get changed into one of our robes, it may save your clothing." She said, producing a cotton robe from the same cupboard.

"If you put it on and pop yourself on the bed, I will give you a quick examination and see how along we are."

"It's still hurting." Helen said, sounds of fear now invading her usually confident tone.

"Yes it does hurt." Patricia agreed. "But not for long. It's the most natural thing in the world and always forgotten once baby comes along." She stopped, raising a hand to her mouth in consternation. "I'm so sorry."

"Don't be, I'm sure you've used that line a thousand times."

"I'm sorry Helen. It won't be for long and I will give you as much pain relief as you need."

Helen bent over as another shockwave of pain shot through her. "We better hurry up," she hissed through gritted teeth. "I think its coming."

Jane . . .

"Dog?" Freddie shouted as he walked into his house.

"Here dog, where are you?" he donned some white gloves which sat in their usual place by the door. "Hope my house is clean you lazy bitch." He shouted again. Rubbing his fingers along the tops of the wooden furniture as he walked deeper into the house, Freddie grimaced as he saw a smudge of grey on the tips of his white fingers.

"Dirty fucking dog," he whispered.

"Hello Freddie," Jane was kneeling in the doorway of the dining room, scrubbing brush in hand as she had been cleaning the white door frames.

"Look at my gloves," he spat at her, "You've been a bad dog."

"I'm sorry Freddie, I've been at work. I've only just started the cleaning."

"Talking today she is," Freddie muttered to himself as he walked around the dining room, rubbing his fingers over the chairs and tables and tutting as he brought his hands up to check them.

"Dirt everywhere."

"I am doing it Freddie. I promise it will be all done in a few hours."

"No sleep for the doggy until the house is clean." He said, still not looking in Jane's direction. Jane began frantically scrubbing at the door frame again. Freddie walked up to her and bent down, gently taking Jane's hand in his. Jane stopped scrubbing and sat back on her haunches, smiling up at Freddie as he held her hand in his. He reached out and stroked Jane's cheek. "Daddy may be having people over tonight."

Jane's heart sank. "Ok Freddie, would you like me to get some canapes and drinks out on the table for when you come back?"

"Yes dog, that would be nice, make sure you're clean and looking pretty, my friends might want to play."

"Please Freddie, not today. I have my period." Freddie grabbed Jane's face in his hand and squeezed hard, squashing her cheeks and mouth very painfully.

"Dogs can't speak." He said quietly. He pulled his hand away from her face and walked away from her, whistling. Jane watched his back as he walked away and scolded herself for being so gutless earlier on. Why hadn't she just gone with Lorraine when she had the chance? Jane knew that she had been right though, the only way she would ever escape his clutches was if he was dead. She imagined taking a knife and plunging it in between his shoulder blades, deep, twisting and turning the blade as Freddie begged for his life. She wouldn't stop until the knife worked its way through to his body and thrust out of his neck.

A look of determination fixed itself onto Jane's face. Maybe she *would* do something about her shitty life today. Maybe she *would* kill that fucker and maybe her baby would actually have a chance at life. Maybe, just maybe.

Helen . . .

"Here's your baby Helen." Patricia said, handing a small bundle over into Helen's embrace. "He's beautiful." A tiny face was visible under a woollen hat, eyes closed, mouth slightly open. Looking down at the face of her son, Helen experienced a warm glow which spread from her middle where her muscles quivered gently and up to her face. She tingled all over with the love that burst from her.

"Hello little man," she whispered and brought the baby up to her nose so she could breathe in the scent of him. "Yes he's beautiful," she agreed and smiled at Patricia. "How long?"

"It's hard to tell, maybe a few hours."

"Can I look?"

"He's your baby Helen; you are most welcome to do whatever you need to do. You can bathe him, change him and cuddle him; I think he would love that."

"He's too small for all that; I'm not bathing him, that's ridiculous."

"It's just a way of having some time together," Patricia said quietly, "But he seems quite happy just being with you." She gently caressed the tiny baby's face with her index finger. "Little cherub," she soothed.

"Can I have some time alone with him?" Helen snapped.

"Of course you can," Patricia handed Helen a small white box. "There's some stuff in here which you may find useful." She smiled. "There's a camera and some ink with card so you can take hand foot prints. Little memories."

"Pointless."

"It may seem that way now, but trust me; at some point in the future you will be glad you did it." Helen threw the box to the floor beside the hospital bed.

"I'll leave you two alone." said Patricia, backing out of the room. "Just press the orange button if you need anything. Are you sure there's nobody I can phone for you?"

"All I need is to be on my own."

Helen watched the door close behind the kindly midwife. "Don't actually have anyone." She said to the door and then turned her attention to the little baby lying in her arms.

"You look so normal." She said to him, "so perfect, but you're not are you? My fault. I made you wrong, it's all my fault, I'm sorry."

Helen copied Patricia's caress, using her index finger to gently stroke the pink cheek of her son. She traced the lines of his face, over the bump of his perfect nose and along the line of his tiny lips. The baby didn't react to her touch in any way. She could only be sure he was alive as she felt the warmth from his body and the fluttering breaths from his chest. Helen moved her finger up to the baby's brow and began to remove the green woollen cap. She wondered who had taken the time to make the little article and gave thought to all the other babies whose head it may have sat on before in the premature baby unit and how many tears it may have soaked up as parents sat holding their dying babies, or cried with joy at their new addition to the family; such a simple piece of material which had such an important place in the first moment of life.

Her finger pushed the hat up and off the baby's face. "And there it is," she said, a tear forming in the corner of her eye. "The missing piece of the puzzle and the most important bit, I'm so sorry."

Helen looked down at the baby's head where the skull should be; there was nothing. It was like his head just ended at the top of his eyebrows.

The doctor had told Helen the baby had a condition called anencephaly, "Baby has developed a brain stem and so its body can perform the very basic functions, whilst your umbilical cord feeds it and keeps the body hydrated." The doctor had explained. "But once baby is born it will only live for a very short time. I'm sorry to tell you the baby will not be able to feed or to respond to your touch; neither will he be conscious of his surroundings. The comforting thing is that the baby will not be able to feel any pain either as there is no brain there. Baby won't be aware of anything. It's up to you how you want to proceed; we can terminate the pregnancy, or you may choose to go full term. Similarly you can let nature take its course; there is a high miscarriage rate in these circumstances. I'm sorry Helen; I wish it was better news."

Helen hadn't realised she was pregnant until she had been eighteen weeks. Grief had prevented her from noticing the changes which had been going on in her body. Her first shock and delight at being pregnant had tragically ended in more grief and heartbreak when she had lain on the bed and sonographers had gone from professionally enthusiastic to quiet consternation.

"My fault?" she had asked.

"It's not known why it happens," the doctor had assured her, "Some suggest that taking folic acid before getting pregnant and throughout the early stages of pregnancy can help to prevent it."

"Which I didn't so *it is* my fault."

"No, no," he reassured her, "There have still been cases even when a woman does that. Its just nature I'm afraid. Nature can produce the most intricate things; humans are probably one of the most complex beings which nature has created, but it doesn't have a hundred percent success rate. Sometimes the sums don't add up right; instead of adding up, nature subtracted. We as humans can hope to help the equation, but life is a difficult sum and sometimes two and two don't make four."

"I was never very good at maths." Helen had said. "Get rid of it."

"Get rid of you," she whispered at the baby boy, "How could I have even thought about doing that?" she pulled the hat back over the baby's brow and blew gently onto his face. Still no reaction came, no flicker of an eye or movement of the lips. Nothing which showed her son to have the feelings she wished he could have.

Helen reached for the picture of Brian which lay on the bedside table. She brought it up to the baby's face.

"Your son Brian," she said, "He looks like you." She kissed the picture. "He'll be with you soon." Laying the photo back onto the table, Helen said, "Daddy will look after you." She smiled. "I suppose I need to give you a name."

Helen thought back to Brian and his travelling. They had spoken about having children once he had got over his travel but. "One day I'll stop moving," he had grinned. "Then we'll have a football team."

"I'll be so old by then you'll be lucky if I can manage *one* child." Helen had grinned back.

"What name would you give it?"

"Kimani." Brian had stated.

"Oh let me guess, African?" Helen had replied sarcastically.

"Of course, you know I love Africa. It means 'adventurous traveller', the Kikuyu tribe use it as a surname."

"So our little boy gets a surname as a first name?"

"And why not? You can just call him Kim if you don't like it." Brian had shrugged.

"Kim." Helen said out loud. "Welcome Kim, I see you. Haban Jambo," she said in Swahili; a term Brian had used with her often. Helen brought the baby up to her face again and kissed his tiny lips, then settled down on the bed holding him close to her body.

"We will lay together little man and I will see you safely into the arms of your daddy. Don't be afraid, mummy's here."

Session Three . . .

"Good morning everyone."

"Hi Marc," Alice smiled, "How are you?"

Marc smiled kindly at the young woman before him.

"I'm very well thank you Alice." He glanced over at Lorraine who smiled brightly back. "Very well indeed."

"I have had a telephone call from Helen. She suffered a miscarriage last night so I'm afraid she won't be attending any more of our sessions."

"Oh that's very sad to hear," said Verity.

"Are you actually joking?" Jane asked aghast. "That's exactly what she deserved; she is a horrible, horrible woman."

"No one deserves that." Amelia mumbled.

"Come on, that just isn't a very nice thing to say." Said Verity.

"Let's just stop and think about this for a second." Lorraine said, "She's actually been really lucky."

"Lucky?" asked Alice, "Lucky how?"

"Well she's had the choice taken away from her now. She's had the *guilt* taken away from her. You can't help it if you have a miscarriage. Nature has taken over and now she can be the angel in it all."

"How so?" Alice asked once again.

"Well think about it," Amelia agreed, "What happened to your baby Helen?" She said in an affected accent, she then turned and replied to herself in sarcastic Helen fashion.

"Oh sadly I lost the baby. I was all set to have the little cherub and nature took over, oh woe is me." She rubbed her eyes, "Lucky bitch looks like a poor victim instead of the heartless uncaring cow she actually is."

"Oh," Alice looked shell shocked, "That *is* actually lucky." She retracted into her own thoughts, weighing up the odds of the same fate befalling her before tomorrows scheduled abortion.

"I don't think we should make any assumptions." Marc counselled. "Helen hadn't given us her story yet, we really don't know anything about her."

"We know she's a sour bitch who has jumped on every one of us in this room and made us all feel bad." Amelia said. "She said she was going to kill her baby just as if someone may say 'I'm going shopping.' It was all a big game to her. "

"Some books have very hard covers," Marc said silently. His statement brought silence to the group; each woman's face registered different emotions.

"Profound," Verity broke the silence.

"Just food for thought," Marc offered.

Verity snorted, "Well I am done thinking about Helen. Does anyone want to hear my story? I think I'm ready to tell you all." Heads nodded and Marc signalled to Verity to carry on.

Hello my name is Verity . . .

"Ok, well hello, my name is Verity." Smiles shone back at the middle aged woman.

"You may be able to tell from my voice that I'm pretty 'well off' as they say. I was actually dreading saying that in front of Helen, can you imagine the come backs?" Verity sighed. "Anyway, yes if they were to look at the rule book of class, I was born with a silver spoon in my mouth. High class, almost royalty; there are Barons and Ladies in my family and yes, I have met the queen."

"Oh what's she like?" asked Alice, face shining with the joy of youth.

"Old," Verity said solemnly.

Alice giggled. "Is she nice?"

"Yes, and very funny actually. I usually bump into her at Royal Ascot. Every June she goes there to watch the horse racing. It's an amazing event; the highlight of my calendar year. So colourful with plants and flowers everywhere. There was even a horse made out of flowers one year. Each day Queenie comes in a different colour and of course the people; oh the people. The women wear the *most* beautiful outfits and also some of the weirdest. I saw a woman with a fish on her head once."

Alice laughed out loud. "Seriously?"

"Seriously. Yes I love going to the horse races and I own my own horses. Not racers; just ones which I keep as pets and ride on. Anyway getting back to my story. I have never had any children. I can't say why exactly, I was very busy when I was younger; really enjoyed being a socialite and travelling between countries, doing 'the circuit' as we like to call it. Due to my high social standing, it is expected that I am involved in some sort of charity events. We like to 'give back'." Verity spoke in a jovial manner and constantly used her fingers to make imaginary quote marks in the air whenever she was using the same old clichés attributed to her society.

"So I did what I had to do. I hosted events, coffee mornings, blah, blah. I was the original lady who lunches; still am actually. My charity functions are well known and loved in my circles. Jane, your dad regularly attends my themed nights, he's a great contributor."

"That's because it's tax deductible." Jane sneered.

"Well yes darling," Verity shrugged, "That's the *only* reason most of the upper class are so enthusiastic." She smiled, "you don't think they really give a damn do you? Everyone is out for themselves at the end of the day. The men are tirelessly making money and keeping it out of the tax man's grasp whilst the women back them up with their 'selfless' charity work. My husband is a millionaire, comes from old money. He is well known and very well respected; I love him as I'm supposed to. We do everything expected of us and very rarely do we come to blows. It's a very convenient marriage and he's a good man. He's never violent or even loud; I have a lot of respect for him myself." Verity stopped and picked at a thread on her top.

"The only problem with my husband is he is so God damned *boring*. Honestly, every day of my life now is pretty much the same. I have been hosting these events for over twenty years, been to countless lunches, coffee mornings, tea dances, balls and brass band functions, snore, snore.

Sex is *so* mundane and robotic with him, it's just another thing which we do. Missionary style, on, bang, off. It wouldn't surprise me if he goes off to a gangbang when he's away on his business trips. He just must be getting his rocks off elsewhere. I am tempted to look into his private closet, I bet it's just chock full of whips and gimp masks."

Jane flinched at Verity's gimp mask comment.

"Sorry dear," Verity looked chagrined. "It was just meant to be a joke. I wasn't thinking."

"No, no it's fine, honestly."

"I know it *sounds* ridiculous, but I've read the newspapers and to be fair, I've been getting my kicks elsewhere too. It all happened just like something out of a Jilly Cooper novel. I employed a stable hand, Junior; again with the charity head on. It was to offer help, to give people from deprived communities a chance. For ex-prisoners to get rehabilitated and give back to society. I am so full of it, it's unbelievable." Verity shook her head in disgust.

"We all try and outdo each other and this was my way of beating my friend Binks, who had a one armed gardener and a transvestite chauffeur."

Guffaws of laughter hit the room.

"I'm not even joking," said Verity. "So Junior came to my stable, he's from 'The Ends' as he liked to call it.

Croydon to the rest of us. God he is handsome. So black, his skin shines. I think he has Kenyan heritage, you know, like a Masai warrior? Honestly his skin is almost purple it's so dark. I just love it, so smooth, mm, delicious. He's young too, twenty two and he's been in a little bit of trouble with the 'five oh' as he calls them. He got arrested a couple of times for gang related crimes and they gave him the opportunity to leave it all behind him before it got too bad and to come and work for me. Oh boy does he work for me. The muscles on him are so delicious and I just *love* his accent."

"A bit of rough?" Amelia asked sceptically.

"Well why on earth not?" Verity was indignant. "He's willing and so am I. well I don't need to go into great detail, but I will say that my love for horses grew and I have spent much more time in the stables lately. You can guess the rest, I came up pregnant. For a mad moment I considered that I may keep the baby, but how do you explain a chocolate coloured baby to your lilywhite husband? No, I've never had a baby; I'm far too old to go through such a massive change in my life, not just physically but emotionally as well. And of course financially, I will be a social outcast and the poor bastard baby will never know a happy day in his life. No one knows; it's just a matter of one more day and the indiscretion will be rectified. Then I can get back on the pony as it were. You probably think I'm disgusting and I probably *am* disgusting, but that's the way it's going to be. That's the way it *has* to be."

"I understand." Said Amelia.

"Really?" Verity looked hopeful.

"Well yeah. It's not that much different to the reason why I'm doing it, or why Alice is doing it." Said Amelia. "A baby just isn't right for our lives at the moment. I have my job, you have your life and Alice has the whole world ahead of her. A baby would destroy it right now. None of us are very far along, by Friday we won't be pregnant anymore and we can go back to our lives. When things are different, later on in life, then there may be a time for babies."

"Well not for me at my age," said Verity. "I'm over fifty so this would be my last hurrah as it were."

"Do you think you can live with that?" asked Lorraine. "I mean we're all younger. Whatever choices we make now we can have a chance at a baby later. You can't, this really is your last chance."

"Darling, every month of my life I've had a chance at a baby and I've spent the last thirty years making the decision to not have one. Just because I've accidentally got pregnant this month, doesn't mean my decision is going to be any different. It's a slip up, a mistake and I'm happy to correct that mistake. If you must know it's not my first mistake, there was the butler and my personal assistant in previous times."

Alice gasped.

"Yes I know, I am a little embarrassed to admit this will be my third termination. But it's not like I go out to get pregnant, sometimes you get caught up in the moment, or your pill doesn't work for whatever reason. Hell even the condom splits sometimes. I don't use termination like a contraceptive, but when the usual doesn't work then I have to put it right. I'm at peace with it. I won't be changing my mind."

"That's understandable," said Amelia graciously.

"Thank you for sharing Verity," said Marc. "Are there any comments."

"I just wondered why they sent you for counselling?" asked Jane. "I mean we all have a dilemma about our pregnancies; the doctor refused my abortion unless I attended this session. He said that speaking to other women like me might help me to be comfortable with my decision, or help me to change my mind as it was obvious to him that I didn't really know what I wanted to do. But you seem so sure, so comfortable with it all, why are you here?"

"I think they saw me as some sort of serial abortionist; the terminator." Verity laughed, "He also saw my age, the fact I had no children and he decided that he didn't want the lawsuit if he failed to tick all the psych boxes. I didn't mind coming, like I said my life is quite boring and this is a bit of an adventure for me. Sorry if that sounds heartless." Verity looked embarrassed, but Jane smiled.

"No I like your honestly," Jane said, "It's been lovely to get to know you. To get to know all of you. This has been an adventure for me too. I know one day I will have the strength to leave Freddie and then maybe I'll give Junior a call."

"I'm not giving Junior up darling. He's all for me, but I think he's got a brother."

"Has he got a sister?" asked Lorraine to much laughter.

"Ok ladies. Thank you all," said Marc. "We would be hearing from Helen next, but obviously she's not here. Let's all have a tea break and then we'll come together again and I will go through what's going to happen tomorrow. If you wish to tell the group whether a final decision has been made or give us an update before we leave today, then you are very welcome to do so. I will see you all in fifteen minutes. Lorraine can I see you outside please?"

"Yes sure." Lorraine jumped from her chair and followed Marc out of the room.

"I wonder what they're up to." Amelia said to Verity.

"He wants her baby," said Verity.

"What? Really?" Amelia and Alice gathered around Verity at the refreshment table.

"How do you know?" asked Alice.

"She told me this morning. Went around to visit his wife last night and hear their story. It's all very tragic apparently."

"Is she going to do it?" asked Alice, "Give them the baby?"

"I don't know, but she is definitely thinking about it. I mean she's a lot further along than us, her baby kicks her; she knows it's alive in there. We just have the knowledge that there could potentially be a baby, but it's just cells. I think I'd be different if I felt something moving inside me.

"Well she needs to make her mind up quickly, I mean, it's the abortion day tomorrow." Said Amelia.

"Will it hurt?" asked Alice, "The abortion I mean."

"Oh no dear, not physically anyway," said Verity. "They make you kind of drowsy and then it's all a bit of a blur really. It's afterwards that the real pain starts; guilt is a very powerful emotion and you *will* feel guilty.

Even though we all know it's right for us and we keep talking about cells and such like; the fact remains we are doing just what Helen said - killing a baby."

"Stop Verity, this isn't what a young girl needs to be hearing." Cautioned Amelia.

"I'm sorry Alice,"

"No, it's ok. You're right, I know what I'm doing and I know there are lots of people out there who believe that its wrong and a sin, but I have to do it. It's the right thing to do; for me and my family and especially for Kieran."

"A very mature attitude Alice," Verity put her arm around Alice's shoulders. "A very mature attitude indeed. Now, let's have some lunch, I could eat a horse."

"It's not lunch time yet," giggled Alice.

"Oh well tea then, potato, patata; whatever, I'm still hungry."

Discuss . . .

The ladies sat on their plastic chairs waiting for Marc and Lorraine to return. Both came into the room, Marc trailing Lorraine. Lorraine looked angry and Marc looked upset.

"Not going to plan." Amelia whispered to Verity.

"Well would you have a baby and give it to someone else?" Verity whispered back.

"People do it all the time," shrugged Amelia.

Marc cleared his throat as he sat down on his chair, sharing an annoyed look with Lorraine who turned her head away from him.

"Hope you all had a good break," he said in his gentle way. "Now tomorrow is the day when you are all scheduled to have the termination of your pregnancy." He looked in Lorraine's direction again and his angered face became almost pleading. "Some of you may have decided during these sessions that termination isn't right for you and some may now be more confident in going ahead with the termination as planned. Does anyone want to share their thought with the group as to how they intend to go ahead?"

"I will." A voice came from the door. The group turned and gasps came from the women when they saw Helen walking into the room.

"Didn't think we'd see you again," said Amelia. "I'm sorry for your loss."

Helen didn't come back with a comment; instead she looked at Amelia kindly and then went over to her and hugged her. Amelia looked like someone who had been caught in the rain. As though she was trying to get away from the wet clothes which enshrouded her, a look of disgust on her face. Helen broke free and smiled at Amelia.

"I'm sorry for being such a bitch." She said, and then turned to the rest of the group. "I'm sorry to all of you for how I've been; especially you Jane."

It was Jane's turn to look uncomfortable. "It's ok." She mouthed.

"No, no it's not ok. I have been a complete bitch to everyone in this room. I have laughed at you, tormented you and criticised you for your decision to have an abortion. Nobody deserves that. We've all gone through different things in our lives and we all have reasons why we don't want to have the babies. I should not judge you because your reason is different to mine. I shouldn't decide who is right or who is wrong for what they are doing. You have all sat here and just listened, yes you have given an opinion, but you haven't judged. I *have* judged. I have hated you for the decisions you are making, because if I had had a choice there is no way I would ever have thought about having an abortion."

"Well you were going to have one." Said Alice. "Amelia said you would do this."

"Do what?" Helen asked.

"Be the victim now that you have miscarried." Amelia spoke over Alice. "You had a miscarriage and now you can claim that you never wanted the abortion in the first place. That you were never going to go through with it. You are just one of the victims."

"Now you have come here to laugh at all of us." Agreed Jane. "What's the joke today? Who are you going to harass and bitch about today? You've missed Verity's story . . ."

"Long story short, got done by the stable boy." Verity laughed.

"Yes, what do you think about that?" Jane asked sarcastically. "Rode him like a donkey she did and now she's sucking out the little baby like it's a pile of rubbish."

"Jane, please." Verity looked shocked at Jane's harsh words.

"Oh I'm so, so sorry." Jane looked ashamed, "I just got carried away in the moment and it's what she does to me. I didn't mean to be mean Verity. I'm so sorry."

"Is that what you all think?" Verity asked the room.

"We haven't got time for all this," Amelia harrumphed. "We have all been through our reasons; Verity yours is no different to mine, or to Alice's. It's just not the right time. No one can judge us for our decisions, after tomorrow this will all just be a distant memory and we can get on with our lives as if nothing happened. There are only *two* people in this room who should even think about having a baby and that's Lorraine." Amelia turned to Lorraine who was trying to shrink back into her chair.

"Lorraine, you are so far along in your pregnancy that you are going to have to give birth to this child aren't you? I mean it can't be as simple as them sticking a pipe up there and sucking it away, it's a fully formed human being. I heard of one baby being born a week before the abortion limit date and it survived. Seriously, it was given only a one percent chance of surviving the birth, but once it had done that then the odds changed and it just got stronger and stronger. That baby is alive today and so could yours be. I know that Marc has asked you to give the baby to him."

"Please, I don't think that's any of your business." Marc interjected.

"Women talk," Amelia shrugged. "I thought we were all here for the same reason. Marc wants your baby Lorraine. I don't know his circumstances; why he wants it, what he can give it, how his living arrangements are etc. But I do know this. If you give birth to a dead baby you are going to have that image with you for the rest of your life. You are going to know that you killed that little baby and that you could have saved it. For the short time I have known you, I don't think you could live with that. You have shown me that you are kind, sensitive and loving. You gave up on your staunch butch lesbianism to allow your body to be treated as a vessel so that your partner could have a baby. This is no different; this is you being a vessel for Marc. There is no love there and the reasons are obviously different, but the outcome can be the same - someone who wants a baby gets a baby. You get to be the heroine and baby gets to live. If you want my true opinion, don't kill your baby."

"Well thanks for that Jeremy Kyle," said Lorraine.

"I'm sorry, I had to say it. There could be a chance of happiness there and I'm a great believer in happiness." Amelia turned to Jane. "And you Jane, you should keep your baby. If there was ever a time when someone should triumph through adversity, it's now. You *so* deserve to have a good life. I mean ok you were a pretty vacuous person before you met Freddie; didn't exactly light up the world with your altruism, but you weren't evil. You don't deserve what has happened to you. You are a perfect example of what happens when bad people seek to destroy others. Freddie is evil; he doesn't deserve to walk on the planet. Your baby could be the good that comes from all this bad. You deserve to have some happiness in your life. You should have the baby and Freddie needs to be dealt with. I could deal with him, run the fucker over with my car; that would put a stop to him. I could make sure that he never hurts you again."

Amelia breathed heavily with the emotion of her soliloquy. She looked around the room at the women who looked at her open mouthed. Helen was the only person with a slight smile on her face; still standing next to Amelia after their awkward embrace.

"Oh my," Amelia said. "Sorry, it must be hormones. Of course I would never do anything like that."

"Even though he deserves it?" Jane asked.

"Well, he *does* deserve it," Amelia smiled, "But I'm not going to do it to him, even though I wish I could."

"I think we would all like to deal with Freddie boy," said Lorraine.

"This is not the appropriate forum to start discussing that kind of thing." Said Marc. "Jane, are you ok? Do you wish to say anything to Amelia?"

"No, she's entitled to her opinion; I wouldn't mind running him over either." She smiled.

"Lorraine?" asked Marc. "Do you wish to respond to Amelia?"

"No."

Marc's heart thumped in his chest. He thought maybe Amelia had helped to make Lorraine's decision for her. Since Lorraine had visited the house and met Eleanor, nothing had been certain. He had thought the meeting went well. They had been very honest with Lorraine, told her all about the pregnancies; even about Eleanor's stint in the home. 'We have to be completely honest with you.' Eleanor had said to Lorraine. Marc was starting to wonder if maybe they should have left out the bit about Eleanor's mental health. Who would want to give their baby to someone who had become so unhinged? If Lorraine would only speak to him about it, he could get some closure on the situation, but every time she went outside to speak with him, she would just say that she was considering her options. Marc was silently screaming inside. His longing to hold a child in his arms was a physical pain. His arms ached with their yearning. Pictures of smiling babies would flash in his head; holding a baby, baby walking, baby laughing and baby calling him daddy. If his yearning had become so bad, he could only imagine at the ache inside of Eleanor. Lorraine could make all of that go away; she could turn the pictures into a reality. She could make

Eleanor whole again. It was killing Marc not knowing how this was going to turn out.

"Ok, thank you for your input Amelia; if you are ready we can go through the process of tomorrow."

"Don't you want to hear my story?" asked Helen.

"Do you wish to give it?" asked Marc.

"I didn't come back for the fun of it. I mean I know I've lost the baby, but believe it or not, I have actually developed feelings for all of you. I want to tell you my story. I think I owe it to all of you after the horrible things that I've said. I want to get through to the end of this; I want to see you all through to the end."

"How nice of you." Said Jane sarcastically.

"You've said lots of times that you can't *wait* to hear what I've got to say," said Helen. "So don't you want to hear it?"

"I do." Said Alice.

"And I." agreed Verity.

"We all do," said Marc. If you would like to take your seat Helen and then start in your own time."

"Why thank you," said Helen. "I will."

Hi my name's Helen . . .

"Ok, first I want to start by saying sorry to all of you. Alice I'm sorry that I was so horrible about your relationship with teacher man. I really do think that he has sucked you into believing that he loves you. It is very easy for men to convince women of their love for them, they say all the right things; stuff you want to hear to make you feel special. But they are just words Alice. If he really loved you he would have waited until you were old enough to have a baby, to get married and to move in together. I think that he just wanted to have sex with you, told you what you wanted to hear and then used you. The fact he's run off to Coventry or wherever he's gone just seals the deal for me; he's not here supporting you and not standing up to take any responsibility or blame. Time will tell what the truth is, but I hope you're prepared for the reality, which is that he's probably onto the next girl by now."

"I didn't think this was about me." Alice complained.

"No, you're right," said Helen, "But I didn't give my true opinions before and I wanted to give them now; a fresh start if you will let me."

Alice thought about it for a second. "I suppose so, we're all in this together after all and you have just . . ." she nodded towards Helen's now empty stomach.

"Thank you Alice. You are very kind."

"You're probably right anyway." Alice shrugged. "I can't get in touch with him at all now; he seems to have disappeared off the planet. His number is blocked and no one seems to know where he is. You are *all* right, he has just used me. I know I'm doing the right thing now. I'm going to have the termination tomorrow and I'm going to get on with my life."

"That's lovely to hear." Smiled Helen. "Amelia, I owe you an apology also. It is not for me to judge whether you are right to choose your job over a baby. Every person is different and has different feelings and instincts. I have no right to judge you because you choose to terminate. No right at all and I'm sorry."

"Thank you." Amelia mumbled.

"The same goes to you Verity, I haven't heard your story but I can guess from your stable boy comment, forbidden love?"

"Something like that."

"Yes, well that's up to you and how you choose to play your games is your business and nobody else's. If I had heard your story yesterday I probably would have called you a snooty bitch baby killer."

"And today?

"Today is today and I'm sorry for what I *would* have said."

"Ok, thank you for that."

"A pleasure. Lorraine, I have never met a woman such as you; you have put your life on hold to give your girlfriend a most precious gift. She has thrown that back in your face and now you have to decide whether you want to keep the baby you never really wanted, hand it over to Marc over there, or terminate and never let the baby exist.

Lorraine looked up at Marc accusingly. "I'm not an idiot Lorraine," said Helen, "It's so obvious. I don't hold any opinion over this. I don't think I have any right to. It's your life, your body, your baby. Only you can live with the consequences of what you do. Your only real decision is which consequence would be harder to live with. Consequence one; you have terminated a healthy baby who never asked to be brought into all of this mess. Deep inside you every day you will question whether you made the right decision. Deep inside you, you may even long for the baby that could have been. Consequence two, you have given birth to a baby and put it in the arms of a couple who desperately want one. You will see the baby grow, loved and cared for, but you will never be its mother. You need to look at both consequences and ask yourself which one you can live with, then you will know what decision you should make."

"I am thinking about it," snapped Lorraine.

"Yes, that's all you can do, but tomorrow you will have to go one step further than thinking. Tomorrow is do or die."

"I know that." Lorraine snapped again, "I will make the right decision, just leave me to it."

"I am sure you will." Helen agreed. "Jane, I owe you the biggest apology of all. I thought that my life was hard, that I had suffered some tragedy in my life, but you are just one big tragedy."

"Oh thanks a lot." Jane looked up from her usual floor stair. "That makes me feel *so* much better."

"I didn't mean it in a nasty way, I'm trying to explain." Helen threw her arms up in the air. "Oh for fucks sake, I'm sorry ok? And you're not a shrew."

"Yeah well you're still a bitch." Jane smiled.

"Yes and I love it." Helen smiled back. "Anyway, now that I've apologised to you all, I guess it's time to tell you my story. Sit back, this may take a while." Helen shuffled in her chair, she could feel blood leaking into her knickers, reminding her of the life which dwelt there just 24 hours previously. Her heart tugged at the thought of little Kim's face; she could still feel the warmth in her arms of where he lay yesterday. Wrapping her arms around herself, Helen began her tale.

"Hi, well my name's Helen. I also must go back a few years so that you understand how I have come to be sitting in this room. My childhood was blessedly happy, I had the most amazing parents; parents who loved and cherished me, their only child. We had some beautiful times and I will never forget just how happy my childhood was. As with all things, this can never last forever. One day my dad didn't come home. I was about fifteen and going through the usual teenage tears and tantrums. Mum would always say to me, 'You just wait until your father gets home.' And I *would* wait; I would wait for him so I could tell him just how horrible mum had been to me that day and he would smile at me and say, 'Just give her what she wants Helen, it's the only way to keep her happy.' One day after another row over something ridiculous, like the length of my skirt, I sat and waited for dad to come home, just like I always did; but he didn't come.

He died; killed by a lorry. He used to cycle to work as he worked in London and said it was much easier. Mum always used to say it was bloody dangerous, but he obviously had to go to work and always said that he'd be careful, but there's no accounting for lorry drivers is there? He never came home.

That was just the beginning of a steep slide into absolute crap. Mum tried hard to keep it together, but it's really hard when you lose a soul mate and the only person you can lean on is your teenage daughter who is going through her own personal tragedy and really hates you at the moment anyway. She turned to the ever faithful bottle of wine and I didn't really see a sober mother for the rest of my teenage years. Luckily dad had left behind some money and I was able to be pretty much self-sufficient through the wine years as I like to call them. Our family is traditionally a one child family; all through our family tree, every couple just had one child. It's great at Christmas, very cheap, but not so good when you need family. There just isn't anyone around. Once the grandparents have died and then your father, it's just mum. I hung around for a while after my teens were over, but we really didn't get on. I couldn't get over the fact my dad had left me; no fault of his own of course, but, my mother had also left me and that *was* her choice.

So I got my own little flat, went to work and pretty much forgot about my mother. I met a lovely guy called Brian. He was just the most wonderful guy, a little bit like my father which is probably why I liked him so much. We got on so well that we married and we were thinking about starting our own family one day. I was even going to break with tradition and make sure that I had more than the one child; hell I was going to have at least three."

"What happened?" asked Alice.

"I'm getting there," said Helen. "So when I got to about twenty five, there was a knock on the door. I answered it and there was this woman standing there. She was old, frail; you know when you see the white wispy hair? Sunken cheeks, eyes which seem glazed with milk somehow. Her skin was yellow; not sun-kissed yellow; bad liver yellow. 'Hi Helen,' she says, 'I'm sorry Helen.' She says. It was my mother. She had come to tell me that she was dying also. Her liver had been ravaged by the alcohol that she had drunk and she had Cirrhosis, but that wasn't what was killing her. Cancer had a hold of her stomach and bowels, she had only a short time to live and she wanted to make amends. Brian told me I should take her in, give her a chance and of course I wanted to as well; like I said, my childhood had been great.

Mum moved in with us and we would talk for hours and hours. Reliving all the wonderful times we had as a child. We talked about my dad and about stuff we had all done together. Over the first few days of her being there, we had wiped away all the bad things that had happened and we were living on the memories of the past. It was so wonderful to have my mother back. She may have been in a different body to the strong beautiful woman I remembered her as, but I could see her in there. Under the layers of wrinkled and yellow skin, I could see my mum. I could feel her love for me; it was great to have her back.

Brian said that he was going to start fundraising. He didn't really know how he could help my mum or me through the cancer. We all knew that she was going to die, it wasn't an 'if', it was just a matter of when. He signed up with the cancer charity and began going all around the world on long treks, raising awareness of cancer and making money for the charity. I was so proud of him; he had always had a wanderlust, one which I had never understood. We had spoken about going away together, but I only wanted to go for a week to packaged hotels with blue swimming pools and cheese toasties by the bucket load. He wanted to live with the tribes of Africa, pray at the temples in China and meet the Buddhists who sit on mountain tops. This was his opportunity. I was so busy with mum and so caught up in reliving my youth and remembering my dad that I was glad when he went. Yes I missed him, but he was doing it for a good cause. It kept him busy and it kept him away from the death which lingered by the door just waiting for mum to take her last breath.

Surprisingly mum took quite a long time to go. You would think that was a good thing, having her around for longer, but it isn't. All it is, is a chance to watch the person you love, slowly disappear in front of your very eyes. They stop being functioning human beings and just become like babies. Getting out of the bath is hard; going to the fridge is hard. Making a cup of tea is impossible because the kettle is heavy and the water is hot. Getting dressed can't be done, brushing hair is impossible because it's hard to hold the brush in the air. There just isn't any strength. Then it becomes hard to eat or drink; lifting a cup to the mouth is an effort. Eventually even fucking talking is an effort; all they do is lie there and breathe. That's all that we become when we have cancer; just a bag of breath. I sat there and watched her, watched her breathing. In, out, in, out, all day long. I held her hand; I spoke to her about life and what I wanted to do with it. I never saw Brian for months; of course I knew it was more than his fund raising keeping him away. Who wants to watch death?

On her last day, I kind of knew she was going to die. We had a visit from the Macmillan nurse who would always come and check her pain relief, ask if I was ok, did I need anything. On that day she came and gave mum an injection, like she always did, but this time she said to me, 'Not long now.' She patted me on the shoulder and asked me if I would like her to stay. She had never done that before. I said no, but I now knew that this was the day that mum and I had to say goodbye to each other. I sat by her bed and said, 'Bye mum.' Well what else do you say? And then again I just sat there and watched her breathe. In, out, in, out, in, out... no more in. I had been breathing along with her, you do that. You match their breathing, willing them to take another breath, god alone knows why. And I realised that I wasn't breathing anymore; there was nothing to match, she had just stopped.

Brian couldn't come back for the funeral, he was stuck somewhere in Kenya so I buried her alone. Then I just got on with my life again, the same way I had done when my dad died. I just got up the next day and carried on living as if the last few months hadn't happened. I went out and got a new job, then came home every day and had face time with Brian. It's like mum had never happened.

Brian came back eventually. He was sorry that he had been away, but I understood. It didn't matter, it wasn't his problem and hey he was fundraising money for cancer charities, doing his bit for the people who were still suffering so much loss in their lives. He carried on like that for a couple more years, going off and coming back; the last time he came back was just like any other, we had our dirty weekend like we always do, but this time I had to tell him that I had cancer."

"Oh my god." Amelia gasped.

"I know right?" Helen shrugged. "I was offered a genetic test about eight months ago. It was the first real contact I'd had with the doctor since my mum had died. I had been feeling a bit tired and kept getting bruised really easily, it seemed like even the slightest knock would result in a blue arm. I also had the shits like you wouldn't believe, couldn't go too far away from a toilet, if you know what I mean. So I went to see the doctor and he told me he would like to do some blood tests. He asked me about mum and how I was coping and then suggested that whilst he was doing the tests, he could check for the probability of me getting the same kind of cancer. 'It's quite unusual to get it so young,' he told me, meaning mum, she was only fifty you see. That's why it was so shocking to see her looking so old when she came to the door. I mean who has white hair like that in their fifties? Well I let him do the tests; he assured me it was highly unlikely that I had the bowel gene as it wasn't in the family, but just to put my mind at rest, blah blah. Well turns out I did have the gene. Not only did I have the gene, but I had the bloody cancer as well; Hereditary nonpolyposis bowel cancer"

"Oh that's so sad," said Verity.

"Yeah tragic," Helen spat back. "Yes poor me, now I'm fucking dying with the same cancer that my mother had. Not only did she bring herself back to me, but she brought the cancer with her. I swear it's like it was contagious or something. I had spent so much time around it, washing her, feeding her, taking away the dirty sheets and towels. It's like it infected me, jumped into me and now it's eating me alive."

"There's nothing they can do?" asked Amelia.

"No, I wouldn't let them. What's the point? I'm only going to die at the end of it, I'd rather have a relatively pain free existence until death comes. I don't want to lose my hair or be stuck on a chair having chemo pumped into me. I don't want to sit in a cage whilst they zap me with lasers that are only going to corrupt my heart or my kidneys. I'm dying anyway; I might as well just go out looking pretty."

"How does Brian feel about it? Did he run away again?" asked Alice.

"Brian, yes well that's the biggest tragedy of my life," admitted Helen. "Brian was obviously shocked when I told him, but he picked himself back up again and said that he was going to be there for me. He was going to help me get through it and we were going to face the cancer together. He almost convinced me that I should have the chemotherapy, say yes to the radiation treatment and maybe even an ileostomy bag. First of all he had to do one more charity trek. He had already committed to it and couldn't let all his followers down; he had a blog where he put all his achievements up and people could congratulate him and make donations. Over a hundred thousand pounds he raised."

"What a trouper," said Verity.

"Yes, good old Brian," agreed Helen. "Well his last trip was to Sierra Leone. He never came back."

"Why?" asked Alice.

"Ebola," Amelia told her.

"Yes, that's right. Would you fucking believe it? Could my life actually get any worse? Brian contracted Ebola Virus. I couldn't even get his body back. He literally spoke to me on the Monday, told me he had a bit of a cold and was finding out about coming home because there had been an outbreak and people were talking about quarantining the whole place. I started to call the Home Office and ask them what they were doing to repatriate people who had become caught up in it out there. Thursday morning I get a call back from the Home Office to tell me that Brian's cold had been more than just that and that he was dead actually and had been buried immediately to prevent a spread of the virus taking place. I couldn't get any of his stuff back, not even a pair of fucking socks. It's like he never existed. All I have is my memories and of course I did have his baby growing inside of me."

"That surely was a joy?" asked Verity.

"Yes a fucking joy." Helen spat again. "That's why I was at an abortion therapy group. That's why I was going off to kill it; it was bringing so much joy into my life."

"Isn't it a part of Brian, a bit of him to keep and to live on?"

"And who was going to look after it? I'm *dying*. There's no one else in my family who would want to look after little orphan Annie."

"Could have been adopted." Offered Lorraine. "You all seem to think its good enough for my baby."

"I couldn't have done that. I couldn't have done anything with the baby."

"Why not?"

"Because it wasn't right. I don't mean right as in good or bad; I mean right as in whole. I didn't have a whole baby growing inside me."

"You can't have half a baby growing inside you, can you?" asked Alice.

"No, no it's not that." Helen started to feel agitated, "please just let me explain. I don't know if it's a consequence of having cancer, or because I didn't take folic acid. I wasn't expecting to get pregnant as I have always been on the pill, but I suppose when you are taking so many pain killers and your body isn't working right, then the pill kind of goes wrong. But when Brian came home that last time, we had our fun like we always did and obviously some of his little swimmers got through. Well I was actually so happy when I found out I was pregnant. You are right Verity I thought it was Brian's way of staying with me. It also justified my reasons for not having treatment; I didn't want to damage the baby in any way and I did hope that I could stay alive long enough to see the child into the world. I didn't really think past that. Didn't consider who would look after the baby once I had died, I guess I just thought that I would get through it, you know? Get over the cancer, maybe go into spontaneous remission and live happily ever after.

Obviously with my luck that was never going to happen. The twelve week scan came up and off I went, Brian's photo in my hand so that he could be there too. I sat excitedly waiting to see my little baby's picture on that fuzzy screen, but all I saw was pain once again. My baby had no brain."

"What?" Jane gasped this time.

"Yes, sounds ridiculous doesn't it. Anencephaly it's called; Google it. It's real. There are many babies born this way but they rarely survive and if they do, they are just like my mum. Breathers. Just bags of bones and breath. I had a decision to make; keep the baby and hope for a swift death once it was born, or put it out of its misery and have the abortion. I don't think there was much choice really; of course I had to ease his suffering. Of course I had to have an abortion. They made me come here because of all the loss I have suffered, just in case I can't cope you know? But I can cope. I will just carry on like I always do. Pick up and move on, that's the best way to deal with death."

"How was it?" asked Alice. "The baby I mean. Did you see it?"

"Him. I saw him."

"Him. A boy?"

"Yes a little boy; A beautiful little boy. And he was *actually* beautiful." Helen looked around her at the women who stared so intently at her. "He had big blue eyes, and all the right fingers and toes. There was just that one bit missing; the most important bit, but the only bit. I held him. Held him whilst he breathed; breathed with him again until there was no more. I watched him go into the arms of his daddy, my son. Kim."

"I'm sorry Helen," soothed Jane. "Sorry for your loss."

"I'm not sorry. I'm glad he's gone. He should never have *been* in the first place. I am dying; I could never look after him. He's better off where he is."

"What are you going to do now?"

"Now? Now I'm just going to carry on. I'm going to wake up each morning and go to bed each night. I'm going to be a complete cunt to whoever I meet because it suits me to be like that. I'm going to hate anyone and everyone. Hate my life and hate the shit that life has thrown at me and then I'm going to die. I have nothing to leave behind, no legacy. I haven't done anything for anyone, there's no hundred thousand pounds which I have raised for charity. I've just been a run of the mill human being with a shit life. That's what I'm going to do."

"That's so sad," said Jane.

"Sad? Yes. Tragic? Yes. Changeable? No." Helen shrugged. "That's just life."

"Thank you for sharing with us Helen," said Marc, "And thank you also, for coming back. It's very kind of you to come back here and share your story with us. It's kind of you to show that you have feelings for the women in this room. You have helped everyone here."

Heads nodded.

"Yeah right, did your degree in psychology teach you that? Of course people are going to feel better about their lives when they hear how shit mine is. Glad I can be of service right?"

"There is always someone worse off." Alice said, "My mother says that."

"Yeah well I am that someone." Helen laughed. "Let your mum know that you met rock bottom and she was a bitch. I'm going for a fag." Helen got up from her chair and stomped out of the room.

Discuss . . .

"That's so sad," Alice said.

"Yep," agreed Lorraine, "It's always the way; all the people who shout and scream, who abuse and bully . . ."

"Are the ones who have the most to cry about?" chipped in Amelia.

"Poor thing," Verity sighed. "I hated her yesterday."

"Me too," agreed Jane, "kind of still do really."

"Do you?" asked Alice, "She was the first person to cuddle you yesterday. I think she's a really nice person who has had a really hard time and is just lashing out. "

"The girl's grown up," said Lorraine. "Alice you sound like a much more mature person since Monday."

"I've learnt a lot," smiled Alice.

"We all have," agreed Lorraine. "So what happens now?" Jane asked Marc.

"Now we can stop and have a discussion about our final decision; tell each other if tomorrow is still going ahead or if you feel that maybe you have changed your mind," Marc glanced hopefully at Lorraine, who shifted uncomfortably in her chair. "Or you don't have to say anything; tomorrow is another day. This is a very important decision you all need to take in your lives; if you get to tomorrow and decide that you no longer wish to carry on, then you can walk away at any point. The fact of the matter is this is your body, your life and your decision. Does anyone wish to offer to the group how they feel right now and what their plans are for the future?"

"I'm definitely going ahead with tomorrow," said Alice. "I've realised I was really silly; he didn't love me. I've just been used."

"You really have grown up," smiled Lorraine.

"You don't all need to keep saying it," Alice flushed, "But you're right, I feel different. I have my whole life ahead of me. I may even have a career one day and be a successful businesswoman. I have *plenty* of time for a baby and I need it to be with the right person. Someone who treats me right and who wants the best for me."

"Go Alice."

"Thanks Verity, what are you going to do?"

"Oh there's no option for me," said Verity. "I will be going ahead with the termination and then I'm jumping straight back in the saddle as it were."

Jane and Amelia laughed. "Verity you are incorrigible," said Amelia.

"My mother always said that," laughed Verity. "How about you Amelia? What do you want to do?"

"Well I'm totally single now. My whole career ahead of me; I'm going to go onwards and upwards. I mean, I know the bosses daughter now," she said, winking at Jane.

"Good luck with that," Jane sneered, "You will have Freddie to contend with."

"Well with any luck I'll get higher than that guttersnipe and expose him for what he really is. I might be able to get to your father and let him know what has been going on," offered Amelia.

"Professional suicide," said Jane, "Don't waste your time. I would actually appreciate it if you could just forget you ever met me. Knowing me is going to get you nowhere in that company and if Freddie knew I had made a friend; my life wouldn't be worth living." Jane's voice had got progressively higher during her speech and her hands scratched frantically at her forearms.

"Don't worry Jane," soothed Amelia, "I would never tell on you. My lips are sealed; I promise. Come on now, calm down." She leant over and patted Jane on the knee, then took hold of her hand to put a stop to the scratching. "Come on Jane, calm down; breathe easy, it's going to be okay."

"It will never be okay," came Helen's voice as she re-entered the room.

"Back again?" sneered Jane.

"Yes Janey, I'm back again, I just can't get enough of the drama."

"Let's all just stop this," said Alice, "Please; we should be supporting each other."

"That *is* why I'm here," said Helen, "Sorry Jane, I can't help sounding like a bitch, it's just second nature to me now."

"It's okay," Jane said, removing her hand from Amelia's touch, "its okay Amelia, I'm okay."

"What are you going to do?" asked Amelia, "Are you going ahead with the abortion?"

Jane's tears, which always stood ready at her eyes, began to fall once more. "Yes I have to, I don't want to, but I just can't see any other way."

"You could try leaving him again," Lorraine offered.

"Like I did yesterday?" said Jane, "It was a pathetic attempt. *I'm* pathetic."

"I'm not going to disagree with you," shrugged Lorraine, "It seems so obvious to me, pack the bags, leave; simple."

"I can't."

"Yes you can Jane," Lorraine shook her head in exasperation. "You just *leave*. We can contact your dad; let him know what's been going on. He gets rid of Freddie, you get your life back, baby gets a mummy; happy days."

"Do you think the baby doesn't need a father?" asked Jane.

"Come on, you're talking to a lesbian here. I don't think men are necessary for *anything*; no offence," she smirked at Marc.

"None taken."

"You are perfectly capable of bringing up a baby. I mean even if you're shit at it, you've got so much money that you can pay for someone to look after it."

"And what about Freddie?"

"What about him?" asked Lorraine, "He can fuck off back to the stone he crawled out from under and go and lick his own fucking floors."

"That just won't work. You all don't know Freddie like I do. He will *never* leave me alone. Even if you could convince my dad otherwise, I don't think it would be long before he manages to inveigle his way back into my dad's good graces again; especially with a baby on the scene. When he gets me back? He will kill me."

"He can't kill you if he's dead," Lorraine said.

"Well that's hardly going to be the case," said Verity.

"I'd run him over," said Lorraine. "I'll pick the biggest car in my fleet, a nice limousine and I will run him over, it will be my pleasure."

"Nice idea," said Amelia, "Just like mine."

"Yes, nice idea," Jane said bitterly, "But you are hardly a murderer Lorraine."

"Don't underestimate me," Lorraine said, "I fought my way through three care homes. I'm hard as nails and ruthless as they come."

"Really?" asked Helen, "How *is* that baby that kicks inside your rough and tough shell?"

"What's that got to do with anything?"

Helen sat forward, "You gave up everything for a woman who went off with a man. You dropped your defences for love. You are no tougher than Alice over there," she said.

"You don't know me" Lorraine countered.

"I've heard enough to know that you won't do that," said Helen, "anyway what *are* you going to do with your little bundle of joy? Still intent on murder there are you?"

"Wow you just can't help yourself can you?" shouted Amelia. "Half an hour ago you were all apologies and now you've gone back on the bitch trip."

"I'm sorry," Helen looked suitably ashamed. "I can't help it, it's the only way I've coped until now and it's hard to be something different."

"Yeah well you don't need to be here anymore, so if you can't be constructive . . ."

"Constructive? What is constructive about offering to kill Jane's husband?" Helen guffawed. "It's *the* most ridiculous thing I've heard. You might as well tell her to stand up to him and knock him out. Gold plate his testicles. You are offering her a solution which you just won't deliver. It's the most un-constructive load of bullshit I've ever heard."

Now it was Amelia's turn to look ashamed, "Well we have to do something." She said.

"*We* don't have to anything. Jane is the only person here who can sort out her own problems. She's right in what she's saying. We have sat here all week talking about ourselves; 'poor me, poor baby,' blah, blah, blah. We've patted each other on the back and spouted crap about how everything is going to be ok, sympathised with each situation. Some of us are here for entirely different reasons," Helen looked pointedly at Marc. "Shameless in our own quests for something else in our life.

Marc stared uncomfortably at his clipboard.

"But the bottom line here is once all is said and done, we will go back to what we were doing before. Alice, you will go back to being the ditzy blonde schoolgirl; too mature for boys her own age and naïve enough to believe the sexual advances of a paedophile are love."

"No, that's not true," denied Alice, "I won't be doing that again."

"Believe what you like Alice, when Mr Summers, or whoever the next guy is, winks at you and tells you you're gorgeous; it will be all smiles and laughter. Although I do believe you won't be stupid enough to get pregnant again."

"Believe what *you* want, I don't answer to you. I have made my mistake and learnt my lesson. It doesn't bother me what you think, you are nothing to me." Alice said; red-faced.

"Ooh, she *has* grown up," Helen laughed. "I hope you prove me wrong Alice, I really do. Anyway, as I was saying . . ."

"Because you do so love the sound of your own voice," sniped Jane.

"True," Helen smiled sweetly back at Jane. "Amelia," she said, turning her head to look at the curly haired career woman, "You will continue to fuck your way to the top. You will probably even fuck Freddie if it suits you."

Amelia took in a sharp breath of disgust.

"Whatever Amelia, keep up the good work." Helen quickly moved on before Amelia could protest. "Lorraine, well when all is said and done, I hope you decide to give your baby to Marc over there. I can see his yearning, it eats him up inside. It probably keeps him awake at night and I can only imagine what his wife is like. I said before I don't know what the story is, but if you don't want that baby and they do then why not? Life is precious - it would be nice to see a balance between murder and salvation in this room. Verity you disgust me . . ."

"Why on earth . . ." Verity began.

"Yeah blah, blah; I'll tell you why you disgust me. I know I have gone back on saying 'it's ok', but as I talk about everyone else's reasons, I realise that you actually do disgust me. You play around in the stables, cheating on your husband; offering your vagina to any stable boy who might wish to dip into it. You think you can do it with impunity and you *were* getting away with it until you fell pregnant. Who gets punished for your promiscuity? An innocent child is the answer. People like you, who use abortion as a form of contraception, disgust me. You will go back to your Jilly Cooper days and if you make the same mistake again? The same thing will happen. You need to grow up and at least acknowledge that you have done wrong, it's not all jolly hockey sticks, clear out the womb and carry on; you have created a life and now you are going to end it."

Silence reigned in the room. Each person digesting what Helen had said and no one eager to continue the debate; Marc wrote on his clipboard then gave a silent cough before speaking.

"Helen, we are grateful that you came back here today and we are also grateful for your honesty."

"I'm not," said Verity.

"I am sorry," said Marc, "I am grateful for your honesty Helen; it is important that everyone gets a chance to give their opinions and for others to digest it.'

"I haven't finished yet," said Helen. "I am still to say my piece about Jane."

"I don't want to hear it," said Jane.

"Well tough because here it comes," Helen stood up and faced the rest of the silent group. "Jane, you are a victim. There are many nasty things I can say about that, but I'm not going to, because what I think is important here is not what you are but who you are. You are a mother. There is a baby growing inside of you who needs you. The baby needs you to be strong and to protect it. It needs you to make a secure and loving home for it and needs you to love it. Before you make your decision I beg you to consider what I have just said. Freddie is just an arsewipe, he is a scared little boy who bullies to make himself feel better; he may even benefit from becoming a father."

"You don't know him."

"Yes that is true and I am probably completely wrong there but, I'm not wrong about you. You can be a mother, you can love and cherish your boy and you can do it without Freddie. People in this room can help you; they can help you get away, they can help you regroup and make a new life for yourself. Hell, there are even people in here who seem willing to commit murder in order for you to get what you want, but that doesn't surprise me considering what you are all about to do tomorrow."

"Really?" Alice said sarcastically, "You are *still* going on like that? Unbelievable."

"Oh fuck off all of you. Do you know what? I don't know why I came here again today. I thought that I could maybe help. I have nothing left in my life; nothing. I have no mother, no husband, no baby, no days left in my life to enjoy. I could be dead this time next week, that's all I have to look forward to. There are no plans to make except funeral plans and do you know who will be at my funeral? No one. Not one single solitary person. I don't even have to make any fucking plans because nobody will be there. I can just leave myself to die and the council can put me in the communal graves. So excuse me if I don't feel sorry for any of you. Excuse me if I can see what you can't. Pardon me if I can see how ridiculous some of you are being and excuse fucking me if I tell you Jane that you *can* have that baby, just stop being a victim. Lorraine, you can give that baby away and carry on with your car business, I know the one it is, I've seen all the limousines outside, nice place, lucky you." Helen said sarcastically, "Shame about the baby hey? Amelia, sleep your way to happiness, good luck when you realise that it wasn't what you really wanted. Alice I hope you pass all your exams and go on to be something great in spite of your stupidity. Marc I hope you get what you want, I truly do and Verity? Fuck right off. Goodbye all of you miserable pond life, I'm . . ."

"Going for a fag?" Jane asked.

"Exactly," said Helen.

"Good riddance," Jane mouthed as Helen walked from the room. "It's so hard to feel sorry for someone, when they are *such* a bitch."

"I hear that," agreed Amelia. "Listen Marc, there doesn't seem to be much point in carrying on does there?"

Marc looked up from his clip board, "Yes absolutely we should carry on," he said. "This forum is for *all* of you. Helen has said her piece, she is going through a lot of turmoil in her life and although she has said some very hurtful things to all of you here today, you will have helped her a lot. Sometimes when people are facing death, they need to vent. They are angry and confused as to what is going on and it is easier to take out their anger on people around them. If Helen had someone at home then maybe she would never have come to this meeting. Today she had no need to come here, she has sadly lost her baby; but she came. She needed to be around people who knew her, needed to speak to people who may understand her. She may seem as though she lost control of her temper and her situation, but believe me; it will have been very cathartic for her to be able to release her tension with us. You have all given her a gift, albeit unwillingly and she will be able to go home and deal with her problems a little better now."

"I didn't see it like that," said Jane. "You are so right; she must be going through such utter desperation. There really is nothing left for her and the poor woman just lost her baby. Oh I feel just dreadful that I let her get to me again and that I didn't see what is now plainly the case. I didn't see a woman screaming for help, I was too busy looking into my own life and problems. Helen needed the cuddle which she gave me yesterday. She needed me to console her, all of us to console her and we didn't." Jane began to cry, "I am so sorry Helen, so sorry."

Tears twinkled in the eyes of all the other ladies in the room. "We must go and find her," said Amelia, "We must go and give her that hug that she needs; can you tell us where she lives Marc?"

"I'm sorry, no, that's confidential," said Marc, "But it's possible she will come to our session on Friday. We are the only people she has right now, so maybe she will think about you all tomorrow and what you are going through and then decide to come and see you on Friday."

"I hope she does," said Jane. "I am going to be her friend whether she likes it or not and I'm going to be her family; no one should die alone."

"I too will do that," said Verity, "I will go to her funeral and lament her passing. I will be her friend."

"Yes so will I," agreed Alice.

"And me," nodded Amelia.

"Oh well if you're all doing it," smiled Lorraine. The women sat in quiet companionship, brought together by the plight of Helen and their own personal battles. A friendship grew amongst them, something almost tangible which each one could feel warmly in their bodies.

"So do you wish to carry on?" asked Marc, breaking their quiet reverie.

"Not really," said Jane, "I have to go and prepare for tomorrow, Freddie may be home earlier today so I can't be late. To answer your question at the beginning of the day, I have no choice, I am going through with it and I really don't want to hear any more advice on the matter."

"Same," said Verity. "I am going through with it, life must go on."

"Yes," agreed Amelia, "It was valuable to be here, it has sorted out my mind and made me realise my relationship wasn't what it should be. I know I'm a career woman and I intend to keep on with my life."

"I already told you what I was doing." Alice said.

"Lorraine?" asked Marc.

"I still need time to think about things," said Lorraine. "Marc I will come and see you and Eleanor tonight before 10 o'clock and I will give you my answer then. I have some things to do and some other people in my life who I need to speak to; like the child's father. Please be patient with me until then."

"Of course Lorraine, I completely understand," said Marc, feeling very unprofessional and uncomfortable with speaking so openly to Lorraine about such a delicate matter. "Well I will end the session there and leave you all to say your goodbye's to each other. Tomorrow you are all booked in according to the notes and letters that you have. I will not be present at the hospital; it is not my role to be involved in the termination process. There is a final session here on Friday; I don't expect to see you all here, some of you may feel like you don't wish to return after the termination has happened and that's fine. Just know that this room is available to you all on Friday morning and you will have access to me should you wish to discuss what feelings you have post-termination. Thank you all for your time and your honesty and good luck in whatever you decide to do." Marc rose from his chair and walked silently from the room, giving a last hopeful look in Lorraine's direction.

Lorraine watched him leave and then turned to the four women who still sat in their chairs. "I've got an idea I want to share with you," she said, "I think I can help Jane . . ."

Home . . .

Jane walked through her front door with her ears alert for any sound which may tell her that Freddie was in the house. Others may think of the place where they live as home, but not Jane, this house was at the very least just a house and at worse, her prison, her torture cell, her potential dying place. Jane wasn't allowed to call out in the house so she didn't bother shouting to see if Freddie was there, instead she walked quietly through the many rooms, taking care not to brush up against any doors or bump into any furniture as she went. An eerie quiet was in each room - every item perfect, gleaming, oozing opulence. She stood still for a few minutes, enjoying the peace and hoping it would continue and that Freddie wouldn't bounce out on her like he tended to do when he was feeling particularly nasty. At any turn in her journey through the marble floored home, he could jump out from a doorway and grab her hair, resulting in either a terse comment and a slap to the behind or, when he was feeling friendly, rape.

Having made it safely to the kitchen, Jane stood for a few more minutes, listening to the silence echoing back at her from the walls. After a few minutes she heaved a huge sigh of relief and began to feel a little more comfortable in her own environment. She went over to the kettle, checked there was enough water inside and then put it on to boil; looking forward to her cup of tea before she had to think about what may happen tonight. She allowed her mind to empty and her eyes to just concentrate on the bubbles she could see forming in the clear strip running up the front of the kettle; small at first then growing ever bigger before finally exploding out of the water. When the water was ready, the small switch clicked off and Jane picked up the kettle, only to realise she had forgotten to get herself a cup or anything else that she needed to make herself a drink. 'Silly cow' she chided herself, then set about finding her tea cup in the cupboard above the kettle.

A loud screech from the house telephone caused Jane to jump violently; dropping the cup to the floor and causing it to smash, pieces of china flying in all directions. Jane crouched down and began to pick up the pieces; she knew she should answer the phone, especially if it was Freddie, but she just didn't have the strength in her today to do that. She waited for the answer phone to come on and listened quietly as Freddie's cocky voice came over the loudspeaker.

"Hi honey, I'm here with your father, we've had a really busy day today and have been very successful."

Freddie was using his 'I'm with your father' voice, Jane noticed; the one which said 'I'm a great bloke and your daughter's a nut job'. He always put on the voice the same way he put on his fake persona whenever he was around her father.

"So we're off to The Regal to celebrate, even your dad's coming along, isn't that great? He won't be here for long though, has to go back home, getting old bless him"

"Cheeky blighter." Jane heard her dad say to Freddie and the both of them shared a laugh; she could just imagine her dad giving Freddie a friendly punch on the arm whilst beaming proudly at his favourite son in law.

"Anyway, after that I'm going to the Marmot club, you know the one we like to go to together?"

'Yeah because you always take me out,' Jane mouthed sarcastically, typical Freddie and all his bullshit. Freddie continued his soliloquy into the answer phone, "So I'll be back quite late, although I might bring our friends back with me so wait up ok honey? Love you, bye."

Dread, fear and anger permeated every part of Jane's body when she heard the last and final words of Freddie, 'love you'.

"Love you," she said quietly back, "I did Freddie; I did." She continued to clean up the mess on the floor, retrieving a dustpan and brush from under the sink. Holding onto the anger and trying to push out the fear and dread from her soul, Jane made her cup of tea and then sat down at her kitchen table to await the night's happenings. Freddie was going to have a very different night to the one he was planning; she knew that but he didn't. The time had come for Freddie to get his comeuppance; Lorraine had finally convinced her with the plan she had concocted; everybody was on board and it was just a matter of timing so that everything turned out alright. Thinking back to their confab in the grotty counselling offices, Jane went through everything they had planned; she had told Lorraine that Freddie would probably be at the Marmot club; he always went there on a Wednesday night because that tended to be the day most deals were struck in her dad's business. Dad hated to sign contracts on Mondays because it was the beginning of the week and he didn't believe people were on their 'A' game on a Monday. It was the same with a Friday; people were too busy waiting to have fun at the weekend. *'No, Wednesday is the day when all good business gets done,'* her father would always tell her.

"It will never work," that bloody Helen had snidely remarked as she had returned once again to the room. Jane couldn't understand why Helen just kept on reappearing in that room. She had been a complete bitch since the day she had started there, sniping and being hateful towards everyone in the room. She'd lost her baby which was very sad and when Jane had heard Helen's story she had started to feel a pang of guilt for hating Helen so much, but that didn't last long because as soon as Helen had told her story she had gone back to being the same bitch she always was. Jane could understand that Helen didn't have much reason to be nice though; dying was the only thing left on the agenda for Helen it would seem and Jane could empathise that maybe she wouldn't be so nice if that was hanging over her head.

Everyone in the room had ignored Helen when she came in, fed up of her interrupting and no longer needing to involve her in their business now that the session was over.

"It really won't work," Helen insisted. *"Lorraine you haven't got the guts and Alice, why you're getting involved*

I don't know, you're far too young to be involved in all that caper. As for you Verity, it's just jolly hockey sticks for you isn't it?"

"It's really none of your business," said Verity.

"Well Amelia it is your business isn't it?" Helen said, "I mean if it all goes wrong that's your whole career out of the window. Surely it can't be a good thing for you to get so involved in Jane's life when the two people who can influence your promotion are the targets of this insanity?"

"Some things are more important than a career," Amelia said.

"Oh my gosh," Helen guffawed, "So rescuing Jane from her husband so that she can have her baby is more important than your career, however, the life of your baby is not? Double standards; absolute hypocrisy; totally fucking gobsmacking."

"Fuck off."

"I will fuck off; you're all a bunch of idiots. I heard everything you planned; it's a complete load of shit. Good luck when the police come knocking."

Knocking over a chair and slamming the door behind her, Helen had finally left them all alone. They had all stared at each other for a few minutes; Jane didn't know what any of them were thinking at that point, but she supposed they had kind of decided it was too late to turn back now the decision had been made, so they had all agreed to carry on. Jane prayed this was going to work, she couldn't see a life with Freddie in the future and desperately wanted to keep the little life growing inside of her. Something told Jane that the baby was a girl and that if she could just have her to herself then it would never be influenced by Freddie and his evilness. If the plan didn't work and she remained Freddie's dog, then she would have no choice but to abort. Jane knew that the baby wouldn't be the only one who lost their life; she was determined that she would leave Freddie and if death was the only way, then death that would have to be.

Home . . .

Marc pulled up outside his house once again, he had spent the rest of the afternoon in his office at work, speaking to his boss about the counselling sessions; Shirley had asked if the sessions were having any value; 'Do they have any significant effect on the decisions being made by the women?' she had asked him. How was he supposed to answer that question? 'Well yes, I am about to be a father.'? Rather than answer Shirley he had told her that the week needed to finish; the women had to have their terminations, or not and he needed Friday to go ahead so that he could evaluate the benefits of the session, if any. 'But is there any reason why we shouldn't go ahead and book in for next week?' she had pressed him. 'We need to know if this is somewhere where we should be using our budget, or if it is really no help at all.' Marc knew that a promotion for Shirley was riding on the success of these sessions. It was her idea to bring women together before termination and she had staked her career on it being successful. Marc liked Shirley, he liked the fact that she actually chose to do something new and innovative within their department to take it forward, instead of making cuts and saving the NHS money, which is what most people did to win their promotions these days. 'Schedule another one,' he had said to her. 'It's definitely helping these women; I think it's a good idea. We may even have prevented the need for further counselling sessions as they are coming to terms with the termination before it happens rather than dealing with the after effects of it. Of course we won't truly know until a few months have passed, but I think I can say, professionally, that they are a success.' Shirley had been thrilled, telling Marc to go home half an hour earlier than his usual 5:30. 'Wow, so generous'. He had quipped, but was glad he may get some time to himself before Eleanor got home that evening.

He saw that Eleanor was already home; she had been home before him every day this week, always eager for the news of his day. Work was no longer a priority for Eleanor; where she had previously thrown herself into her career; it was now a distraction from what her life could possibly become in the very near future. He took a moment just to sit and look at the home they had so lovingly created together. He imagined the insides of the house, no longer perfectly refurbished, but with little indications of a child living inside. The wallpaper slightly picked, the walls a little bare where they have been scrubbed clean of the crayon drawn haphazardly over it. He could see in his mind the muddy footprints left on the light grey carpet which ran up the stairs and could imagine the dog hair that must surely follow the child wherever it went. He and Eleanor had always spoken about getting their child a dog; a true friend that he or she could always rely on. Something warm and loyal where they could bury their head and cry, knowing that there was always love around them.

"Please let it happen," he murmured to himself, "Please let Lorraine come here tonight, please give Eleanor what she wants. God, please, please give her the one thing that I can't." Marc saw the curtain twitch and Eleanor's slim face peek out from between the curtain panels. She had been sitting and waiting for him to come home, as she had every other day. He could see her concern, knew she was wondering why it was taking so long for him to get out of the car and also knew that she probably thought he was dreading giving her bad news so was hiding away. In order to allay her fears, Marc sprang out of the car, plastering his face with an inane grin and waving to the twitching curtain. Eleanor opened it fully and grinned back at Marc, hope drawn all over her face. "Yes?" she mouthed through the window. Marc realised his grin said too much and he pulled back into a smile, shrugging his shoulders at Eleanor and walking towards the door. 'Let me in,' he mouthed and she left the window, curtain falling silently back into place.

Breathing deeply and considering his next words, Marc waited the short time for the door to open, still smiling, still offering the 'everything is going to be okay' face.

"Hello handsome," Eleanor smiled as she opened the freshly painted door, painted a bright blue this time, yet another distraction from childlessness.

"Hello my beautiful wife," smiled Marc back. He looked into her hazel eyes, bringing his hand up to her chocolate brown hair, noticing for the first time a few strands of silver which twinkled like glitter in her hair. "How was your day?"

"Never mind my day," Eleanor brushed his hand aside impatiently, "Come on Marc, tell me what happened."

"Can I come in first?"

"Yes, yes," Eleanor grinned, "Sorry Marc, I'm just so full of anticipation." She let him go passed her and both walked into the back kitchen. Marc started his usual ritual of coffee making and avoidance, knowing that Eleanor sat looking at him, her eyes boring into his back, waiting for the answer that was going to make both their lives change.

"How was Lorraine today?" she asked him.

"Same," Marc shrugged; he put the coffee pot down and turned to Eleanor. "I don't know Ellie, I just can't call it. She said that she would be coming around here tonight, but I'm not sure if that is to make any agreement with us. Whenever it's been discussed at the group . . ."

"Discussed? What? The other people there know about it?" Eleanor asked, looking a little shocked.

"Well yes; I mean, she didn't get up and say, 'Marc wants my baby.' They all worked it out for themselves and obviously they are there to discuss what is going to happen to the pregnancies and how they are coping with what is going on. Lorraine is a part of that group and inevitably they ended up speaking about it."

"What do the others think?" asked Eleanor.

"I'm not sure," said Marc, "They seem to have conversations without me there. Whenever I leave the room for a coffee break or for lunch it's obvious that's when the real discussions take place. That's what I would expect from any group, it's my function to get them talking and even though they know it's my job to be there, it's usually the case that the group forms their own bonds and choose to talk without the facilitator being around. The only thing I've had with regards to Lorraine and I, is the sniping which comes from Helen." Marc shrugged. "I do get the feeling though, that they have said she should do it."

"Why do you think that?"

"Well I have heard them say it," smiled Marc, "But that doesn't mean anything, it's up to Lorraine at the end of the day and every time I even try and get her to look at me, she turns the other way. We did go out and discuss it this morning . . ."

"And?"

"And she just said that she needs time. You know how scared she is that she may be consigning the child to the same type of life that she had. She's been through the system Eleanor; she's been beaten, molested and bullied through every childcare facility that she's been in."

"We would never do that."

"She doesn't know us. She doesn't know that we are nice people or that we have so much love to give that we are willing to just take in a baby from some random woman." said Marc, he walked over to Eleanor and placed his hands on her shoulders, looking down at her pretty face, so full of hope. "All she knows is that I'm a counsellor and you're a solicitor. She knows that we have tried to have our own babies; she knows that it sent you on a very tormented path and she knows, well she can see how desperate we are to give a baby a home. But she doesn't know what will happen once she hands that baby over. She doesn't know how she's going to feel when she gives birth. What if she wants the baby? What if looking into the eyes of her child makes her suddenly yearn to be a mother herself?"

"Well we would have to let her keep the baby."

"There's no 'have to' about it Eleanor. That's what would happen. But Lorraine doesn't want that. She doesn't want to look into the eyes of her son and daughter and feel like she wants to keep them. She wants to have the life that she's got now. She wants to drive her limousines and have her lesbian lovers. She wants to be free from any ties and not have the responsibility of bringing up another person. She doesn't want to fail as a mother, she is frightened."

"But we could help her," insisted Eleanor, "We could take on the responsibility and we could make sure that the baby had everything it wanted. We *want* to do that. Can't she see that?"

Marc felt frustration bubbling inside him; to Eleanor it was so cut and dried, she was so certain of her need for the child that she just couldn't consider how Lorraine must be feeling. To her it was simple; Lorraine was at an abortion clinic because she didn't want the baby growing inside her. Eleanor *did* want the baby, so Lorraine should just give it to her. Marc knew this must be a symptom of the mental breakdown Ellie had had when she lost her own children. The desire for children had never left her, even in her darkest moments; the only thing that was at the forefront of Eleanor's mind was the need to hold a baby in her arms. Marc couldn't comprehend this; to him having a baby was important, yes, but it wasn't everything. His desire was more about making *her* happy than having a child.

"I don't know what to say to you, I can't force her to do anything. I have told Lorraine that we are here for her. I have told her that we are willing to take on her baby, to love it and to treat it as our own. I have also told her that she can be a part of the baby's life, that she can be like an aunty or a big sister to it. I have given her all the options Eleanor, I have tried my hardest, but I can't try any more. Tomorrow is the day that she has to ultimately make up her mind. Her appointment is scheduled for the morning, should she decide that she wants to go ahead with the abortion"

"She can't do that; she *must* come to us." said Eleanor.

"We can't make her."

"We must, please ring her Marc; ask her when she's coming here." The doorbell broke into their conversation. "That must be her," said Eleanor, jumping from her chair and brushing Marc's hands from her shoulders. She walked quickly to the front door and opened it, revealing Lorraine standing there.

"Hi Lorraine."

"Hi Eleanor, can I come in?"

"Yes of course, you must come in." Eleanor opened the front door wider, "Careful of the paint, it's still a little wet."

Lorraine carefully walked into the hallway, minding the door as she stepped foot into the hallway.

"Have you made a decision?" asked Eleanor, unable to wait for the formality of small talk to go ahead.

"Will my limousine be alright out there?" asked Lorraine.

"There aren't any parking restrictions at this time of night," said Marc, "Limousine?"

"I have to pick someone up in it later," Lorraine said, "One of my drivers has let me down so I said I would do it; I can't let my clients down, there's plenty of competition in this industry."

"I'm sure there is," said Marc, "How does she drive?"

"Yeah, nice," nodded Lorraine, "not like those stretch limos, they're a nightmare to get around corners and to park." She smiled.

"I bet they are,"

"Oh for God's sake," Eleanor said; then looked immediately ashamed. "Sorry Lorraine. I'm so sorry, I know it's hard for you, please come in and let's talk."

Lorraine walked with Eleanor and Marc into the back kitchen and sat where asked to sit. She waited quietly whilst Marc continued to make the coffee he had started and accepted a cup of white coffee from him. She was stirring sugar into her coffee when Eleanor began to speak to her again.

"Lorraine, thank you for coming here. I know we've had long conversations last night, you've met me and met Marc. We've spoken about the reasons why we don't have children and why we feel like we can help you . . ."

"Stop, please stop. I'm not one of your clients Eleanor; you don't have to speak to me as though we are going into a business transaction. I get it. I understand that you and Marc are a desperate couple looking for the one thing in your life which is going to make it better. I get all of that." She paused. "I also, am desperate. I have got myself pregnant for somebody else, someone who has treated me like shit and dumped me. Someone who came into my life and I thought was going to be there forever. Someone who convinced me to turn my back on my butchness and allow my body to be used so that she could have a baby. Let me be clear on this; I don't want a baby. I don't want to bring up a child and I don't want to have the responsibility of someone else's life in my hands. I don't want to have a baby and then put it up for adoption or into care because I have been that child and I have had a really shit life, to put it mildly."

"We know; we can help . . ."

"Please let me finish." Lorraine supped her coffee. "But I also don't want to have an abortion. I have really thought about this and I have listened to the tales of the women who we have been with this week," she said looking at Marc, who nodded in agreement. "I have heard what they've got to say and I've sometimes agreed with them and sometimes not agreed. There is one woman there who should absolutely have her baby. She should be allowed to get on with her life without fear or harassment. She deserves to be happy and to have the baby which she blatantly wants to have. There is another woman there who has been through so much in her life; so much stress, heartache and pain. She has lost so many things in her life, including her baby and she still stands strong; oh she's a complete bitch and we all actually hate her, but I also admire her, she is courageous and says it how it is. She has made my mind up for me."

"How?" Eleanor asked.

"She has just helped me to come to the decision that I am going to have the baby. I feel it kicking inside me, getting stronger and stronger each day. My body tells me in every waking moment that there is a life inside of me. It's not a foetus or a bunch of cells, it's a person. There is nothing wrong with it, it is strong and healthy and I think probably a boy." Lorraine smiled. "I have no right to murder this child. I have no right to take away the life it could have just because my life isn't turning out the way I wanted it to." Lorraine took a deep breath. "I am going to have this baby."

Eleanor smiled through tears of sadness. "I am happy for you Lorraine and I understand."

"Understand what?"

"I understand that you want to keep your baby."

"That's not what I'm saying," smiled Lorraine. "I am going to have this baby and I am going to give him to you."

Silence hung in the air, time paused and everything stopped, the last words echoing around the small kitchen. Eleanor heard them reverberate around her brain.

"You are going to give him to me?" she asked, "To us?"

"Yes I am." Lorraine nodded, her mind finally made up. "I wasn't actually sure that was going to be my answer until I sat here just now. In fact, I didn't really know *what* I was going to say until the words came out. Listen, I have been a vessel since the day I got pregnant. I was having this baby for somebody else in the first place. That hasn't changed. I am still having the baby for someone else. It maybe the completely wrong decision; you are, after all; complete strangers to me. That isn't uncommon though is it? I've been looking it up online and surrogacy is between strangers, the only difference is that they get paid to do it." Lorraine put her hand up, "I'm not asking for payment, I earn plenty with my car firm, I don't need your money and besides, you're going to need it with this little one on the way." She patted her stomach. "I do have one condition though."

"Name it," Marc and Eleanor said in unison. "Yes, name it," said Marc, "We will give you anything."

"I do want to be a part of the child's life. This is the thing I've fought with myself about. Having the baby has never been an issue for me; it's how the baby will live that I need to be sure about. I can't be scared that he will go into Care. I can't be frightened that he might be unhappy or scared in his life. I need to know that he's okay."

"Of course you do."

"I have to be able to say to myself each day, 'he's okay, everything is alright,' I need to know that he is having a good life. I can't do that from the outside, I have to be a part of his life."

"What are you asking for?" said Marc, "Joint custody?"

"No, nothing like that. I just want to be someone in his life. An aunt, a godmother, something like that. I need to know that you're not going to move away and that I can have access to him whenever I want. I don't mean to take him away from you or to even have him for the day, just access. You know?"

"We could draw up a contract," Eleanor's law training kicked in. "We could make a contract with you Lorraine, one that prevents us from leaving the country without your permission and one which allows you to have access to him. Even one that gives you the rights to make decisions with us about his life."

"Let's be clear," Lorraine stopped Eleanor once again. "I know the law on this already; I know that I am the person that has the rights to say what happens to him anyway. Even if I hand him over to you, I would be the one that legally would be able to make *all* the decisions about him. If I thought you were ever doing the wrong thing with him, then I would have to step in and take him from you."

"That can never happen." Eleanor pleaded. "Please Lorraine, you can't give a baby to us and then take him away if you don't agree with what's happening to him. If I pick the wrong school or put him in the wrong clothes am I always going to be wondering if you are going to knock on the door and take my child away? I don't think I could live like that. How could a child be happy in a place where his mother is always on edge that he is going to be taken away from her?"

"No Lorraine, Eleanor is right. I know that at this moment she would probably agree to anything so she can have a baby, but she is completely right when she says that is no way to bring up a child. We have to be certain in our parenthood so that we can make decisions and look after him, or her, in the way that we see fit."

"It's getting complicated already," shrugged Lorraine. "Although I don't think I mean choosing schools and clothes and stuff like that. I think I mean that if I see that he is unhappy then I want to step in." Lorraine picked up her coffee cup once again and looked into the fluid inside, searching for an answer she couldn't find. "I really don't know how I want it to play out. I mean I know that if I give the baby to you, I have to do it wholeheartedly. I have to be sure that I am taking a step back and allowing this child to not be mine. The more I talk about it, the more I'm talking myself out of it again. It would just be so much easier if the child wasn't here; if I had the abortion and got rid then the problem would go away."

"This is just going in circles Lorraine," Marc said exasperated. "I know it's a difficult decision for you, I know you are finding it hard to make it and to take that final step, but two minutes ago you were certain it was what you wanted."

"Yes, I was certain," agreed Lorraine. "The only thing is, when I was having the baby for my girlfriend, I was also having it for me. I don't mean that I wanted a baby, but I knew that I was going to play some part in the baby's life. We would bring the child up together, I would be like a father figure to it and I would be involved in making decisions like schools, days out and stuff. I kind of want to still have that involvement, even though I don't want to do the whole bringing up baby thing. I'm so confused. I don't know what to do."

"Why don't you move in with us?" Eleanor said.

"What?" both Marc and Lorraine said.

"Move in?" asked Marc.

"Yes, move in." Eleanor gestured at the kitchen around her. "We have the space for now and when the baby comes we can move. All of us, together, into a bigger house. You can have your life Lorraine; you can come and go as you please and live exactly how you want to live. It would just be like you were lodging with us. It will help you get to know us for the next twenty weeks until the baby is born."

"And then what?" asked Lorraine.

"Then when the baby comes you will know. You will know what you want to do. You will either decide that we are the wrong people to bring the baby up or that we are the perfect people. You will have heard our arguments, lived our lives with us. Seen how we are with each other, know that we love each other."

"I will be intruding."

"Yes, you will, but that's what you need to do." Eleanor said. "You need to be with us, to learn about us and to become part of the family, because if you do give us your baby, that's what you will be anyway. We will all be a family. Marc, you, baby and me." Eleanor embraced Lorraine. "We can do this Lorraine; we can make a home for this little one." She put her hand on Lorraine's stomach.

"He just kicked," smiled Lorraine. "I could feel him, strong little legs."

"He wants this." Eleanor agreed. "He wants us to try. What do you think Lorraine; do you want to be a part of our family?"

"Two for the price of one?" Lorraine asked.

"Yes," laughed Marc, "What the hell, it's been quiet around here for such a long time, I could just do with some more people to talk to."

"I always wanted to be adopted," grinned Lorraine, "Didn't think it would happen after I became an adult though."

"Right, that's sorted." Said Eleanor. "We're probably all crazy, but what the hell, we will never know until we give it a go will we? I can't believe we're all going to be parents." The light which shone from Eleanor's face told Marc that the decision, for her at least, was the right one. Lorraine seemed to agree; she looked content with the decision which had been made, so much so that she even put her feet up on the chair next to her and relaxed into her coffee drinking. They sat for another hour going through the whys and wherefores of how it was all going to work. A decision was made about a moving in day for Lorraine and an agreement was made to always talk about how they were feeling and to be honest and upfront about whether things were working between them. With every minute that passed Marc began to also agree that the decision was the right one.

Once all the plans were in place and a date set for Lorraine's move into the home; next week after she had made arrangements to put her flat up for rent. Lorraine got up and said thanks to Marc and Eleanor. "I am surprised by what has happened here," she said, "But I'm also very happy. It seems too good to be true and something is probably going to go wrong, but fuck it, life's too short not to take chances."

"Agreed," smiled Eleanor. "Thank you so much Lorraine. Thank you for coming and thank you for talking to us. Thank you for listening and thank you for understanding. Thank you, thank you . . ."

"Enough with the thank you. Is she always like this?" Lorraine asked Marc, grinning. "I can't be listening to 'thank you' all day long."

"No, she's really not," Marc grinned back. "But you'll get to know her and love her just like I do."

"Oh you don't want me to love her," laughed Lorraine. "You wouldn't be able to handle the competition."

"Now, now."

"Only joking." Lorraine walked to the front door and opened it, "Right I have to go, I have somewhere to be." She turned to walk out of the door and stopped quickly. "I thought you said the car was going to be alright out there." She said.

"It should be, they only tow cars away if they are parked there before 5 o'clock." Said Marc.

"Well it's not alright," grimaced Lorraine."

"What's wrong?" asked Marc, walking to the door and looking out at the empty space where there was once a limousine.

"Well," said Lorraine, "It looks like my car has been stolen."

Freddie . . .

Freddie took a deep drag on his cigarette as he strutted out of the London Nightclub. Blowing a few smoke rings, he turned to the drunk, bedraggled Linette as she stumbled out through the door behind him.

"Come on love, I'm feeling the need," he urged her.

"Alright, cor fucking 'ell, I've only just bought these shoes," Linette complained as she splashed the red soled, crystal adorned, pink shoes in a muddy puddle. Freddie grabbed her by the arm and led her along the street, laughing as Linette stumbled, barely able to keep upright on the five inch heels.

"Come on Linnie, I've got work in the morning, I need to be in my bed and snoring my little heart out by three or I'll be knackered tomorrow."

"Where are we going?"

"Just down here," he pointed to an alleyway which ran alongside the club. "I know a place, come on."

"Give us a drag of your fag."

"Yeah like I want your lips around my cigarette; the only thing you're sucking is my cock love."

"Charming."

Freddie continued briskly along the alley, pulling Linette behind him and then stopped when they came to a darkened alcove set into the Nightclub wall.

"Come on Linnie, get on with it, I'm fit to burst."

"Anyone would think you never got any." Linette laughed. "We only had a shag last night and we had that threesome about two days ago. You are one horny bastard."

"I can't help myself, it's your dark good looks and compelling nature that just want me to fuck you."

"Really?" a dirty blond, doe-eyed Linette tugged on Freddie's arm and pulled him around so she could look into his eyes. "Do you really think that Freddie?"

Freddie snorted, "Don't be daft, you're a dirty fucking hooker Linette. I fuck you because I can, because you have a good suck and a dark hot minge." He grabbed her hair and began to move her head towards his penis, which he was releasing from its cloth prison. "Now get on it Linette, you filthy whore and make sure you swallow; the last thing I need is dirty underwear. The wife just hates washing cum stained pants." He giggled as Linette got to work, gagging with every thrust of his manhood.

Freddie walked along the High Road, sucking on his bloodied knuckles. Linette had got just a little bit too full of herself after the blowie, talking about feelings and possible relationships. Freddie had started to suspect she may be getting too full of herself when she had stopped charging him for sex, but had decided to make the most of it and then put her in her place if she got out of hand. He was quite sad that he had had to teach her a lesson; she had a pretty face really, even if it was always smeared with make-up and hidden under a ton of slap and false lashes. Linette wasn't looking quite as pretty now that his knuckles had given her a make under, but Freddie was sure she would bounce back; her type usually did. He would give her a mercy fuck when she was able to walk again.

He whistled to himself as he strolled along the deserted High Road, he knew that he would have to hurry to get a taxi so that he could get home to bed as he had a very important meeting in the morning. Jane's dad had been with him at the club earlier, the mug. He couldn't believe how easily he had inveigled his way into the family and just taken it over. Jane had always said she had a strong bond with her father, some bond; all it had taken was a few words in his ear and he now thought she was an absolute fruit cake, due to be sectioned at any minute. He was frightened to even go to the house as Freddie had told him tales about Jane's behaviour. *I can't bear to think of my little girl like that,* he excused himself from the whole situation, preferring instead to let the great Freddie 'look after' her. Guilt and a sense of duty now led Jane's father to pretty much give Freddie anything he wanted and tomorrow morning was a meeting which may just seal the fortune that Freddie had been hunting since he started this whole thing with Jane. He might give the little dog a pat on the head when he got home; she was the key to his future after all.

Freddie looked left and right but could see no sign of any traffic let alone a Taxi, he marvelled at how such a vibrant and busy city such as London could turn into a ghost town, particularly when he needed to get home. Crossing the road, he swaggered along the street and his mind turned to thoughts of a kebab. He knew in London there must surely be a twenty four hour shop open somewhere so he was determined to find one, buy the big dirty meat filled wrap he wanted and then hail a cab home.

When Freddie took his next step onto the tarmac, he heard the sound of a car coming up the road behind him. Hoping it would be a taxi, he turned with his hand in the air, ready to hail his ride home. Bright lights blinded Freddie and the sound of the car engine deafened him in the otherwise soundless street. Freddie tried to take a step back out of the way of the car, but when he did, the car changed direction and headed straight for him. Drink, drugs and tiredness had clouded Freddie's judgement and he was unable to react quickly enough to get out of the way of the screaming metal giant which headed straight for him.

The car hit Freddie dead centre, causing him to fly along the road and end in a crumpled heap on the tarmac. He groaned, touching his head and body as he felt for any damage that might have occurred, aware that the drink was also, mercifully, dulling any pain he may be feeling. He was vaguely aware of the sound of a car engine once again and hoped that it was now an ambulance coming to see to his injuries.

Freddie began to reach for the phone in his jacket pocket but never managed to get hold of it as the car hit him once again, all four wheels going over his body, breaking skin and crunching bone as arms and legs were carried up into the arches by the turning wheels; pummelling Freddie's body, blood bursting from his veins and spurting over the hard cold floor.

Barely conscious, Freddie's last vision was of a woman standing over him; she bent down and put her face right up to Freddie's ear.

"You are a disgusting human being. You use, abuse and violate women in every way possible. People like you should not be allowed to walk on the planet. I hope you rot in hell, you bastard."

A hard kick to Freddie's face was the final blow which put his light out; Freddie would never know of the baby that was growing in the belly of his woman and would never again lift a hand to hurt his wife. The woman turned and walked away from the scene and from the car which sat, engine idling, Freddie's limbs still entwined in the rear wheel arches. She walked slowly, purposefully and at no stage did she turn to look back on the life she had destroyed. She was determined to focus only on the life she had just saved.

D. I. Turnbull . . .

Detective Inspector Todd 'Todger' Turnbull sat at his desk with his new favourite Sergeant, Stanley Bloom, sat opposite him, dark eyes pouring over the latest burglary statistics.

"Seem to be getting worse," Stanley said morosely, lifting his coffee cup and tipping it right back; hoping to score the last drop of liquid.

"Worse how?" asked Todd.

"Well, our actual reports of burglary have gone down."

"Which is good."

"Yeah, but so have our detection rates."

"Oh, that's bad." Todd pushed his chair back, leaning heavily on the back legs of the chair. "Why do you think that is?" he asked.

"Everyone's a forensic expert nowadays," sighed Stanley. "We have every programme under the sun giving away all our methods of detection."

"Mm," mumbled Todd. "Gone are the days of leather gloves and a crow bar."

"Dummy burglar alarm boxes and Alsatian 'I live here' stickers in the window are no longer a deterrent"

"They'd be better off with a cardboard policeman in the window and a shotgun on the wall." Both men laughed at Stanley's quip.

"It's proving very hard to catch then out at the moment. They're going in with latex gloves, covered shoes . . ."

"Covered shoes?"

"Yeah, you can get these little shoe covers from the gyms and swimming pools nowadays; so your shoes don't make the poolside dirty. The burglars are putting them over their shoes to prevent trainer treads from showing up in the mud outside the windows. We haven't made a plaster caste of a trainer print for months." Stanley sighed. "The little fuckers have even given up smoking on scene and no one's had a dump in a bedroom drawer for a good long while."

"Every cloud . . ." said Todd.

"True. It's not so bad for the victims, but its shit for us."

"Literally," agreed Todd. "Wait a minute," he put the front legs of his chair on the floor again and reached over for the figures which had been sitting on the desk in front of Stanley.

"Stan, where can you get the shoe covers from around here?"

"Well they don't sell them in your local supermarket," Stanley grinned, already guessing where Todd was going with the conversation.

"So where; exactly?" Todd pushed.

"The council swimming pool or every gym which has a pool."

"There are loads of gyms around here," said Todd, "But not that many with pools. What we need to do is check CCTV for the days before or on the days of burglaries. Watch out for anyone who is going in the place but not really staying. Where do they get the covers from once they're in there?"

"Usually just at the entrance to the pool; or in the changing rooms. "

"So they would have to be a member or have paid to get in?"

"Or jumped the barriers; easily done."

"No," Todd shook his head, "Draws too much attention." He ran his hand through his silver hair, feeling the oiliness that had started to come into it since his last shower. He tried to think when was the last time he had a shower, it felt like an eternity since he had last been home and had time to do the usual mundane everyday things that normal people took for granted. Did he go home yesterday? All his days seemed to blur into one, he thought he may have had a shower two days ago.

"Guv?"

"Sorry Stan, so we need to send the boys and girls to all of them; get them to ask for CCTV and for attendance logs. Let's see if we can spot anyone we know."

"It's a bit of a long shot Guv."

"It's our only shot at the moment," grimaced Todd, looking at his watch. "Well that's half the night shift done with no drama. Let's keep our fingers crossed for the other half."

"Why did you say that?" asked Stanley; alluding to the usual policeman's curse when mentioning a shift had been quiet or without drama. "It's going to kick off now."

"Well Stan my man, it has been particularly *quiet* around here this evening," grinned Todd.

"Now you've done it Guv. You've really said the Q word?"

"Quiet," Todd continued. "Really quiet this evening," he opened his arms wide and gestured with his hands, "Bring it on." He said.

The wooden door to Todd's office banged loudly and then the handle clicked a few times as someone the other side attempted to open the door.

"I told you," said Stanley, "That didn't even take a minute. You've cursed us Guv."

"Come in," shouted Todd as the door continued to makes sounds without actually opening. "Oh for fucks sake," he muttered, getting up from his chair and trying to open the door. He met with resistance on pulling at the handle so pulled harder, opening the door and bringing a uniformed officer tumbling into the room.

"What are you doing McIlvenna?"

"Sorry Guv, I thought your door opened the other way."

"And when it didn't open, did it not occur to you to try pushing it?"

"Yes, er, no." PC McIlvenna straightened himself up, blushing red.

"Not intending on becoming a detective I hope?" asked Todd.

"No sir."

"Thank fuck for that, now what do you want?"

"R.T.A. sir, outside the Marmot club."

Todd's blue eyes bore into PC McIlvenna's face. "And why would I be interested in a car accident?" he asked.

"Believed deliberate Sir. An old brass saw it happen, says the car drove straight at the victim; twice."

Todd looked towards Stanley who was already putting on his overcoat. "Sorry Stanley, you were right. It's my fault."

"Bound to happen," Stanley smiled. "Better than sitting her doing the figures anyway."

"True, true." Todd turned to the young PC. "Do you think you can find your way back to the control room or do you need me to hold your hand son?"

"I'll be fine thank you sir. Are you going to come with me and pick up the CAD printout?"

"I think I can manage without that," said Todd. "I know where the Marmot Club is. I can get up to speed when I'm on scene. Is the Duty Inspector there?"

"Yes sir."

"Traffic?"

"First on scene."

"SOCO?"

"On way."

"Great. Okay, tell the control room E.T.A. ten minutes."

"Yes Sir, will do." PC McIlvenna almost bowed as he left the Detective Inspector's office.

Todd grabbed his own overcoat and put it on his large frame, closing the door behind him and Stanley as they left the room. "Got any plans for tomorrow Stan?" he asked.

"Looks like they're cancelled Guv," said Stanley.

"See, that's why I like you Stanley," smiled Todd, wondering when he was actually going to take that shower.

"Well I don't like you too much right now," Stanley countered. "Quiet. Why, oh why did you have to say quiet?" he continued to moan at Todd as they made their way along the dark and deserted corridors of the police station. Todd just hoped it wouldn't be another twenty four hours before they were walking these corridors again to go home.

Fifteen minutes later, Todd's car pulled up at the blue and white police cordon which had been tied across the road. He parked his car at the cordon and got out, joining Stanley at the front of his car before nodding to the uniform that stood guarding the scene.

"Morning." Todd greeted him.

"Morning Guv," said the police officer, nodding in Todd's direction. "Serg," he acknowledged Stanley. "At least it's not raining."

"Yeah, thank God for small mercies." Todd stood at the cordon and took in the scene in front of him, trying to ignore the police staffs that were there. The street itself was cobbled, a typical remnant of London's bygone days. The street lights on this particular stretch of the road were sparse as it was more of a cut through than a main street. The local council had not yet replaced these lamps with the dayglow halogen lights that seemed to be cropping up all over London; instead it was the dull orange glow afforded by the tired streetlamp that stood about twenty metres up from the scene.

Todd could see a light being assembled along with a white tent which would eventually be erected over the scene in an attempt to prevent the elements from disturbing or destroying the one piece of evidence which may lead to the capture of the person who had come to the point in their lives where freedom had no value.

He breathed in the atmosphere; felt the still wind and looked into the sombre light. He could imagine these streets looking pretty much the same hundreds of years ago, but instead of the shiny limousine which stood before him there would have been a horse and cart.

"Strange choice of murder weapon," Stanley broke into Todd's thoughts, coming to stand beside him.

"Not many people killed by Limo," agreed Todd. "Have we run a check on it?" he asked the uniform who stood quietly nearby.

"It's a rental vehicle Guv," said the PC, "Recently stolen; got the report about eightish last night."

"Last night being the night we're still in, or the night before?"

"This one Guv, just a few hours ago."

"Any sightings previously?"

"Too early for that information Guv. We can run a report on the A.N.P.R cameras if you wish?"

Automated number plate recognition technology had been a real godsend to the police. With so many cameras everywhere, it made the job of finding stolen or wanted cars that bit easier.

LISTEN TO THE SILENCE...

"Not an easy car to hide, even for a few hours," Todd said, "Should get a good lead from that."

He turned his attention to the body which lay haphazardly on the floor in front of him, legs still twisted up into the rear wheel arch of the limousine; other limbs at odd angles to the body which lay there. From the way the other limbs had also obviously taken a journey into the wheel arch of the car, it was obvious to Todd that the person had been hit more than once.

"They mean to kill him." Said Stanley, seeing where Todd was now looking.

"Yep, look at his face." Todd drew Stanley's attention to the dark haired face which lay sideways on the cobbled street; his cheek and eye no longer in the correct position as they had been dragged and torn by the road when the car had hit the body, slamming it into the floor. A dead eye stared back at the detectives as they surveyed the scene, daring them to look away; the other eye too mangled to be recognised as an eye, hanging from its socket by the purple veins.

"Nice looking guy," said Stanley. "I think he's winking at you Guv."

"Not funny Stan," Todd always felt uncomfortable with the macabre humour that went with the job.

"Do we know who he is?" he asked, turning to the PC once again.

"Freddie Farnham." said the PC, "Son in law of Brian Knox."

Todd whistled when he heard the name which was synonymous with the large corporation.

"Did he work for the company?" he asked, already searching for the possible motive.

"Board of Directors apparently," said the PC. "We have a statement from someone who was with him."

"The brass?" guessed Todd.

"Yes sir, although she stated he doesn't pay her. They have been in a relationship for some time apparently."

"Where is she?"

"Sitting in the meat wagon Sir." The PC gestured to a large white police van parked along the street. "PC Baynes is with her and so is the paramedic.

"Was she hit as well?"

"Not by the Limo Sir. By him." The PC pointed at the mangled body which lay silently before them. "Done quite a job on her he has."

"Right, get hold of that hire company and find out just who hired this car before it was stolen." Todd ordered. "Tell the SOCO to do what needs doing; I've seen enough from here. Get the photographer on the job and tell that lot," he pointed at the police officers still milling around the edge of the area, "to get their size twelves off my fucking crime scene."

"Yes Sir."

"And if I see one photo being taken by anyone other than the photographer, you are all sacked."

"Yes Sir."

"Come on Stanley, let's talk to loose knickers. See what she has got to say for herself."

They walked along the pavement and as they neared the white van, could hear the sound of sobbing coming from the open doors at the back. A female PC stood at the door to the van, notebook in her hand; talking gently to a lady who sat on the hard black benches within a caged area. Her dirty blond hair was bedraggled and she held a pair of pink shoes, splattered with muddy drops of water. Blood covered her face and stained the front of her dress. A green suited paramedic was holding a bandage to the lady's nose which had a gash across the bridge. Her eyes were swelling as she sobbed and blood seeped from wounds to her cheeks and forehead. She sobbed in between protestations of pain every time the medic attempted to patch up her nose.

"That fucking hurts," she shouted, pushing the medic's hand away. "Leave it," she said, "I've had worse.

"You need stitches love," the calm tones of the experienced medic cut through her tears. "Let me help you and then I can leave you alone and go help someone else okay?"

"No, fuck off. I don't need your help," she screamed at him. "I told you, its fine." She tried to get up and push her way past the open doors of the van, but the female PC put down her notebook and took the lady in hand, pushing her back onto the bench.

"We need to speak to you Linette; you're not going anywhere right now."

"Why not?" Linette protested, "I aint done nothing. Why can't I get out?"

"You have witnessed an accident," explained the PC, we need a full statement from you."

"It was no accident love; I've already told you that. Unless you accidentally reverse over someone after you've already knocked them over and then get out to kiss them goodbye. Yeah if you accidentally do that

243

then yeah it was a *terrible* accident." She sniffed loudly, grabbed the bandage from the medic and wiped her nose with it. "Fucking silly cow," she muttered to herself.

"Do you want treatment or not?" asked the medic. "If you don't, then sign this form and I'll leave you alone." He offered her a clipboard with a form on it and his pen. Linette took it from his hands, signed the form scruffily, dripping blood on it and then handed it back.

"Now fuck off."

"Gladly," he said, then turned to the female PC. "Keep an eye on her," he said, "If she shows any signs of concussion, she'll need to come in. I mean really we would like to take her in for observation, considering its all head injuries."

"Not a chance," spat Linette.

"But in the circumstances . . ." he left the rest of the sentence unspoken, shut up his bag and moved away from the van, muttering, "ungrateful bitch" to himself as he went.

Todd and Stanley had stood back as this exchange had gone on, but now moved right up to the open van door, taking up the space where the paramedic had once been standing. Todd addressed the PC.

"Good evening, PC?"

"Baynes Sir," she said, blushing when she saw Todd's face. He had a handsome, silver fox appearance which always proved quite a hit with the ladies. Todd rarely used it to his advantage, but he had been known to turn on the charm when necessary; tonight though was not one of those occasions.

"PC Baynes, thank you for watching . . ." he turned to the lady inside the van who was still wiping her bloody nose. "Linette isn't it?"

"How do you know that?" she asked, "I've never seen you before."

"I just heard PC Baynes here use your name. Although you do look familiar to me now," Todd tried to place where he had seen Linette before.

"Ever paid for the pleasure?" Linette smiled at him through bloody teeth. "Good looking man like you, you shouldn't need to pay for it. I'd do you for free."

"Did you do Freddie for free? Todd asked.

"Freddie," Linette gasped, standing up to leave once again and being pushed back by PC Baynes.

"He's dead ain't he?" She cried, "Definitely dead?"

"Yeah I'm sorry love, he's dead."

She sobbed loudly. "I liked him."

"Is he one of your regulars, Linette?" Todd asked.

"Yeah, but not in that way," she shrugged. "I always did him for free but he would look after me, you know? Buy me drinks and show me a nice time in the club, V.I.P. when I was in there. You don't get that very often."

"Isn't he married?" asked Stanley.

"Like that means anything," Linette rolled her eyes and shook her head. "She's a right nutter apparently, completely gone in the head. He only stays with her because she's the bosses' daughter. He goes in the club too, nice old fella."

"Does he know about you?"

"Are you on the same planet as me? Of course he fucking does." Linette shook her head once more. "Old boys' club love, they're all at it. Mind you the father only ever wants a cuddle, misses his wife I reckon. She's dead you know?"

"Mm, can I come in and have a chat with you love?" asked Todd. Linette moved herself into the corner of the cage.

"Help yourself luvvie," she gestured to the empty bench opposite her. Todd climbed into the van, dropping his head very low to avoid banging it on the steel cage door. Stanley followed him and PC Baynes turned her back on the group, guarding the van, but leaving the detectives to their business.

"Ok Linette, do you want to tell us what happened tonight?"

"Where do you want me to start from?" she asked.

"From the beginning is always good for us," said Stanley.

"And you are?" she asked both of them.

"Sorry," said Todd, "Detective Inspector Turnbull."

"Detective Sergeant Bloom," said Stanley.

"I'll talk to the organ grinder, not the bleeding monkey then," she said, giving Stanley a disdainful look before turning to Todd. "It all happened very fast Inspector," Linette said, her demeanour changing to that of poor innocent victim. Her eyes widened and she pushed her chest out. Todd could see the pout forming indicative of the typical flirtation he always seemed to encounter, even in the direst of circumstances.

"Ok, so tell me," Todd urged her.

"Well we had been in the club. Freddie was pissed, but not hanging, you know?"

"Yeah."

"He told me to go outside with him, 'cause he was feeling frisky I suppose; not that it usually makes a difference. Anyway I went out with him and we went down the alley."

"Which one?"

"The one just up the road there, to the left of the club."

"Ok."

"Yeah, I nearly broke my fucking shoe in a puddle; not that he cared. We went down the alley and I started to give him a blowie and then all I did was ask for a bit of loving and he went mental. Called me a whore and a slag and then knocked ten tonnes of shit out of me." She wiped more blood from her nose with the stringy piece of tissue she still held in her hand.

"Has he ever done that before?" asked Stanley. Linette looked immediately sheepish.

"Well yeah, he has. It's a job hazard ain't it? I'm like a super ho; I heal super quickly. I swear I'm made of rubber." She laughed. Todd had heard this many times before from the prostitute community; he was sad that they had such a low opinion of their selves and treated violence like a part and parcel of their profession.

"You don't have to put up with that kind of violence," he voiced.

"Yeah I know, I should be going to the prossie union and arranging a strike or something," she said sarcastically, "But what's a black eye when you get top class champagne and the odd pair of designer shoes? I see it as a service to their wives, what they do to me here; they're not doing to them at home."

"Really?"

"No, not fucking really," Linette wiped her nose again, smearing blood on to the back of her hand. "Anyway do you want to hear what happened or not?"

"Yes, sorry Linette, carry on."

"Well to be honest I think I passed out for a little while. Not very long, but I know one minute he was hitting me and the next minute I was on my own on the floor. I felt dizzy and obviously my face was pissing blood, so I kind of stood up slowly and thought about what to do next. She stopped to wipe her nose yet again, this time the blood was more congealed and a small clot appeared on her hand. Linette picked it off and flicked it onto the floor near to Stanley's feet. She smiled at his obvious distaste and carried on. "Then I heard this shout, more like a scream or an 'aah', you know? I thought it may be Freddie although I didn't actually know. Then I heard like a thump."

"Any screeching of tyres?" asked Todd.

"No, not really," Linette shrugged, "Not that I noticed anyway. Well I heard the thump and then like a moaning sound so I just peeped my head around the corner and I saw Freddie rolling around on the floor. I was going to go over to him, but then I saw that Limo coming at him again. Backwards it was going and fast. I had to hold onto my mouth to stop myself from screaming."

Todd looked quizzically at Linette.

"Well I don't want anyone to know I'm there do I?" she said, "I don't want to die do I?"

"Fair enough," he agreed, "What happened then?"

"Well I watched the car go over him again. The noise was sickening. I could hear his bones knocking inside the wheel arch, loud breaking noises; don't think I'll ever forget that sound. Then it stopped and this woman got out. She walked over to Freddie and then bent down to talk to him. She was well close; I mean she could have even kissed him."

"Did she kiss him?"

"I don't know, I'm just saying she was close enough to him that she could have."

"Did you hear what she said?"

No, they were too far away. But then she got up and kicked him in the face and walked off that way." Linette pointed in the direction which led away from the alleyway she had been standing in. "Thank God she didn't come in my direction; if she had seen me, I would be a dead woman by now."

"What did she look like?" Todd asked.

"Oh I don't know," Linette's demeanour began to change again. She was beginning to close off, unwilling to get any more involved in the situation.

"How did you know it was a woman?" Todd pressed her.

"Actually I don't," Linette said, "My face was full of blood; I've probably got it wrong."

"You were quite clear a few minutes ago?" said Todd.

"My head's hurting me now," said Linette, leaning back onto the metal wall of the cage. "I can't do this anymore, I'm sorry, I feel sick."

"Linette is would really help us if you could help out. Freddie has been murdered in cold blood. We will keep you safe if you help us out; protect you from any problems."

"Yeah, yeah I've heard all that shit before. Listen mate, I have to live in this world. You know no one talks; it's the rules. Come on. But I will tell you this; I would not be surprised if his wife was the one behind the wheel. He's told me all about her and what a looney she is. She probably lost it and decided to kill him. I wouldn't worry though; her dad will probably have her shipped off to a desert island somewhere before you lot can nick her. Money does a lot you know?" she winked at Todd. "Goes a long way the British pound does. She's like Teflon mate; nothing will stick on her, mark my words."

Vomit suddenly exploded from Linette's mouth and the left side of her face seemed to drop. "Oh," she exclaimed, "I feel weird."

"Pc Baynes, get that ambulance back here now," Todd shouted out of the door. "Linette, I think he's done more damage than you realise mate. We need to get you looked at right away."

"My head hurts," she mumbled and began to slump where she sat. Todd put his arms around Linette and Stanley helped him to move her to the floor of the van, her back now lying in the pool of vomit she had just produced.

"Oh God, get her out of the van," urged Todd and they both picked her up once more and took her to the pavement. PC Baynes removed her Gore-Tex jacket, turning it into a makeshift pillow.

"Get her looked at," Todd said to PC Baynes, who was already talking into her radio, calling back the paramedic.

"Right, Stanley, we need to get around to Freddie's house quick, but we need to be careful. We are either dealing with a deranged murderer or a bereaved wife; let's not go in all guns blazing. We'll start off with a belief of innocence, ok?"

"I didn't think there was any such thing," said Stanley.

"There isn't mate," agreed Todd. "Not in this world."

Lorraine . . . home

Lorraine sat at her wooden dining table in the grotty one bedroom flat she had been living in since her girlfriend had turned her world upside down. She had the money to get somewhere better, the limousine business had been doing really well, but she just didn't have the inclination. All of her time had been taken up with the baby. First she had been determined to carry on, despite the mess she was in and then she had been determined to get rid of the baby. Now she was going along an entirely different path and she actually felt quite good about it. Here was Lorraine's chance to give her child something which she could never have hoped to have given it in other situation. Meeting Marc and Eleanor had given Lorraine the courage to carry on. If she was honest with herself she could never have gone through with the abortion.

Had it been earlier, when the foetus was as small as a pea, then yes, easily she could have gone ahead, but for the last few weeks, Lorraine's little visitor had made itself known to her. She had felt movements from very early in pregnancy; around sixteen weeks. Little flutters and now definite kicks and they didn't seem random either. Lorraine could tell when the child was asleep, could feel its energy when she had just eaten and could even feel it reacting to her being in a bath of hot water.

The bond people spoke of was not obvious to Lorraine, but she could understand how it began in pregnancy and then developed into something much stronger once the baby was born.

Lorraine didn't want that; of that she was sure. She couldn't wait to get back to normalcy and start pulling some new women. Lorraine was determined to have a new one each week and have as much fun as she could once the baby went to its new parents. That's how she saw them now. Marc and Eleanor were the baby's parents and she was feeling confident that she had made the right choice.

As the clock on the wall chimed loudly the hour of 3am, Lorraine realised she'd been sitting at the table all through the night. She had been waiting for news of the limo which had been nicked and was always waiting for Amelia to ring and tell her what had happened to Jane last night. Had their plan worked? Was Freddie gone? Could Jane escape the termination and actually have a new baby and a new life out of the clutches of that maniac? All questions she nervously awaited the answer for.

Her clock stopped chiming and almost simultaneously, Lorraine's mobile began to ring, she grabbed it from the table in front of her and quickly answered it.

"Hello?"

"Hello, Lorraine Cheveaux?"

"Yes."

"It's PC Baynes here from Onslow Police Station."

"Ok."

"We've found your car madam."

"That was quick."

"Yes. Unfortunately it has been involved in a road traffic accident which resulted in the death of a member of the public."

"Oh my God," Lorraine gulped. "Did you catch the person who nicked the car?"

"No madam, I'm afraid not. This call is to advise you that you can inform your Insurance Company that the car has been found, but that we won't be able to release it to you until all our investigations have been completed."

"How long will that take?" asked Lorraine.

"At the very least, a week," responded the police officer.

"Ok, thanks for letting me know. Sorry about the dead man."

"Pardon?"

"I don't know how to say it; sorry. I'm just sorry for all that has happened. I know it's not my fault, but I can't help feeling a little guilty that my car has killed a man."

"I didn't say it was a man Miss Cheveaux."

"Or woman? Not a child, surely. Please not a child." Gasped Lorraine.

"No ma'am, it was a man. Maybe someone you know? He could have been involved in the theft of the vehicle. Do you know Freddie Farnham?"

"What?" Lorraine couldn't believe what she was hearing.

"Freddie Farnham."

"No, I don't know him," lied Lorraine. "Thank you for your call PC?"

"Baynes."

"Thank you for your call PC Baynes, what do I do now?"

"The Detective Inspector may wish to take a statement from you in due course."

"Ok that's fine, is that all?"

"Yes, thank you for your time."

"Thank you, goodbye." Lorraine took a deep breath once she had put the phone down. Freddie Farnham? Wasn't that Jane's husband? What had Amelia done? This was not what they had planned to do.

Lorraine hoped that Freddie's death was a very timely accident and that she hadn't become involved in something way more than she had agreed to. She began to search through her phone for Amelia's number; it was time to ask some serious questions.

Jane . . .

A loud knocking on the door broke Jane out of her silent reverie. She jumped so violently that she dropped yet another cup on the floor. She stood still and listened; *was that Freddie?* She hoped with all her heart that it wasn't and that it was Amelia. Jane couldn't move, she was frozen to the spot, waiting for some sign to tell her just who was at the door.

"Mrs Farnham?" a male voice intruded into Jane's silence.

Jane turned her head sharply towards the sound of the man's voice. That definitely wasn't Freddie.

"Mrs Farnham?" the door knocked again. *Could it be the police?* She wondered. Her body started to shake; Jane still couldn't decide whether to stay frozen to the spot or to move her body.

A loud knocking continued at the front door and then a shadow came across the kitchen window where Jane was standing. She moved her head so she could see out of the corner of her eye and saw a stocky, dark haired male; his dark eyes twinkled at her and he smiled, giving a small wave.

Jane broke out of her frozen stance and gave a little wave back; the dark haired male held up a black wallet to the window with a badge and a photo card on it. Jane knew this was a police badge, she had seen enough of them in TV programmes. The male motioned for her to open the kitchen door. She jumped into action and went over to the door, opening it a small amount and sticking her nose outside.

"Can I help you?" she asked, noticing another taller male with silver hair come up behind the stocky one.

"Detective Sergeant Bloom," he smiled at her. "Sorry, we tried the front door, maybe you didn't hear us?"

"No, I heard," apologised Jane, opening the door wider and indicating to the broken china on the kitchen floor. "I just dropped my cup and got a bit stuck."

"Oh dear, that's not good, let me help you clean it up." DS Bloom made his way into the kitchen passed Jane. She stood to one side and hung her head, taking up her default position of staring at the floor. The silver haired man opened up another police wallet and pushed it under Jane's nose.

"Detective Inspector Turnbull," he said. Jane looked up into a handsome face looking back at her. "Sorry to disturb you at such a late hour; were you sleeping?"

"Uh, no, just, uh, sitting." Jane shrugged. "I'm waiting for my husband to come home."

"Ah, Mrs Farnham, I'm afraid we're here because of your husband."

"What has he done?" Jane asked.

"Would you like to sit down Mrs Farnham?" asked Todd. "You might feel more comfortable if you're sitting down." He nodded to Stanley to bring over one of the kitchen chairs, which he did; gingerly stepping through the broken china which still lay on the floor.

Jane sat down in the wooden chair, she held onto the seat with her hands, trying to keep herself and her fear firmly in place.

"What's he done?" she asked again.

"I'm afraid, Freddie, has been involved in an accident. There is no easy way to tell you this, so I am just going to say it straight away." Todd always hated this part of his job. "Freddie was hit by a car this evening and died." He continued to talk before Jane could give any reaction. "We don't believe it to be an accident; we have a witness who tells us he was hit once and then the car reversed and went over him again."

"Oh God," Jane uttered, staring ahead of her apparently stunned. Inside, her head was experiencing hundreds of conflicting thoughts. Her emotions ranged from shock and upset to sadness, but the overriding feeling she had was of complete joy. Her mental shackles sprung open and dropped to her subconscious floor. Streamers flew across her vision and fireworks banged and cracked in her ears.

"She's fainted Guv," Stanley said as he grabbed Jane before she toppled onto the floor. He noticed her slump as soon as she had received the news.

"Forgot to breathe," agreed Todd. "Just sit her on the floor Stan, she'll catch her breath in a minute and wake up." He helped Stanley move Jane to the floor, they slid her over to the wooden cabinet doors and propped her up against the fitted kitchen.

"Some gaff," Stanley whistled. "They've got a bit of dosh," he said.

"Money isn't everything," sighed Todd. "Especially now, the poor cow," he shook his head.

Jane suddenly gasped and came to, fluttering her eyes and grabbing onto her clothing; ensuring she was fully covered.

"It's ok Mrs Farnham, you're ok, you fainted." Todd offered.

Jane looked up at him. "Did you say Freddie is dead?" she asked. "Is he really dead?"

"I'm afraid so." Todd nodded. "I'm sorry for your loss."

"Ha," Jane guffawed, "Sorry?" she stopped herself from speaking more, realising that she was maybe coming across as perhaps a little too happy.

"Mrs Farnham . . . uh . . ."

"Jane." She offered.

"Jane, we need someone to identify your husband's body."

"So it's not him?" she asked, a feeling of dread once again assuming position.

"No, we are pretty sure it is Mr Farnham. We have an eye witness who was able to give us his identification at the scene," said Stanley.

"Who?" asked Jane, knowing full well it would probably be one of the tarts from the club.

"I believe it was a member of the club he attends." Todd chose to use tact at this point. "Someone he has met before and has spent time with in the club, so we're pretty sure it's him, however, we do need formal identification." He paused to let that sink in.

"Do you think you are able to do that?" he asked.

"No." Jane shook her head. "No, I can't do that."

"Does he have any other family members who are able to do it?" Todd asked. It wasn't uncommon for close family members to shy away from seeing their freshly dead beloved.

"He's an only child," said Jane. "He hasn't seen his parents for years. I don't even know how to contact them. I'm not even sure he had any contact with them ever." Jane realised that she had never really been told anything about Freddie's history. He had always glossed over that part of his life when they were courting and after they were married, normal conversation just didn't take place. In fact, Jane realised, she didn't actually know Freddie at all.

"I'm sorry Jane, but if we can't find anyone else, then we must urge you to help us do this. It's the only way to help Freddie."

"Help Freddie," Jane echoed. She was still having a party in her head knowing that she would never have to see his hateful face again. A sudden thought hit her.

"Dad," she said. "My father can do it, he's Freddie's main person at the moment. I'm sure he'll be devastated that he's lost his favourite boy."

Todd was used to a range of emotions which people experienced when they found out their loved ones were dead. He had seen the darkest of despair, screaming madness, utter hopelessness and just sheer devastation, cross the faces of those he had delivered this kind of message to. This was not the case with Jane. He couldn't read her emotion; it didn't seem to have a place in the dark places that victim's family's thoughts usually inhabited. If he had to put a name to it, he believed she almost seemed relieved and very possibly happy at the news that he had just imparted.

"Are you ok, Jane?" he asked.

"Uh, yes." She smoothed her hair, shook her head from side to side, to remove the jubilant dancers inside and then became very business-like. "My father will be able to identify Freddie. They work together you see; quite closely. In fact, he was with him earlier on this evening. I will give you his phone number and address." She got up from her chair and reached for one of the kitchen drawers, which housed some paper and pens.

"He will be devastated to lose his right hand man." She turned to offer Todd the paper she had written on. "Maybe you can remind him, he's got a daughter, when you see him?" she smiled.

Todd looked at her questioningly.

"Sorry," she said, silently chiding herself. "We haven't spoken for a while."

"Jane," said Todd. "I get the feeling there's something you're not telling me." He motioned for her to sit down again, which she did. "I have delivered messages like this to, sadly, lots of people in my time and I have to say that you don't seem to be surprised that he is dead, or indeed, sad. Do you want to tell me anything about your situation?"

Jane shrugged.

"I can assure you, I will find out in the end. It is my job after all." He shot her a knowing smile. "I don't want to have to come back here and ask you back to the police station; if there's anything you know right now, it's in your best interests to tell me."

"Yes," agreed Stanley. "Mrs Farnham, your husband has just been run over by a limousine . . ."

"Limousine?" exclaimed Jane, becoming more animated. "Oh my God."

"Does that hold some relevance to you?" asked Todd.

Jane gathered herself together. "No," she lied. "No, not at all; I mean it's just such an unusual thing to happen isn't it?" she babbled. "I mean, killed by a limousine. It's not a bus or a car is it?"

"No," agreed Todd; although he believed the limousine had a far greater meaning to Jane, by the way she was acting.

"Well he always did have expensive taste. I suppose Freddie would be pleased that it was a limo and not a double decker bus," Jane smirked. She could really do with a drink right about now, but her mind wandered to the little bundle of cells inside her womb. That little bundle now had the chance to grow and multiply; cells moulding themselves into fingers and toes, electricity shooting across the fabric of the mind that is made out of millions of atoms. Life was being made and Jane wasn't going to have to stop it any more. *I'm going to be your mum* she thought, *we're free*. She couldn't suppress the smile that began to spread across her face.

"Mrs Farnham?" Todd asked quizzically. "Is something funny?"

"No," Jane chided herself again, "I'm sorry," she said. "The truth is Freddie was a pig. He treated me like a dog; literally. I know it seems like a weird reaction, but I'm very happy he's dead. I'm free."

"Free?"

"Yes, free. Free to be a human being, to sleep in a bed, to make a mess, to spend my *own* money. Free to love my father, to have friends." She stood up and spread her arms out wide. "I'm never going to be hit, patted on the head; raped." She looked Todd in the eye, when she said the last word. "Free." She said once again.

Todd finally understood. This wasn't a wife who had lost a husband; this was a victim who had been set free from her tormentor. Freddie Farnham was bad. Freddie Farnham was an abuser. Whoever had committed this offence, even if it was Jane Farnham herself, they had freed her from a life of torment.

"Mrs Farnham, where were you this morning between midnight and 3am?" asked Todd.

"Home," Jane smiled. "Home, I'm always home."

"Is there anyone that can confirm this for me?" he asked.

"No one in particular," shrugged Jane. But I do have CCTV," she pointed towards a door at the back of the kitchen and began to walk towards it. Jane opened the door and inside was a small pantry, filled not with consumables, but with a bank of monitors; each displaying different parts of the house and gardens outside.

"You don't live in a place like this without security," said Jane. "You can go through these tapes and you won't see me leaving." She smiled up at Todd. "I didn't kill my husband, Detective Inspector," she said. "But I'd like to shake the hand of the woman who did."

"Woman?" Todd asked, "I never said it was a woman Mrs Farnham."

"Woman, man, what's the difference?" Jane asked. "He's dead and I was home, I really can't help you any more Detective, I'm sorry." Jane felt the old confidence of her youth coming back to her. It had been locked away deep inside for the whole time she had been married to Freddie, but now the box was open. Arrogance, confidence and a sense of self-worth bubbled up inside her. It warmed her bones, surrounded her womb and washed Jane's wretchedness away. The old Jane was coming back. This Jane was strong, this Jane was bold and this Jane was going to be the best mother a child could have.

"I'm sorry Detective," said Jane, "I'm feeling tired and emotional. I've just lost my husband after all. Thank you for coming to tell me. I will give you my father's number and I'm sure he'll be happy to go and identify Freddie's body." She reached for the pen and paper again and wrote her father's mobile number on it, then handed it to Todd.

Todd took the paper, folded it and put it into his pocket. He looked at Stanley who was already looking for an exit.

"Thank you for your time, Mrs Farnham," Todd said. "I have some more enquiries to do and I may be back to speak with you again."

"Well I'm not going anywhere," smiled Jane. "You are welcome to come here whenever you like, I've got nothing to hide."

Todd nodded and made his way out of the kitchen, behind Stanley, towards the front door. He would send an officer around later to collect the CCTV footage. Whilst he believed it was entirely possible that Jane Farnham was at home and didn't commit the murder herself. He had a feeling that she knew more than she was telling him and could very well be more involved in his murder than she was letting on. One thing he knew for sure was, even though she had obviously suffered at the hands of the man whose body lay broken on the cobbled floor; his job was to bring the murderer to justice and he intended to make sure that was exactly what he would do.

Amelia . . .

Amelia was in a panic. The plan they had to frame Freddie just hadn't taken place. Lorraine's car had been stolen, Verity didn't turn up when she was supposed to, Amelia hadn't known what to do at that point, go to the club and go ahead or stay at home and hope everything was going to be alright. She had decided at the time to just stay at home. Once Lorraine had contacted her and told her that the car was gone, it had just pushed everything else out of place.

Amelia had to get her stuff ready to go to the abortion clinic, but had still heard nothing from the other women as to whether Jane had walked out on Freddie anyway. That stupid bitch Helen had been right in the end. Of course they wouldn't be able to save Jane from her bastard of a husband.

It had all seemed so obvious when they were in their little counselling room. Verity was supposed to go along to the club; she had some contacts in there who moved in the same circles as Jane's father. It was her job to get into a conversation with him and be present when Freddie got caught with a prostitute. Amelia was to find the prostitute and pay her to take Freddie on, not just to have sex with him; it was obvious that this was nothing new to Freddie or his father in law; but to entice him into starting something violent. The idea was that Amelia would discover Freddie as he was about to hit the prostitute and then she would cause a scene. Verity would already be ingratiated with Jane's dad and she would talk him into seeing what a bad piece of work Freddie really was. The fact that Amelia worked in the same company as Freddie was supposed to be an extra bonus, because this wasn't something that could just be buried. At the back of her mind, Amelia had seen her career going down the pan, it had been a very dangerous decision of hers to get involved in anything like that, but somehow she had found herself in the middle of everything. In the meantime Lorraine was supposed to be helping Jane move out and back into her father's house, to greet him there and tell him what Freddie had been doing to her. He would have seen it for himself and then would believe that Jane wasn't mad, but had been enslaved by Freddie and needed to be freed.

It all seemed so simple when they were talking about it. Even when Helen had completely destroyed them, laughing at their plan and telling them it was so ridiculous; they had still believed it was a possibility. Anything was possible if they all pulled together; they had all agreed that it was going to work.

It had been a relief when Lorraine had told Amelia the car had been stolen; it was like fate was telling Amelia to stay out of Jane's business and keep her job. The job that was so important to her, she was about to terminate an unwanted pregnancy.

"So stupid," said Amelia as she packed a dressing gown for herself. The clinic hadn't told her to pack anything, they told her she wouldn't need any pyjamas and that slippers would be provided, but it seemed weird to be going in for a surgical procedure and not taking the obligatory hospital clothes. She continued to pack, putting her slippers in anyway; she would feel more comfortable in her own slippers. Her mobile phone rang and Amelia dropped everything to answer it, when she saw Lorraine's name appear on the screen.

"Hi Lorraine, what happened?" she asked anxiously.

"You will never believe me." said Lorraine.

"Tell me," she insisted.

"Well, you know my car was stolen?"

"Yes."

"You really won't believe that this is what I'm going to say."

"Lorraine, please, what happened?"

"The car was used to kill Freddie Farnham."

"What?" Amelia was aghast.

"I'm serious. The fucking thing was driven to where he was at the club last night and when he went to cross the road, it ran over him."

"Oh my god."

"Yes and then it ran over him again." Lorraine's voice broke.

"Again?" said Amelia, "Oh my God."

"I know," said Lorraine.

"Who did it?" asked Amelia.

"What do you mean who did it?"

"Oh come on Lorraine. We were planning to stitch him up last night. We were all talking about being there; it was our little mission to get Jane away from him so that she could have that baby."

"Yes, I know, but the car got stolen," said Lorraine.

"Got stolen and used to kill over the very man that we were trying to stitch up," Amelia shouted. "Come on Lorraine, don't you think that's more than just a coincidence?"

"Well it wasn't me," said Lorraine. "I was at Marc and Eleanor's last night when the car was stolen."

"How long were you there for?" asked Amelia, becoming suspicious. "I've only got your word for it that the car was nicked."

"What? I didn't do it," insisted Lorraine. "I couldn't do that."

"Where was Verity?" Amelia asked.

"I don't know, I haven't spoken to her at *all*." Lorraine sighed. "I don't know what's happened to her, but when I went to call her last night; I couldn't get through to her. I thought she must have changed her mind about going to the club and just didn't want to answer her phone to me."

"But she was just as interested in helping Jane out as we were," said Amelia.

"Yeah well people change their mind . . . a lot."

Both women went quiet for a short while, searching for answers to the hundreds of questions which were going through their minds.

"Have you changed your mind?" asked Amelia.

"About what?"

"About your baby of course," said Amelia. "Are you still going to give it to Marc?"

"It's not like that," said Lorraine. "I'm not just giving it away. It's not like it's a puppy or a car."

"Well what are you doing then?"

"We're coming to an arrangement." Lorraine said, "A mutual arrangement where we are all involved with the child."

"Like aunts and uncles?"

"Kind of," agreed Lorraine. "I know that I don't want to be a full time mother, but I also know that I don't want to just put my child into the care of another person. We will co-parent, but the child will live with them."

Amelia could not understand how Lorraine could come to this arrangement with a couple who she had only met in the last few days. She understood that Lorraine was under pressure to make a decision as soon as possible. She only had until the twenty fourth week of pregnancy to decide whether or not she wished to terminate her pregnancy. Lorraine was obviously pregnant. She had a pregnant belly and complained that the child kicked her. It must be a completely different scenario for her, where life was apparent.

Amelia still had no symptoms of pregnancy other than a slight feeling of sickness in the morning. She couldn't imagine a child inside her, couldn't link a person to the cells that were growing in her belly. For her it was just a transaction, a mistake that needed rectifying. But for Lorraine, it surely felt like an act of killing. There was something inside her which she knew to be alive, potentially a living human being that could come into the world and grow into the next Prime Minister or someone else. Amelia didn't think she would be able to terminate quite so easily if she was as far gone as Lorraine, so she supposed the decision then had become easier for Lorraine. Keep the baby, help

Marc and be part of the child's life. Still, Amelia reasoned, hormones are a funny thing; maybe Lorraine's hormones had got the better of her and she had also made the snap decision to help Jane with her Freddie problem. Maybe Lorraine's car hadn't been stolen after all and she had gone on a midnight drive to mow down the person who was treating Jane with so much hatred.

"Lorraine, I hope you haven't done anything silly." Amelia voiced.

"I swear, Amelia, my car was stolen from outside Marc's house. I didn't do anything."

"Have the police been in touch?"

"Only to tell me that they've found my car and that it had been used in the hit and run," said Lorraine.

"Did they know that you know Freddie?"

"*I don't* know Freddie," said Lorraine.

"Have they spoken to Jane?" Amelia kept pushing.

"I didn't ask, funnily enough," said Lorraine. "Oh yes, Mr Policeman, can you tell me how the wife of the man I don't know is? I mean I don't know her either, I just thought I'd enquire."

"Alright, alright," Amelia stopped her, "It's just a little bit frightening and I'm confused as to how I've got myself involved in all this. I just want to get on with my fucking life." She became angry. "I've gone from doing a simple termination, where I had a boyfriend and a good chance of working my way up the company; to possibly being involved in the murder of my boss? For fucks sake, remind me never to accept counselling from anyone, ever again."

"I'm sorry Amelia. Listen; good luck for today."

"Good luck?" Amelia shouted down the phone, and then remembered what she had been getting ready for. She put her hand on her flat stomach. "Oh, good luck, yeah thanks." She muttered. "Bye Lorraine."

"Bye."

Amelia put the phone down and shut her bag, she checked her watch and realised she was now running late for her appointment. She hoped she got there on time and she hoped that Lorraine was telling the truth about not being involved in Freddie Farnham's death. She quickly thought of Jane and wondered how she must be feeling; was she relieved or upset? One thing Amelia did know; if it was her in Jane's position, she'd be having a party right now.

The Day . . .

Verity arrived at the large white house in West London. Such a pretty house with a bright blue double door on the front, she wondered at how it could be the gateway to a health clinic. Her feet crunched on the gravel and she looked around the imposing doorway for a method of entry. Finding 'reception' handwritten on a bell, she pressed it and then pushed both doors on hearing a buzzer, fumbling around until the right one finally opened up at her push.

Verity took a deep breath and walked into the clinic, not knowing what she would find at the end of the corridor. She walked into an open reception with a pleasant looking lady sitting at a low counter.

"Good morning," the lady smiled at her, no judgement in her eyes. Verity found herself beginning to relax a little.

"I have an appointment." She said.

"What's your name please?" the smile remained on the lady's face and seemed genuine.

"Verity Roebottom." She found herself giving clipped responses, unable to feel completely comfortable in her surroundings. Usually she would give a little quip about her surname 'Roe as in fish eggs, bottom as in bum', that kind of thing, but it didn't seem appropriate here.

"Ok Verity, thanks very much, come with me please." The lady got up from her chair and still smiling, motioned for Verity to follow her through a door. Verity followed, finding herself in an area which housed a very large and impressive staircase, a blue sign with 'clients and staff only' being the only clue that it led up to where all the action happened, she supposed.

The lady took Verity into a large waiting area, blue chairs dotted around the floor in twos, already housing some couples who were intent on each other, or girls sitting alone looking at their telephones.

"Gosh, there's a lot of people here," said Verity.

"Yes, I'm afraid we're running a little behind today," said the kind lady as she placed Verity's notes at the back of a larger pile of notes hanging in a little tray on the wall.

"Expect to be here for at least three hours. Take a seat where you can." And the lady was gone, shutting the waiting room door behind her. Verity looked around and her attention was caught by a waving hand in the corner. She smiled at Alice who sat on her own near the window. "Hi," she mouthed and then walked over. Suddenly she felt a lot better about where she was, finding someone who she knew was going through the same thing as her was reassuring. Knowing that she had to make things right for Alice was even more helpful; Verity always worked better when she was helping someone else with their problems, rather than having to face her own.

"Alice, you are going through with it?" She kept her voice low in the large room.

"Yes of course," smiled Alice. "I'm quite looking forward to having it all over and done with, then I can get on with my life. Did last night work? I wish you would have all let me be involved."

"You know we couldn't do that to you Alice, anyway you're too young to go to nightclubs, you would never have got in."

"Well, did it work? Is Jane ok?" Alice persisted.

Verity looked a little ashamed as she said, "I don't actually know. I wasn't there."

"Why?" asked Alice, "What happened?"

"Well my husband came home last night and for the first time in a long while, wanted to talk to me."

"What's so different about that?"

"Well it just is. We spend so much of our daily lives just getting on with things you know? He has always told me that we are just a convenience, has let me get on with things. I mean we've been polite to each other, I have a lot of respect for him, but we never really talk." Verity shrugged her shoulders. "Last night he came home and sat with me in the parlour. He began to talk to me and first of all I was a little indifferent to it, I mean you know how boring I find him?"

Alice nodded.

"Well he just talked about his day and then mentioned a mutual friend he had bumped into. We sat and talked. It was so unusual, so pleasant and so unexpected that I just got caught up in the moment. I know that's frightfully poor of me, I mean there's a poor girl who is going through such a terrible time in her life and I just forgot all about her."

"Well you haven't really known her that long," Alice soothed.

"Yes I know that," Verity agreed, "And I suppose, in my heart of hearts, I didn't really want to go there. Helen was right, it was a stupid plan. If Jane wasn't going to leave her husband on all the other occasions she had the chance to, why would she do it just because we told her to?"

"But wasn't her dad going to be there? I think the plan was that he got involved and kind of took that choice away from her," said Alice.

"Well I just don't know," Verity shrugged. "I've probably been a complete cow and stopped Jane from ever having a life, but do you know what? It's probably for the best. We could have made her situation much, much worse. You just don't know when you get involved in these things, how they're going to end."

"Yes I guess." Alice looked out of the window at the green grass and apple tree, heavily laden with small red apples. Her belly rumbled, reminding her she hadn't eaten since nine o'clock last night. She checked her watch and wondered just how long she would be stuck at this place.

"I'm a little frightened," she admitted to Verity.

"Me too," Verity admitted back. They both sat in silence, gazing out at the garden and watching the little birds that hopped around on the lawn. Verity hoped that Jane was ok and that things had happened as planned last night. She supposed if anything went wrong, then they would be seeing Jane's face come through the door any minute. As she looked to the door, she saw Amelia walking through it, guided by the same lady from reception. Amelia immediately noticed Alice and Verity and strode purposefully over to them.

"Where were you last night?" she demanded of Verity. Before Verity could respond, Amelia continued to talk.

"Doesn't matter now, everything went wrong anyway."

"Why, what happened?"

"Oh Lorraine's car got stolen, you didn't answer your fucking phone and I bottled it." Amelia looked as ashamed as Verity had done earlier. "To be completely honest with you guys, I didn't want to put my career on the line. I mean you both know the reason I'm here, once I had time to think about things, I just didn't want to go through with it."

Alice and Verity nodded, both understanding exactly what Amelia was saying. Being in the counselling sessions had been like being in a little bubble; everyone sharing and supporting. It was easy to get carried away and plan things. When they left the room and returned to reality, the plans weren't so clever or doable.

"It doesn't really matter now anyway." Amelia said, a worried smile wiping itself across her face. "Freddie is dead."

Alice and Verity both gasped loudly, causing others in the waiting room to turn and look at them.

"Sorry," mouthed Amelia to the room and then turned in to the two ladies before her. "Yes Freddie is dead, he was run over last night and here's the rub . . ." she paused for a little while.

"It was Lorraine's car that did it."

"What?" Verity asked. "Lorraine?"

"Well she says no. Lorraine did ring me last night and tell me that her car had been stolen. Apparently she was at Marc's house, you know, discussing the baby and stuff. When she went outside, the car was gone."

"That's a bit of a coincidence," said Verity.

"You're telling me," said Amelia. "I mean what are the chances of that? Not only does Lorraine's car get stolen, right at the time we are supposed to be using it to collect Jane, but that car then goes on to kill the very man that we are all trying to get rid of." She left that statement hanging in the air.

"You don't think that Lorraine?" Alice said quietly.

"I wouldn't put it passed her," said Amelia, "I mean, she is quite hormonal and all that."

"Hormones do not cause you to go out and murder a man." Verity said with finality.

"Oh yes they actually do," Amelia countered. "You read all the time about mothers killing their babies and stuff like that. It's entirely possible."

"But why would she?" Alice asked.

"Why does anyone do anything?" shrugged Verity. "There's no accounting for humans."

"What if it was Jane herself that did it?" said Amelia. "It would make sense."

"I can't see that," countered Verity. "She's put up with it for so long, why would she suddenly take control. I thought yesterday, that even if we all managed to play our part in this, then Jane may still not

278

leave her home. Look what happened the last time Lorraine went back to her house with her. She point blank refused to leave. What's to say that wouldn't have happened again?"

"What if when Lorraine told her the car had been stolen, she decided enough was enough and she was going to go and kill him?" Amelia opined.

"But it was Lorraine's car that killed him. She would have had to have already made that decision and gone to take the car." Verity countered.

"Could have been Helen," voiced Verity.

"Don't be ridiculous," said Amelia, "That cow wouldn't do anything to help Jane."

"It's possible," insisted Verity. "She knew the plan, knows where Marc lives; remember she said she only lived up the road from him? She could have seen Lorraine's car and decided to go and sort it out herself."

"And kill a man?" asked Amelia.

"She is quite ruthless."

"No one is that ruthless unless they've got a reason to be." Amelia shook her head. "The woman had just gone through a miscarriage. No, not a miscarriage, a still birth and she's got cancer. I can't see how she would get involved in something like this."

"Maybe she's got nothing to lose," said Alice.

"And maybe we're barking up the completely wrong tree." Amelia said. "No, I don't think it would be her; she's too much of a bitch."

"I can't think of anyone else." Verity sat back in her chair. "It's bizarre."

"Alice?" an enquiring voice came from the waiting room door. Another kindly looking lady, this time in a peacock blue nurse's uniform, looked into the waiting room. Alice stood up and began to walk over to her. "Wish me luck," she whispered.

"See you on the other side," said Amelia. "Be brave Alice."

"I will; thanks."

"Are you going to the meeting tomorrow?" asked Verity.

"Yes, I need to see this through right to the end."

"Ok, Alice, we will see you then. Good luck."

"Thanks."

The two elder ladies watched the young girl walk out of the room, knowing that they would be following that exact same route when their names were called by the lady in blue.

"Will it be ok?" asked Amelia.

"It has to be," said Verity, taking Amelia's hand. Both women sat in sisterly solidarity, waiting for the voice that would begin the next part of their journey.

Helen . . .

"Hi, my name is Helen . . .; I was told to come here when things got bad." Helen sagged against the counter of the hospice she had just arrived at. The young, kindly looking, man who had been sitting behind the reception desk smiled at Helen with a half-smile and a concerned look.

"Do you have a lead nurse here?" he asked.

"No," confirmed Helen. "To be honest, I haven't been to any of my appointments. I just couldn't be bothered with all the crap." She gasped as a sharp pain hit her ribs. "I could probably do with some pain killers," she grimaced.

"Ok, let's get you to a chair," the guy came out from behind the reception desk. "I'm Derek."

"Derek? That's a funny name for a young black man." Helen snorted.

"Named for my grandfather," he smiled back at her, unperturbed by the insult. "He was a good man, I'm proud to wear his name."

"Wear his name; that's a good way of putting it," smiled Helen. Another sharp pain hit at her ribs and she took in a sharp breath. "You're very good looking Derek, too good looking to be working in a place for the dying."

"Don't worry Helen, I go out at night and use the looks God gave me." Derek winked at her. "But you know; man has to pay the bills."

"Are you a nurse?"

"Yes."

"How old are you?"

"Twenty six."

"So a young black man, named Derek, who is a nurse; could be the last person I ever speak to in my waking life." Helen muttered to herself.

"Is that a bad thing?" smiled Derek.

"No, no, not at all," Helen shook her head. "I'm just taking everything in. I know that I might not be here in a few months."

"Trying to make sense of it all?"

"Something like that." Helen nodded. "The problem is, nothing made sense before I was dying, so why I think it's going to make sense now, is beyond me."

"Well we can have a long chat later, it's my night shift so if you want to have a discussion about life, I'm up for that." He grabbed Helen as another wave of pain hit her and she bent over in agony. Guiding her to a pastel green sofa next to a bubbling fish tank, he grabbed some papers off the reception desk and handed them to Helen. "I need you to fill these in Helen," he said, "Or have you got someone with you, who can fill them in for you?"

"No one." Said Helen.

"Anybody coming later?"

"No. I have nobody," she shrugged, "They're already dead."

"Well then it's lucky you now have me." Derek sat beside her on the sofa and took the papers back from Helen. "Right let's fill these in; they will let us know about your illness, treatment you've had already, who your lead doctors are etc. etc. I can then contact the hospital and get all your medical records sent over and we can find you a room. I do believe my most favourite room is available; it looks out onto the garden and there's such a lot of wildlife around here, it's a beautiful room."

"Wildlife?"

"Yes, you know, squirrels, foxes and birds."

"Crap."

Derek laughed, "You are still on the outskirts of London, it was never going to be lions, tigers and bears."

"Maybe I'll see God coming for me," said Helen, "Or the devil; I'm not sure which one will be coming."

"Many a devil has come here," said Derek, "But they all leave in the hands of God."

"I'm not so sure that will happen with me."

"I've watched many people leave this world, Helen, and they all go the same way; peacefully. Not one soul has left this hospice screaming and not one soul has looked like they were in the Devil's hands."

"Well young Derek, I think maybe you are going to experience something new with me."

"Always up for the challenge; now let's get these forms done and get you settled in a room. I think the first thing you need is some pain relief?"

"No, the first thing I need is a cigarette."

"Those things will kill you."

"Hilarious Derek, Hilarious." Helen and Derek laughed together and Derek began to ask her questions about the illness that was ultimately to send her away from the world she lived in.

Amelia . . .

Amelia woke up in a daze; what had just happened? She looked around her, to see a few women sitting on dark blue beach chairs. Beach chairs? Was she at the beach? Everyone was wearing a blue sarong, although had their normal clothing on top.

Alice sat beside her, blue sarong around her middle, cup of tea in her hand and was dunking a biscuit into the brown liquid. She smiled at Amelia, when she noticed her looking at her.

"Hello sleepyhead," said Alice. "It took you ages to wake up; I've eaten five biscuits while I've been sat here."

Amelia felt a heavy pain in her abdomen, a reminder of what had just happened to her. Her memory and mind came back into focus.

"Oh, it's been done," she commented.

"Yes," agreed Alice. "Me too." She smiled. "I'm so relieved it's over. It wasn't as bad as I thought it was going to be. A little embarrassing isn't it? I mean it's not often that you walk around with your bits hanging out and then going into that theatre place was a little bit scary. There's a lot of people in there isn't there? I mean two doctors, two nurses, and all that equipment. But I can't remember anything after he asked me what my name was; it was like one minute I was getting onto the table and the next minute I was lying here on this chair. Wham, Bham, done. No more baby, just like that. It's kind of weird when you think about it. One minute you're pregnant, feeling sick and scared and then the next minute you're not pregnant. You're just back to normal again, like nothing ever happened. I wish they had something better than these biscuits though, I don't like the custardy ones. I much prefer the chocolate ones. Why are you crying?" Alice snapped out of her ramblings when she saw a tear escape from Amelia's eye. "Amelia? Are you ok?" she asked.

Amelia didn't know how she felt. She thought she should be feeling the same as Alice; relieved that it was all over. It's what she had wanted; she didn't want to be pregnant. Did she? She put a hand to her stomach where now there was just a dull ache. Just a few minutes ago there had been a life in that belly. Little arms and legs kicking around, the next Prime Minister or leader of a large organisation and now there was nothing. Now there was just an empty womb and Amelia. Had she done the right thing? Should she have gone ahead and had the baby? Where she had been really certain of her decision this morning; now she wasn't so sure.

"Just hurts a little," she told Alice, who was still looking enquiringly over at her."

"It's like a heavy period," agreed Alice. "But it will all be gone soon and then you can go on and get to the top of that company. I reckon I will be reading about you in the news; 'Amelia heads multi-million pound contract.'" Alice put the words in the air with her hands and then gave a small clap. "I'm going to pass all my exams now." She continued. "I'm not going near another man until I have got all my grades and I'm going to really make something of my life, you know?"

"Yes Alice," Amelia smiled. "I think you will. You've definitely done the right thing."

"Oh I know that." Alice nodded her head strongly. "It would have been so stupid of me to go ahead and have a baby at my age. I thought I may feel a little bad after, you know? But I don't. I feel like a weight has been lifted off my mind. I'm just going to forget all about this now and get on with my life. Just like you."

"Yes." Amelia nodded along with her, but something wasn't right inside. She knew she should be feeling the same way as Alice, but there seemed to be this yearning inside her. Her body mourned the loss of its cargo and her mind was asking her, 'where has the baby gone?' Amelia knew that hormones could be playing a part in how she was feeling. The nurse had told her that it will take time for the body to settle and hormone levels to calm down. Tears sprang forward again and Amelia let them flow, in the hope they would make her feel better.

She turned to the sound of Verity's voice, who was being wheeled through to the beach chairs. Verity was singing loudly, 'Land of Hope and Glory' while her eyes were closed and her legs were open; blue sarong hanging off her knees. The poor nurse who pushed the chair, frantically grabbed at the sarong before it fell to the floor; another nurse rushed to help keep Verity's dignity intact, although Verity didn't seem to mind, her singing getting louder as she pushed the nurse away from her.

"Was I like that?" Amelia asked Alice, a sinking feeling in her gut as she thought that she may have been so ridiculous.

"No," said Alice. "No, you are very quiet. Most of the women have been," she giggled. "It's only Verity."

Verity continued to struggle with her singing and the nurses struggled with her sarong, as they moved her from wheelchair to blue chair. "Fuck off," Verity lashed out at the nurse.

"A few more minutes and we'll leave you alone." The nurse took everything in her stride, grabbing Verity's arm and placing it back beside her. She adjusted the blue sarong once again and then placed a heat pack on Verity's stomach, before backing off to the nurse's desk. The nurse smiled over at Amelia and Alice as she passed by, "You're awake," she said to Amelia. "Cup of tea and a biscuit?" she asked.

"No thank you." Amelia refused.

"Need to have something to eat and drink before we can let you out of here," said the nurse. "I'll make you a nice cup of tea."

"Coffee, please." Amelia couldn't stand tea.

"Coffee it is," the nurse smiled again. "Sugar?"

"Two please."

"Oh I couldn't have two sugars in my tea," said the nurse. "Biscuit?"

"Ok."

"I'll get you a nice one," the nurse winked as she went over to the tea making equipment; so normal, so nice and so non-judgmental. Amelia looked around her at the women in differing states of recovery; some talking quietly to each other, Alice happily dunking biscuits in her tea and Verity still mumbling along to some song or other in her sedated sleep. The only person in this room who cared what Amelia had done was Amelia. The only person to judge her would be herself. She just hoped that she would feel better about what she had done in a few hours, because right now, she felt like she had made the biggest mistake of her life.

Jane . . .

'We are going to be so close you and I," Jane patted her flat stomach. "I'm going to be the best mummy and you're going to be the most perfect little girl. Please be a girl darling." Jane sent every hope and thought through her nerves and veins down to her womb, trying to channel the power to make her baby a girl. It's the only way she could be sure that Freddie would never enter this world again.

The last night had been one of the most joyous events in her lift, but also one filled with a little sadness. Freddie had been her world for so long; literally the only person who gave her any sort of attention. Even bad attention was attention, so when he would give her the odd pat on the head and call her 'good dog'; she had felt a frisson of pleasure. Jane knew that would never happen again. She would never again have to lick the floor, hide in wardrobes or be a sex slave to a monster. Jane was free.

She thought about how Freddie had died; violently run over by Lorraine's Limo, twice. Jane wondered who had done it; it certainly hadn't been the plan she had agreed to. As far as she was concerned, the girls were supposed to get Freddie caught up in some scandal, in front of her father. Something that would make daddy see what a monster Freddie was and that would mean he would be open to Jane telling him what Freddie had done to her and then help her to be free of him. She hadn't even been able to go along with that plan. It was just too frightening. When Lorraine had told her that all bets were off, because her limousine had been stolen, Jane had actually been relieved. All the ups and downs she had been going through in her mind and the determination she had had, to end it with Freddie, had amounted to nothing in the end. She had been ready to go to the abortion clinic in the morning and go ahead with the termination, it had seemed the better thing to do, the *easier* thing to do. When the policemen had knocked on her door and told her of Freddie's demise, well, that had just been the most life-changing news he could have brought her.

After her initial shock at the confirmation that Freddie was dead, Jane had felt the freedom. Now it was her and her baby against the world, she was going to bring this child into the world and even if it was a boy, was going to bring it up to be a human being to be proud of. Jane was determined she wasn't going to let Freddie ever live again, either through his memory or through his child. 'Freddie who?' Jane asked herself and then smiled. She was going to go shopping with *her* cash card and was going to buy herself the best clothes money could buy. It was about time her father started paying her back for lumbering her with Satan himself. Then she was doing hair, make up and shoes; heels whilst she still could. Jane was back and the first thing she intended on doing was going back to the counselling session to see her new friends. She was going to show them the real Jane and thank them for being instrumental in getting her life back; she suddenly realised that those friends had been going through terminations in the last twenty four hours. Not only did these ladies need to see how they had changed Jane's life, but she also needed to be there to see how they were and make sure they were okay with the decisions they had made. She hoped everyone *was* okay and wondered briefly how Helen was doing.

Jane hoped Helen would return to the counselling; even though she had been a right bitch the whole time. When Helen had told her story, everything made sense; how could anyone hope to be happy when they had been through such a sad time. Jane had thought her life to be sad and lonely, but at least Freddie, no matter how evil, had been *someone*. At least Jane had always had the option to go to her father and her friends; it had been her choice not to do so. Helen had nobody. Everyone was dead in her life and now she was dying, probably alone. Jane made a pact to herself to speak to Helen and force her to become friends; she knew it was probably futile, but she would try anyway.

Helen . . .

"I'm frightened." Helen said to Derek, who now sat by her bed reading a glossy magazine.

"Oh speaking now are we?" Derek said. They had come to an agreement to remain in silence, after Helen had told him to fuck off a few times. Derek had arranged for Helen's admittance to the hospice after he had received all her medical notes from her GP.

"I'm sorry," said Helen. "I'm such a bitch."

"Yes you are," smiled Derek, "But that's okay, I love bitches." He winked at her. Helen was coming to the end of her life. Derek had read through all of her notes and seen that she was in the end stage of her cancer. She had refused any treatment from the time she had found herself to be in the state she was; this didn't surprise Derek, he had met many people who chose to leave the world quietly, accepting their fate and allowing the cancer to spread itself through their body, until it ultimately took over. He hadn't come across anyone as young as Helen deciding to do this though. It was usually people who considered their own lives to be over already; they tended to be over seventy, already had all their children, lived their working lives and didn't actually want to spend their old age in suffering and pain. They would usually leave the world content, leaving behind a legacy to be proud of, a family who mourned them, but also celebrated the life that had touched them. Helen seemed different; alone and way too young to just give up. Derek wondered what her story was.

"Want to talk?" he asked.

Helen looked around at the room which she knew would be the last one she ever saw. White walls, wooden cabinets, sink unit, door and glass patio door leading out into a green garden. The garden was manicured, flowers bloomed in every corner. There was a little tree of some kind in the middle with hanging cages on it. Peanuts poked out of the cage sides and little birds flew up to it, pecking away at the contents. Derek had been right about the 'wildlife', Helen spotted a grey squirrel, poking its head out from a nearby bush and then dashing for the tree, scaring the birds away from their own food. She watched it for a little while; saw its cheeks filling with the nuts he was skilfully retrieving from the metal enclosure.

"It's a nice garden." She mumbled.

"Yes, people do like it." Derek agreed.

Helen's attention turned once again to her room. There were no clothes in the wooden wardrobes to the side of her bed. She hadn't brought any with her, there hadn't seemed any point. The room had been thoughtfully decorated, she thought; an attempt had been made to make it look like just any other bedroom. There was none of the usual hospital stuff that you would expect to see; no turquoise blue paper curtains, hanging expectantly on a metal rail; waiting to be swiftly drawn in times of emergency. No machines with bright lights, loud noises and the obligatory green heartbeat, pulsing across the screen. She looked behind her, not even any oxygen sticking out of the wall. It was literally just a bedroom. No, not a bedroom; a *dead* room. This was where people died. They didn't need any machines or oxygen; nothing that would prolong life. This is where Helen had come to die.

"I'm frightened," she said again. Derek reached for Helen's hand, but she pulled it away. "I'm not that frightened," she spat; to which he laughed.

"Is everyone frightened when they come in here?" asked Helen.

Derek sat back and thought for a while, thinking back over the many faces he had seen lying in the same bed as Helen, the many faces that he had seen lose animation and become still.

"No," he decided. "No, not everyone is frightened. To be honest, most people are ready by the time they come here. They have battled; fought with every breath of their body to get rid of the illness they may have at the time. Tried *everything*, but when they come here, the battle is over. This is the place where people tend to say, 'ok, I give up, I've had enough'." He sat forward and took Helen's hand again. "They are ready; that's how most people are."

"I've never been ready." Helen sighed. "I wasn't ready when it took my mother, I definitely wasn't ready when it took my husband and I'm really not fucking ready for it to take me. I had a baby yesterday you know?"

"I saw your medical records remember."

"Yeah, I'm a mother; to a dead baby." Tears formed in Helen's eyes. "I'm a daughter to a dead woman, a wife to a dead man and a mother to a dead baby; how's that?"

"You're still a wife, mother and daughter." Derek offered.

"And soon to be a dead one." Helen laughed. "Full set."

"You could just be really tired, Helen. You're bound to be feeling a lot of aches and pains after giving birth. There are muscles which are having spasms as they go back into place, your hormones are all over the place."

"The pains of that I can feel, on top of the other pain." Helen pointed to her side. "I know that the cancer moved into the bone, it has been splitting my ribs apart for the last couple of months. I can actually feel them crack under the pressure of all the tumours inside there. I haven't been to the loo for a couple of days," she held her hand up as Derek began to speak, "I know, I know, could be the baby; but I haven't had a wee for a day either now I know *that's* not right."

"Why don't you let me arrange for a doctor to come and see you? He could have a look at what's going on and get you the right type of help. It seems silly to sit here and just suffer."

"I deserve to suffer."

"No one deserves to suffer, Helen."

"I do. I've done some very bad things in my life, Derek; I am not a good person."

"We've all done some bad things."

"You won't be able to top what I have done. I am the biggest bitch going. Anyway," Helen shook off the conversation. "I think you may be right, Derek, I think

I do need a doctor." Her face became much paler as she said these words. "I think something's going on inside me and I have to admit that I'm in pain."

"Okay, I am going to go and get the doctor, he can look you over, do a few checks and if he feels that you would benefit more from a hospital, then we can arrange to send you over there." Derek stood up, pleased that he had managed to convince Helen to get some medical attention.

"I'm not going to hospital." Helen insisted. "I know it's my time, Del boy, I just need some pain relief, because even a hard bitch like me can't stand much more of what's going on inside here."

"I will be back shortly honey."

"Derek?"

"Yes?"

"Can you take me to the smoking room first?"

"Those things . . .

"Will kill you, yes I know, ha ha, very funny. Now help me up." Helen offered Derek her hand, which he took and then helped her to get out of the bed she was in. Once standing, Helen faltered a little, holding onto her side where her pain was particularly bad.

"Chair?" asked Derek.

"No, fuck that," said Helen. "I'll get there," she stood up straighter, pushing Derek away from her. "One step at a time," she mumbled to herself as she put one foot in front of the other, all the way to the small room at the end of the corridor which housed most of the dying population of the hospice. "You might as well leave me in here," Helen smiled at Derek as she took a seat next to an elderly lady, "Might as well die doing what I love best."

"Hear, hear," the lady smiled up at Helen. "What have you got?"

"Cancer,"

"C.O.P.D." coughed the lady, waving her cigarette at Helen. "These things really are killing me. I've enjoyed every single one though." She shrugged.

"Same," agreed Helen, lighting up her own cigarette. "I love a fag." As she took in the first pull of smoke, her chest clenched and she found it difficult to breathe. Daggers of pain stabbed her all over and she began to shake. Helen couldn't make the breath come out of her lungs. She kept breathing in and in, with every stab of pain. Derek grabbed Helen by both arms and then leant behind her, patting her on the back. The movement, caused her chest to spasm once more and induced a cough. The cough helped Helen's lungs to get back into action and she coughed loudly, taking in a shallow breath as she did.

"Fuck me," she muttered through the coughing. "I'm not enjoying this one." She put the cigarette out in the ashtray. "I think I'll go back." She held out her arms to Derek once again for him to help her up and then staggered back to her room, leaning heavily on Derek as she went.

"I'm getting weaker and weaker," Helen admitted.

"Yes you are," agreed Derek, "Let's get you back to your room and I will go and get the doctor."

Lorraine . . .

"Thank you for coming down to speak to us Ms Cheveaux," said Detective Inspector Todd Turnbull. "We need to speak to you about your vehicle being stolen and the possible connection you may have to the deceased's wife."

They sat in the interview room of Onslow police station. A drab room, grey in colour, with dirty blue carpet tiles on the floor. The wooden desk in the middle had burn marks on them, a reminder of the days when smoking was acceptable in a police station. DI Turnbull had already issued Lorraine with a caution and done the necessary paperwork needed to start the taped interview procedure. Now he was trying to get to the bottom of why Freddie Farnham was lying in a morgue.

"May I call you Lorraine?"

"Yes you may."

"Thank you. Lorraine, we have been speaking to a few people, who we believe may have been able to help us understand how your vehicle was stolen and how it came to be involved in the hit and run accident which occurred and which resulted in the death of Freddie Farnham."

"I know."

"Now, we have been told that the house you were in, when the car was stolen; was the house of Marc Delgado?"

"Yes."

"Yes. We have spoken to Marc and he informs me that he has been counselling sessions with a group of women in the last week."

"Yes."

"Yes. You were one of those women?"

"Yes."

"Thank you and it would appear that another member of that counselling session was Jane Farnham?"

"Yes." Lorraine started to feel uncomfortable. She knew this looked really bad, but she also knew that she had nothing to do with Freddie's death. At least, she *hoped* she hadn't had anything to do with it. She certainly hadn't agreed to any such thing.

"Thank you. Now, Lorraine, can you explain to me what happened on the night your car was stolen?"

"I'm not sure I understand what you mean?"

"Where were you, what were you doing?" Todd urged.

"Well I was at Marc's house, we were having a conversation and then when I was leaving, I looked out of his front door and my car wasn't parked outside anymore." Lorraine shrugged, there really wasn't any more to tell than that.

"Can you tell me why you were at Marc's house?" asked Todd.

"I don't think that's any of your business." Said Lorraine, turning to her solicitor, she looked enquiringly at him.

"It's up to you if you tell him," the stony faced solicitor offered. "It won't have any bearing on your case."

"My case?" Do I actually have a case? Lorraine wondered. "Okay, well I was just there having a conversation with him and his wife. I really don't want to discuss this with you and don't think it has any bearing on my *case*."

"I won't ask you to elaborate," agreed Todd. "So you were there at Marc's having a conversation. Can you tell me please, do you have a friendship with Jane Farnham?"

"No."

"No?"

"No, we have been going to counselling sessions, as you said, but I never met her before that."

"Never?"

"No." Lorraine insisted.

"Have you spoken much over the last few days?"

"Not really, I mean we're going through counselling, so we all talk, but that's not necessarily with each other. We kind of talk out to each other, but we don't talk *to* each other."

"What is the counselling about?" asked Todd.

"Hasn't Marc told you?"

"No, he has only told us that it was a counselling session. He has a duty of confidentiality so hasn't told us anything more than that. You don't need to tell us either, it's entirely up to you."

"Then I won't. It's my business."

"Okay, that's fair enough." Todd reached for a laptop which was sitting beside him on the desk. "Now, we've done quite a lengthy investigation into Freddie Farnham's last days, to see if we can get a clue as to who may wish him dead, or who would want to cause him harm. In order to investigate this, we retrieved computers from his home." He began tapping buttons on the laptop. "We also looked into his CCTV cameras; is there anything you'd like to say at this point?"

Lorraine felt a sinking feeling in her stomach and pins and needles around her shoulders. Fear was creeping into her psyche.

"No."

"No?" Todd turned the laptop towards Lorraine, so she could see the screen. "I'm going to play you an excerpt from the CCTV, I wonder if you can tell me if you recognise anybody on the screen, please Lorraine. For the purpose of the tape, I'm now pressing 'play' on the CCTV footage which we recovered from Jane and Freddie Farnham's home, yesterday afternoon." Todd pressed play and watched the same footage as Lorraine and her solicitor. Lorraine was very clearly seen on the screen approaching the home with Jane, waiting outside for a short while and then going into the front hallway.

"Now you can see here there are two women?" Todd asked, to which Lorraine nodded. "Can you tell me who these women are please?"

"That's me and Jane Farnham."

"You?"

"Yes, me," agreed Lorraine, becoming irritated with this policeman's manner.

They continued to watch the exchange between Lorraine and Jane in the hallway of the home. Lorraine remembered how she was pleading with Jane to leave

Freddie and had been trying to convince her to get out of the house. Jane just refused to go and eventually kicked Lorraine out of the house. They watched this play out in front of them. Lorraine was just glad there was no sound.

"Seems quite heated," observed Todd. Lorraine just stared sullenly back at him. "Can you tell me what is going on here?"

"What do you think is going on?" asked Lorraine.

"It's not for me to speculate, Ms Cheveaux. I have you here with me and am hoping that you can tell me? I asked you if you knew Jane Farnham and your answer was no."

"No, you asked me if we were friends. I am not her friend; at least I wasn't before I met her this week at the counselling."

"Yet you knew her well enough to go with her to her home and then to have a heated argument before she asks you to leave?"

"I was trying to help her."

"Help her do what?" asked Todd.

Lorraine sighed, "Listen, we have been having counselling for women's things." Lorraine didn't feel comfortable giving this man the full details of her counselling, it really wasn't his business and she didn't want the other women to be stigmatised either. "During the counselling, Jane, told us all about her disgusting husband. How he treated her like a dog, hit her, used her for a sex slave and made her do some really degrading things. We were all shocked by what she had been going through. All of us wanted to help her; I offered to help her move away from him, after all I've got the car and am probably the strongest of all the women in that session. I went to her house with her and was going to help her leave him. We were just going to grab her stuff and she was going to move out. But when we got there, she changed her mind; said that it wasn't as easy as just walking away, she loved him and even though he was a complete wanker, she was going to stay there."

"So that's what you are arguing about?"

"Yes, I was telling her that she shouldn't put up with it, that she needed to leave and she was basically telling me to fuck off."

"Did it make you angry that she wouldn't leave?"

"Yes of course, no one should have to live with such abuse," agreed Lorraine.

"Were you determined to get her away from Freddie Farnham?"

"Yes, we all were."

"So would you have gone to any length to make sure that he couldn't hurt her again?"

"Yes." Lorraine blurted out. "I mean, no, not that."

"What?"

"Not murder. I wouldn't kill him. I wouldn't kill anyone." Lorraine was feeling increasingly uncomfortable in her chair. She felt the baby inside her moving and kicking, obviously picking up on her discomfort.

"Lorraine, as part of our investigation, we have looked into the past records of all the people who have come to our attention." Todd produced a piece of paper, "Here is your previous history; now I am allowed to bring this into the interview as it is has a relation to what we are discussing. When you were a very young girl, thirteen in fact, you were arrested for attempted murder."

The solicitor sitting beside Lorraine reached over and patted her arm, indicating for her to sit still.

"Officer, you didn't offer me this information before we came into the interview," her solicitor challenged.

"Didn't I?" asked Todd, feigning innocence, "It must have slipped my mind. I'm so sorry. Do you need to stop and discuss this?"

"No, we don't." Lorraine said loudly. "Listen, I was in a care home, being raped repeatedly by a man who should have been looking after me. One night it got too much and I poured a kettle of boiling water over him. As you know, because you have my record in front of you, I was arrested for attempted murder, I was eventually charged with actually bodily harm and I was found 'not guilty' by a court because of the extreme provocation I had suffered. That bastard deserved it. Freddie Farnham deserved what he got as well, but *I* didn't do it. I was at Marc Delgado's house with both he and his wife. My car was stolen from outside, how can I have been the person driving the car, when it was stolen from me?"

"We only have your word that the car was stolen," said Todd. He felt a little guilty bringing up Lorraine Cheveaux's past history. She had obviously been through a really trying time in her life and he didn't blame her for what she had done. He probably would never have arrested her in the first place had it been him investigating, but he had a job to do and had to do whatever was necessary to find out who had killed

Freddie Farnham, even if he agreed with Lorraine that he had probably deserved all he had got.

"My car was stolen. I rang the police, you have spoken to Marc, he surely backed that up?" asked Lorraine.

"He certainly said that you told them your car had been stolen," agreed Todd, "But what he wasn't able to do, was confirm that you had actually arrived in a car. Neither Marc nor his wife, Eleanor, saw you actually arriving in a vehicle. They were inside their house and only saw you, once you knocked on the door. Marc and Eleanor never saw you in a car, so cannot guarantee that your car was ever outside their house."

"Oh that's just ridiculous." Lorraine huffed.

"Well from our point of view," continued Todd, "We have a lady who says that she is not friends with Jane Farnham and has never met her before counselling, yet is seen very clearly on CCTV in Jane's home, just a couple of days after meeting and having a heated argument. We then have the same woman who has reported her car as stolen, although we can't prove the car was ever outside the house where it was purportedly stolen from. We then have a man, Freddie Farnham, who was knocked over and killed in the street, by the same car and an eye witness who states it was a woman driving."

"Really?" asked Lorraine, "It was a woman driving the car?"

"Correct," confirmed Todd.

Lorraine took a moment to take this in; a woman?

"It wasn't me." Lorraine said. "I don't know what more I can say to you."

"Well, our investigations are continuing. We now have the names of the other women who were in the counselling session and it is our intention to question all of them with regards to this incident. Are you sure there is nothing more you wish to say to us, considering all of the evidence we have put before you?"

"None of this is evidence," said Lorraine. "It is all fact, yes, but none of it proves that I was the person who ran over Freddie Farnham."

Todd had to agree with Lorraine. It is easy to find guilt in any information if you manipulate it in the right way; police had been guilty of doing just that in the past, but Todd wasn't that kind of police officer. He wanted proof, incontrovertible evidence that a person was guilty. All he had at the moment was a jumble of facts. He just hoped that when he interviewed the other women, some more information would come to light and he'd be able to make sense of it all. His money was still on the wife, she had the most to lose by Freddie being alive and the most to gain from his death.

"Well thank you for coming in to see me today Lorraine; please keep yourself available as we may need to speak to you again. We will be keeping your telephone and asking our lab to go through it to see if there are any messages which may come to light, is that okay?"

"Absolutely," Lorraine agreed, she couldn't wait to get out of this police station and go to the counselling session on Friday. She needed to speak to the women and find out just what the hell had been going on and who was the woman that had driven Freddie Farnham to his grave?

Helen . . .

"A man has died in a hit and run incident in London, reports suggest that the vehicle was a Limousine which was being driven by a woman. A police representative told us they were investigating the matter and were hoping to make an announcement very soon. Freddie Farnham was . . .."

Helen smirked to herself when she saw the news report on the television. Dead, just what the bastard deserved.

"It's the wife," said Derek.

"No it isn't," Helen guffawed. "I know her."

"Do you?"

"Yes, she's a shrew, there's no way she would do it." Helen had a sinking feeling in her stomach. What if Jane was approached by the police and asked if she had anything do with the death of her husband? People always thought it was the wife that did it. If the police had even the slightest reason to arrest her they probably would. Helen was finding it hard to think straight, there was a very definite stabbing pain in her stomach which was relentless and she could feel her body dying from the feet up. A doctor has prescribed her a morphine injection, which would be coming very soon; she knew she had to act fast.

"Derek, can you please get me a paper and pen, I have to write a letter," she said.

"Are you able to write Helen?" Derek asked; concern on his face. "You can dictate it to me if you like."

"No, I have to do this myself," she said, holding onto her stomach. "But make it snappy Derek for fucks sake; I'm in real trouble here."

"No problem honey, I'll be back in a tick." Derek flew out of the bedroom door. Helen hoped he came quickly back and the doctor hurried up with that morphine. *What a shit way to die,* Helen thought.

Friday . . .

Marc sat alone in the room which he had come to think of as his new workplace; at least he hoped it would be. He felt as if this week's counselling sessions had gone really well. When Marc had put the counselling session idea to his bosses at the council, they had been met with resistance. Abortion was such a sticky subject with everyone; not one person having the same view as the other. Even within his office of social workers, who had seen all walks of life, not everyone agreed on the subject. There were some who were entirely against it, stating that all life is life and humans have no right to involve themselves in human nature. There were some who were completely pro-choice, a woman's body is her own, she has the right to decide whether she wishes to go ahead with a pregnancy and should absolutely be able to make that decision at whatever time she chooses to do so. Then there were, what Marc liked to think of as the in-betweeners; those who agreed with women's choice and agreed that abortion should be an option for them, but were also of the mind-set that once a foetus reached a certain gestation, it should become illegal and that the current six month limit was way too high.

Marc had had some very heated discussions in his office since he had brought the idea of group counselling to the table and he had been under a lot of pressure to make the counselling work. He had compiled the beginnings of a report last night to show how the women had been affected by the sessions and what decisions had been taken as a result of them. Today he hoped to get feedback from the ladies and show that the counselling had been beneficial to them. Marc had begun to write Lorraine's name on his report and then stopped himself, how on earth was he going to explain this one to his manager? He thought that maybe it would look as if the counselling had been his way to do his own baby shopping, rather than to help women. In some ways that had been the reason why he had started out with the counselling sessions; his love for Eleanor was so deep and his urge to help her so strong, that the idea to approach women who were terminating, had bubbled up from his churning insides. When he had put the idea forward, however, and had started to read case studies and explore the effects of abortion, he had realised that it was actually a very beneficial thing he was doing for the women and the cause became more important than his own personal mission. Marc could not decide whether to add Lorraine to the report or not, he would face that particular decision when he knew how the rest of his life was going to go.

So far Lorraine had agreed to go ahead and have her child, then co-parent with Marc and Eleanor. Lorraine had seemed relieved when she went to them with her decision; relieved that she didn't have to go through a termination and relieved that she had found the best parents to help look after the baby. Marc had read a lot about surrogacy and open adoption, so he knew that although there were very many happy ever afters, there were also retracted agreements and some very sad non-parents in the world. He had everything crossed that he and Eleanor were soon to become a success story, because one thing Marc knew very well, was that Eleanor would not be able to survive the loss of another child.

"Hello Marc," Alice's young voice happily sang from the doorway.

"Hi Alice," Marc smiled up at her. "I'm glad you came back."

"Why wouldn't I?"

"I don't know," he admitted, "But I've never done this before, so didn't know if ladies would want to come back after their termination. I thought maybe some of you would decide that you just wanted to put it all behind you and forget all about it."

"Oh I do," Alice nodded, "But I had to see how the others got on. I saw Amelia and Verity at the clinic, so I know they're ok, but I didn't see Jane, Lorraine or Helen, obviously. I wanted to know what happened to them"

"I don't think Helen will come back and see us," said Marc, she had seemed so very sad the last time that she had gone to them. Her baby had been lost and her she was losing her life. Marc had felt so sorry for Helen, but admired how strong she was, even if it did come with a shed load of bitterness.

"No, I know, but Jane . . ." Alice walked into the room and sat down, "Did you see on the news?"

"Yes, yes I did."

"Did you call her?"

"I'm not allowed to be involved with my clients in that way Alice." Marc shook his head. "I am here only to listen and to observe, I have no right to call Jane at this time."

"But aren't you from the social services?"

"Yes."

"Well they get involved in everything don't they?"

Marc smiled, "It may seem that way, but we understand that people have their own issues they are going through and are making choices that they shouldn't necessarily be making. But it's a choice they have to make for themselves; I don't have a right to get involved."

"What about my choices?" asked Alice "I thought you may call the police when I told you about the teacher."

"You are fifteen Alice, what has happened between you and he is, illegal and morally wrong, but these sessions are confidential. I would never be saying anything. Besides, you're sixteen in six months' time, hardly a baby."

Alice didn't feel the need to elaborate on just how long she had been seeing the teacher and the fact she was actually fourteen when she started having sex with him. She shifted uncomfortably in her chair. "Still I thought you might say something."

"When you are told something is confidential, then it is," smiled Marc again. "How are you Alice?"

"I'm good," Alice nodded and then cuddled herself; wrapping her arms tight around her upper body. "I'm good." She said again and then looked towards the floor.

"How do you feel?"

"Kind of sad," Alice admitted, "It's like a loss, you know?"

"Uh huh."

"I mean, I don't regret it, I know it was the right thing to do, but I feel . . . empty."

"Ok we can talk through that feeling," said Marc.

"Started without us?" Amelia said as she walked into the room with Verity. "Found the singer on my way in," Amelia smiled at Alice.

"Shut up," Verity went red in the face, "It was the drugs."

Alice giggled, "You were funny Verity."

"Had the absolute ride of my life," laughed Verity, "Those drugs made me so happy, I honestly had the best afternoon; a lot better than the morning anyway. Did you see what happened to Jane's husband? My God, I thought that was just karma. I mean what we were going to do is nothing compared to what actually happened."

Mark raised his head sharply at what Verity had done, questioning her with his gaze.

"Oh reign yourself in," Verity said irritably. "We were going to . . ."

"Verity." Spat Amelia. "Stop."

"It doesn't matter now," Verity insisted, "I'm going to tell him. Besides, he has a duty of confidentiality."

"Tell him what?" asked Jane as she walked into the room. Verity, Alice and Amelia, immediately looked guilty and searched each other as if to ask who was going to speak.

"Jane, we can tell him, there is confidentiality in this room." Verity soothed, "It will do us good to talk about it and get it all out in the open air."

"I agree," said Lorraine, who walked into the room looking angry. "I've been in the police station over all this and my fucking car has been stolen."

"I'm sorry," said Jane.

"You don't have to apologise Jane, it's not your fault," said Lorraine. "But I'd like to know whose fault it is?" She asked of the ladies who had all now taken their seats.

"Don't look at me," said Amelia.

"Or me," said Verity.

"I can't actually drive," said Alice, "And anyway, you wouldn't let me do anything."

Marc cleared his throat. "Can somebody actually tell me what is going on here?"

"I will," said Verity, "The long and short of it is, we had hatched a plan to help Jane get away from her husband. It was probably a very stupid and unworkable idea. I was to go to the club and pay one of the prostitutes there to get with Freddie. I don't suppose I really needed to do this as he was always with one anyway. Amelia was supposed to go to Jane's dad, who is her boss at work and convince him to go to the club with her. We were going to expose him as the beast he is and then convince her dad to go with us to her house and collect her, then it would be happy ever after."

"Sounds just so rubbish when you say it out loud," Amelia voiced.

"It is rubbish," agreed Verity, "That's why I decided not to go ahead. I knew that we would potentially make things worse for Jane and really didn't want to do that. I think we were just so wrong to try and get involved in her life, thinking that we could be her saviours, when life is just so much more complicated than that."

"Where did Lorraine's car come into it?" asked Marc.

"I was just supposed to go to the club and take pictures of him, then be there when the father appeared to take him to Jane's and help her move out." Lorraine shrugged, "Even that sounds silly now."

"You were trying to help," said Jane, "I thought it might work, I was ready for it to happen."

"I'm sorry Jane," Amelia said, "I have to be honest that when Verity told me she wasn't up for it, I felt great relief. When it came down to it, I just wasn't prepared to give up my career and I also didn't think that it would work."

"Its fine," Jane said, "Anyway it really doesn't matter now does it, the bastard is dead."

Jane smiled triumphantly, "I know I probably shouldn't be so bloody happy, but I am," she admitted. "I am glad that he is dead, I don't know who did it; I know the police think that I did."

"How ridiculous," said Lorraine, "I think they actually think that I did it."

"Why would they think that?" asked Jane.

"Uh, it's my car," Lorraine rolled her eyes. "I've got previous history of violence, it's my car and I'm a lunatic lesbian. Why wouldn't they think it's me?"

"Your car was stolen," Jane offered.

"They've only got my word for that, haven't they Marc?" Lorraine looked to him.

"I can't lie to the police Lorraine; we didn't see your car, only you."

"Well whatever, either way, they think it's me. They also want to talk to you three." Lorraine pointed over at Verity, Amelia and Alice. "They probably think it's a conspiracy. The conspiracy of the counselling group." She laughed. "They don't know why we come here; maybe they think we are being counselled because we've all got psychopathic tendencies. They will probably be waiting outside later to arrest us all."

Jane shifted uncomfortably in her seat. "I'm so sorry to put you all through this."

"It's not your fault Jane," insisted Amelia. "It's just one of those things. None of us have actually done anything wrong, so nothing bad will happen to us. Don't worry. Shall we begin?" she looked to Marc, "I do actually have somewhere to be; I've spent a whole week away from work and doing everything on my laptop late at night, I'll be glad to get back to normality."

"Yes of course," agreed Marc, "Alice had already began, do you want to continue Alice?"

"Sure."

The Decision . . .

"So, I had the abortion." Alice looked at Verity and Amelia who had been at the clinic with her. "I was just saying to Marc that I feel empty." Verity and Amelia nodded in understanding.

"I lost my grandma when I was eleven and I remember this feeling," said Alice. "It's like something has gone from inside of you. But not where, you know . . ." she pointed to her stomach. "From here," she pointed to her heart. A tear formed in her eye which she quickly wiped away.

"I'm not sorry that I did it. I know that it was the right thing for me to do. I know that one day I will have a proper relationship, a house and a car; probably a few dogs."

"And a horse?" Verity asked.

"Probably," laughed Alice. "I know I will be okay, but yes, I feel empty."

"Just don't fill that emptiness with doughnuts," winked Amelia.

"I won't." smiled Alice, "That's it really, I'm happy that it's over, I'm looking forward to the rest of my life and I know that, the same as when my grandma died, the emptiness will go away. Time really is a great healer."

Marc finished his report on Alice, writing quickly on his clipboard. "Do you feel the sessions have helped you in any way Alice?"

"Oh yes." Alice nodded her head vigorously, "Before I had them, I was very on the border as to whether I would go ahead. I mean I knew that I shouldn't keep the baby, but I think if I hadn't had the chance to say what I was thinking, then I might have talked myself out of it. I also think that once I spoke about him . . ." Alice was reluctant to mention her teacher's name, "Then I realised that it wasn't love and I had just been used. I could still be with him now, like a daft cow. Meeting you all was the best thing that could have happened. Thank you."

Tick, Marc's pen made a bit line on his paper. He was glad that the sessions had helped.

"Amelia?"

"It's weird," Amelia began, "I started this whole thing, thinking that my career was the most important thing for me. I was prepared to do anything to get to the top of the pile and there was no way that a baby was going to get in the way of that. When I decided to have a termination, I told myself that was the reason I had to have it."

"And now?" asked Marc.

"Now I realise that actually, the reason that I needed to have a termination, is because I was in the wrong relationship. It was a relationship of convenience, it worked for me because I had someone at home, like I thought everyone should, but that's not really what I want. If I am to be completely honest, I think I am gay."

"Hey, hey," Lorraine jumped up, "Welcome to my side of the planet girl." Everyone laughed.

"Shut up Lorraine," Amelia chided with good humour. "I'm glad that I had the termination, it definitely wasn't the right time for me to have a child. I don't actually feel anything where that's concerned; it was just a procedure. It was something that had to be fixed. I don't feel emotional about it, I don't have a physical feeling, it's just something that had to happen and it has." Amelia smiled at everyone in the room. "I feel happy. I am looking forward to what my life is going to bring now."

Lorraine flicked her tongue between her two front fingers. "Lots will be coming your way," she said to Amelia.

Amelia laughed, "You're not my type."

"How do you feel the sessions have been?" asked Marc, "Did they help?"

"Yes, of course." Amelia agreed. "Without them I probably would have remained in my relationship, quickly had the termination and carried on. Yes, I'm glad I came here. Thank you."

Tick, Marc smiled inwardly. He was pleased that things were going so well. "Verity?"

"I, quite sickly, enjoyed myself," said Verity, "But that was just the drugs. I'm like Amelia really. I don't feel anything in regards to the actual termination. It was something that I needed to happen and it did. It was quick, quiet, painless and things can go back to normal for me now. I'm glad I came here, but I don't think it would really have made much difference either way, although I'm glad to have met some new friends."

No tick, Marc could not qualify that the counselling session had been beneficial, but it hadn't been detrimental either. "Jane."

"I didn't go ahead with the termination," said Jane.

"That's why we didn't see you at the clinic," Alice gasped. "What happened? I mean I know what happened with your husband and everything, but what, what happened?"

"Well I was going to go ahead with it. I was sitting at home last night thinking that even if all those stupid plans went right and my dad kicked Freddie out of the business, then I still wouldn't have his baby. I didn't want to have a baby by Freddie Farnham. I didn't want to have his blood running and mingling with my blood to create a life which had his DNA in it. I was all set to go and have the abortion, no matter what happened last night."

"So what happened?" Alice insisted.

"Give her a chance Alice," warned Amelia.

"Sorry."

"It's ok," smiled Jane, "Well, when they came and told me that Freddie was dead, I was shocked. I hadn't planned on him dying you know? I thought I might be getting rid of him and that he would be out of my life, but I never thought about the fact that he wouldn't ever actually exist again. That changed things for me. I had to really think about whether DNA was actually responsible for someone being so very horrible. This is my child inside me, I know it's a girl, I can just feel it." she patted her stomach. "Freddie can't ever touch her, or speak to her, or influence her in any way. My DNA is in her, *my* blood and I am her mother. She is mine and I am hers. I am going to bring her up by myself."

"What if it's a boy?" asked Verity, "What will you do then?"

"It's a girl." Jane remained steadfast in her belief, "I just know it is."

Marc wondered how exactly Jane *would* cope if her child turned out to be a boy. He made a note on his report that she may need further counselling and to ask her permission for a referral at the end of the session.

"Were the sessions helpful?" He asked.

"God yes," Jane nodded, "Yes, this has changed my life. I had never told anybody about my life. I suffered in silence and would probably be suffering still. Freddie wouldn't be dead and I wouldn't be free."

"How do you know that Freddie wouldn't be dead?" asked Amelia.

"What?"

"Well how do you know Freddie wouldn't be dead? We don't know who killed him."

"Well . . ." Jane became flustered, her mouth open and shut like a goldfish. "I hadn't thought of it like that." She shrugged her shoulders. "I suppose I don't know that. It just seems as though without all of this, then that wouldn't have happened."

"Do you know who did it?" Alice asked.

"What?" Jane looked around at the ladies in front of her. "Why would I know who did it? I thought it was one of you."

"Why would we kill your husband?" Verity asked, sitting upright in her chair. "We wanted to help you, but I for one am not prepared to murder anyone. I don't think I'm even capable of such a thing."

"I didn't do it," Amelia agreed, "I didn't even have the guts to take your dad there in case I lost my job. I'm hardly going to go and drive over someone."

"Don't look at me," Alice gulped, "I can't even drive."

"Well," Jane's face became flushed, the redness heating her cheeks. "I don't know what to say; I just thought . . ."

"Thought what?" Lorraine asked.

"I don't know," said Jane, "I don't know what I thought. Someone killed him, a woman."

"Yes. Apparently so," agreed Amelia, "But it wasn't any of us."

"Well, we will have to let the police find out." Jane shook her head. "Anyway, yes I'm glad it happened and I'm glad he's dead. I'm glad I came here and I'm glad I've kept my little girl."

"Thank you." Marc ticked his box on the chart. He really had a lot to say about Jane and how her husband had been brutally murdered, but he knew that wasn't his place, he was here to do a job and nothing more. He also made the same note about a safeguarding referral once the day was over, he felt like Jane might need some extra support in her onward journey, especially if the baby she was carrying turned out to be a boy. Marc hesitated before saying Lorraine's name out loud. He knew that they had agreed what they were going to do with Lorraine and her baby, but he was frightened she was going to change her mind, or maybe already had and wasn't even pregnant any more.

"Lorraine?" He said quietly.

"Lorraine is still pregnant," a big grin broke out on Lorraine's face as she stood and pushed out her already swollen stomach. "This little shit will be looked after by my co-parents."

"Co-parents?" asked Alice.

"Yes, I have come to an agreement that the child will live with a very lovely couple, who are desperate for children and who I know will look after it very well."

Marc blushed as all eyes bore into him.

"I will still be allowed to see the child and make sure that he or she isn't being treated badly. I am happy for its co-parents and happy for me too."

"Congratulations Marc," said Verity. When he looked up at her, she said "We all know. You don't think that loud mouth would keep it to herself do you?"

Marc blushed and looked down at his notepad. "I don't want you to think that this counselling session has been in any way for my benefit."

"It really doesn't matter does it?" said Verity. "Lorraine has what she wants, you have what you want. Everybody's happy and all is well that ends well. Don't worry Marc; we won't be reporting you to any ethics council."

Marc couldn't bring himself to look at the women, he felt so terribly guilty that he had gained so much from the meetings. "Thank you," was all he could think of to say.

"And yes, these meetings have helped me tremendously." Lorraine said. "So there we are, all happy; all done?"

"Yes, I suppose we are," agreed Marc, "Thank you everyone for agreeing to come to these counselling sessions, I feel like they've been a real help to you all."

"Except Helen," said Jane. "Nothing could have helped her."

"I had actually forgotten about her," admitted Alice. "Does anyone know how she is?"

"No, I haven't heard anything," said Marc.

"Me either, but then she's not exactly any of our friends is she?" asked Verity. "She is a very sad and unhappy lady who is not long for this world. It's such a shame that we couldn't have made friends with her, she is going to be very lonely when it comes to the end."

"You reap what you sew." Jane shrugged. "I do feel very sad for her, but if you're just such a bitch, then that's how your life will be. Look at Freddie, his life ended horribly because he was a horrible man."

"Helen could have done it." said Amelia.

"I don't think for one minute that she would do something like that," shrugged Jane. "Why would she feel the need to help me?"

"She's dying, got nothing to lose," Lorraine offered, "Probably would have enjoyed doing it."

"She's a bitch, but she's not a murderous bitch," Jane countered. "It's probably an old prostitute who has done it to him; God knows he's had enough of them. It's no surprise that people don't like him is it? I can't be the only person he's abused."

"Fair point, well made," Lorraine said. "Anyway it's probably something we'll never know, but don't be surprised if the police come knocking at all our doors again."

"Thanks for that," grimaced Verity.

"Just saying," smiled Lorraine. "Come on, let's get out of here. We can go to that café up the road; I will buy you all a nice cup of tea.

"Goodbye everyone, thank you very much for attending." Marc said.

"Bye." All the ladies waved at Marc as they walked out of the door together. Marc was pleased that the five ladies had come together and made true friendship bonds, he was hopeful that the bonds would last and that Jane could become stronger. Luckily, he would still have a very strong bond with Lorraine if all went well, so he knew he would be able to find out how everyone was doing. He looked forward to that.

Helen . . .

"Have you sent them?" Helen asked Derek.

"Yes darling, all posted - they will arrive wherever they're meant to be, tomorrow."

"Thank you."

"That's ok, are you sure you don't want me to call the people instead, give them a chance to come in and say goodbye?"

"No, they're not my friends." Helen smiled. "I don't have any of those."

"I don't believe that."

"No seriously, I'm a right bitch." She lay back on the soft pillow, looked around at the pleasant room, sunlight came in through the large glass panels of the door. A little robin hopped about on the grass outside the door, the flowers moved about in the breeze. "So pretty." She murmured.

"Yep, it's a lovely room." Derek agreed. "Are you ready Helen?"

"Tell me again."

"Ok, well this is an injection which will go onto a pump. It has very strong pain killers inside it and it will help you go off to sleep."

"No pain?"

"No pain honey. Once you are asleep, you won't wake up again. We will keep it topped up and eventually your body will shut down, you know that's happening anyway right?"

"Yes I know, this fucking body hasn't done me any favours at all."

"Are you ready?"

"Wait," Helen held her hand out and Derek held onto it. "Should I speak with a priest or what? I mean, is there actually a God? What if I haven't been doing the right thing all my life? Do you think I will go to Hell?" Her voice was very weak, but the fear in her eyes was strong.

"I really don't know Helen," said Derek, "But I do think that your loved ones will be wherever you're going. You are just following all the people who have gone before you. Wherever they are, is where you will be."

"My baby?" Helen cried soft tears.

"Your baby," Derek agreed, "Your baby is waiting and so is your husband."

"Brian?"

"Yes Brian, and your parents."

"My mother."

"Yes and your dad."

"Don't want to see that cunt."

"Helen!" Derek laughed.

"Sorry. Yes I will go and be with them. Forever." She looked at Derek's face, "Do you think I will ever feel again?"

"Feel what?"

"Anything? Is death a conscious state? Will I know I am dead?"

"Those are the questions that can only be answered once you are truly dead and by then you probably won't care about it." Derek shrugged. He wished he could answer Helen's questions, but there was nothing to say. "I know you won't be in pain anymore." He offered.

"No you don't, you liar," Helen smiled weakly. "You don't know anything because you ain't dead."

"True, but I see you when you die. I have seen many people leave this world and I can tell you one thing that I know is true."

"What?"

"The one thing that I see on everybody's face is peace. No more tears, no more struggles, no more pain, just peace."

"Have you got any pictures?"

"Helen, you are shocking." Derek laughed again. "No, I don't take pictures, I promise, I will treat you with dignity and will clean you, sort your hair out and make you look lovely for your funeral. Might be a bit harder with you though as you're such a state."

"Rude."

"Only messing." He rubbed the back of her hand. "So are you ready Helen? I can see you're in pain."

Helen nodded, "I think I am." She struggled to sit upright in the bed, letting out a loud exclamation of pain when the cancer bit at her side. "I'm ready to leave this fucking shithole."

"Let's not make your last words swear words." Derek soothed, gently pushing Helen back onto the white sheets. "How about we sing a song as I start the pump?"

"Jesus wants me for a sunbeam?" Helen smiled cheekily.

"Anything you want," Derek maintained his calm and quiet responses. "Just ask and I will put a song on for you to go out to, what do you want?"

Helen thought for a while and then said, "Can you play me some of that African music, you know with the male voice choirs? I want to be reminded of Brian as I go, maybe they will wake him up somewhere so he is ready to meet me."

Derek flicked through his online music account and found an African Zulu male voice choir online. He pressed play and the low sonorous voices came through clearly into the room, filling it with sound.

"That's nice." Helen said, "Hit me with it Derek before I change my mind."

Derek pressed the start button on the infuser and watched as the clear liquid began to make its way along the clear plastic line, into the cannula and on, into Helen's veins.

"Good night Helen." He said.

"Night." She said back and closed her eyes, waiting for the medicine to take her out of this world and into the arms of her husband and child.

DI Turnbull . . .

"Guv, letter for you." A young PC pushed a white envelope into Todd's hand.

"This has been opened," remarked Todd.

"Didn't have an addressee on it Guv." The PC shrugged, swiping his brown hair away from his forehead.

"What does that say?" Todd held the envelope up to the PC's face so he could see the writing on the paper.

"C.I.D." The PC offered.

"Exactly, who is in charge of C.I.D.?" Asked Todd.

"You are Guv."

"So why, then, has somebody else opened this letter?"

The PC looked at his shoes and then all around him, searching for an answer to Todd's question. "I didn't open it Guv, I was just given it by the station officer and asked to pass it on to you."

"The Station Officer?" Todd asked incredulously. "Why on earth would the Station Officer be opening post?"

The PC shrugged his shoulders and backed away from Todd, turning back the way he had come, "I don't know sir, sorry." He mumbled before walking quickly away.

"Place is falling apart," Todd shook his head, taking the envelope to his office. He sat in a chair which had once been an upright state of the art, envied chair. Now the chair was leaning slightly to the left, had questionable stains on the worn brown material and was the one which got pushed around the office by people so they didn't have to sit on it. The chair reminded Todd of his own career, except he didn't get pushed around and he knew where every blemish he had, had come from.

Taking the white envelope in his left hand, he pulled out a single sheet of paper. The writing on it was quite hurried, Todd could tell the writer had rushed as there were random gaps between each word and not every letter had been considered. He took time to get used to the writing before he read it properly, but on first glance he realised he had just found a killer.

'To whoever is in charge of the investigation into the death of Freddie Farnham, it was me.'

Ok well that has definitely narrowed things down, thought Todd. He read on;

'My name is Helen Wood, I am currently lying in Woodland Hospice, and if you come quickly enough you can arrest me, but first let me tell you why I did it.

I met Jane Farnham at a counselling session. She probably won't want you to know this, but we were having abortions. My reason is my business, but you can probably work it out as I am almost dead. Jane's reason was her husband. He is a bastard, Grade 1. She told all of us that he has led her a dog's life, literally. To be honest I didn't really like Jane, I thought she was a weak, shrew of a woman who couldn't stand up for herself, but then she told me about the life she had had before Freddie. She's the daughter of a rich man, had led a privileged life and was a confident young woman. Freddie Farnham stripped her of who she was, left her a shell of a human being. She wasn't living a life, she was just existing.

When you are dying, you realise how precious life is; how every minute counts. You look back and you kick yourself for every time you stopped yourself from living. That roller coaster you didn't go on, that flight you didn't take, even that doughnut you didn't eat. None of it means anything when you're dead. Jane is young and pregnant, she could have a whole life in front of her, with a child that she wants and that bastard was stopping it from happening. Jane wanted an abortion because she didn't want to put someone else through what she was going through. She didn't want to bring a life into this world that was ended before it had even begun. I could see the torture in her eyes as she spoke; saw the pain in her body as she moved. I sat and watched her for a few days, wanting to reach out to her and help, but I just couldn't; my life and my illness have left me cold.

One day I heard the other ladies in the group discussing how they could help Jane get out of her predicament. They talked a lot of crap, saying how they were going to trap Freddie in front of Jane's father and let him know what was going on. Poor deluded souls. If there's one thing I know about men, father's in particular, it's that they only believe what they want to believe, or what suits them at the time. Nothing these women were going to do was going to help Jane; in fact they would probably just make it worse.

I didn't have an abortion in the end, my son was born early. He died. I knew it was going to happen, I suppose that's why I was going to have an abortion, so I wouldn't have to face the death, but it happened anyway. When I was sitting there looking at this little life, smelling the smell, touching the soft skin, I knew what it was like to be a mother, even if it was for the briefest of times. I knew that suddenly I could be the strongest person in the world, if it meant protecting the life in my arms. I would fight for him and I would kill for him.

Jane deserves to have that. Jane shouldn't have to go through an abortion because her husband enslaves and weakens her. I knew if Jane could have her baby, then her whole life would be restored to her.

I have nothing to lose. I'm dying; I could already be dead.

I live on the same road as Marc Delgado. I saw the limousine parked outside his house that night and knew it would probably be there, because I had heard a conversation between Lorraine and Marc earlier in the day (they are in the same counselling sessions as me). I stole the car, easy for me as I did a bit of car-jacking in my youth; can't nick me for it now as I'm dead. I went to the club where I knew Freddie was going to be, because they had spoken about that as well. See what I mean? Not very good at planning things are they? I mean, tell the world!

I went to the club and knocked the fucker over and then I drove over him again for good measure.

Case closed.

Good luck getting here before I die.

Helen

Todd put the letter on the table. This was the break he'd been looking for, but he couldn't help feel disappointed. Todd enjoyed investigating crime, looking at all the leads, speaking to all the witnesses and finding evidence. Piecing it all together and seeing what he could come up with, was what made his job interesting. He had been about to go and arrest Jane Farnham again as all leads were pointing to her. History repeats itself constantly and there were countless incidents of beaten wives killing their husbands. Todd didn't blame any of them. In fact, he had been instrumental in ensuring that other women were found 'not guilty' of some of their crimes, due to severe provocation. Todd was a fair police officer; it wasn't all about getting his man, it was about seeing justice done. When a woman took matters in to her own hands and did what they did to these abusive husbands, that was sometimes justice enough in Todd's eyes and he would make no real effort to have them go to prison. He had seen this particular case going in this way, so the letter was an interesting twist on his investigation.

"No one to arrest," he murmured to himself whilst picking up the phone. "Get me the number for the Woodland Hospice," he asked the operator. "Please." He remembered to add.

Jane . . .

Jane could see the police officer getting out of his car on her driveway. She was busy changing the curtains in the house. Now that Freddie wasn't around, she didn't need to have the rigid opulence he so craved. She was going to fit some nice loose drapes, ones which she could pull across the window, or fling open as the feeling took her.

"Shit." She mouthed to herself when she saw Detective Inspector Turnbull look at her, directly in the eye. "He thinks I killed Freddie." She said to herself. "He's come to arrest me." She put her hand on her growing stomach and tried to visualise how she was going to manage in prison with a baby and then what she would do with the baby once it was no longer allowed to live with her in gaol.

"Granddad will look after you," she muttered to the baby inside her. "He was a good daddy to me when I was small, you will be okay."

Even though she had watched the police officer get out of his car and walk up her driveway, Jane couldn't help but jump violently when the doorbell rang. Even though Freddie was no longer around, the smallest reminder of her life with him, would still instil fear into the depths of her. When that doorbell had rung in the dead of night, it would usually be the call for her to become his whore. Not only his, but whoever else may have shown up with him at the time.

Jane let go of the blue material she had in her hand and walked quietly to the door, praying that it was just more questions and not the executioner bearing chains. She opened the large door slowly, peaking around the edge of the door and squinting her eyes in the sunlight.

"Jane?" D.I. Turnbull said.

"Yes," said Jane, not really knowing what else to say or do.

"I have some news, can you come inside please." Todd took Jane's arm as he walked through her front door and led her gently to the large chenille sofa in the living room.

"News?" asked Jane.

"Yes, I've received a letter," said Todd, giving a small smile which barely touched his lips. "It's from a Helen Wood."

"Helen?" What was she doing writing letters to the police? She had probably accused Jane of the murder. "Why would she be writing to you?" she asked.

"Did you know her very well?"

"No, not well at all." Jane stopped and thought about that for a little while, "Actually I suppose I know her as well as anybody can know someone. I've heard her life story, heard about her poor child and of course that she is very sick."

"Dying."

"Yes, dying," Jane confirmed. "She was at the same counselling as me; I was going to have an abortion."

"Yes, her letter told me that," nodded Todd.

"And what else did her letter tell you?" asked Jane, waiting for the accusation to come.

"She has admitted to the murder of your husband Freddie."

"What?" gasped Jane, "What?" she gasped again; "That can't be right, why would *she* do that?" Jane shook her head; she couldn't understand why Helen would say that she had murdered Freddie.

"She has explained everything in her letter," Todd offered the piece of paper, now ensconced in a plastic evidence bag. "Read it, Jane, it might explain things to you."

Jane read the contents of the letter. She could see that Helen had reached the end of her road and was now dying in a hospice. Something inside Jane soared with happiness. Helen had freed her. A dying woman, a complete bitch on the surface, had done the most wonderful thing and freed Jane from her shackles.

"I mean, it's wrong, but I'm very happy." Jane admitted.

"Happy?" enquired Todd.

"Yes, I can't lie," shrugged Jane. "Freddie was a complete pig. Everything Helen has said about him in here is true; he made my life an absolute misery. I was nobody, nothing, empty inside; frightened of everything that moved, because that's what Freddie Farnham had done to me. He took my very soul and ripped it to pieces. I cannot lie, I'm glad he's dead." She read the letter once again, grateful to Helen, but still confused as to why she did it. Helen had seemed like such a selfish person, this was truly a most benevolent deed, if there was a heaven; Helen had just got herself into it, as far as Jane was concerned anyway.

"Are you going to arrest her?" asked Jane.

"I have to go and speak with her, yes," admitted Todd. "But I thought I would come and see you first, no rush is there. Are you ok Jane?"

"Yes," smiled Jane, "I really am just great. I have my life back, will be able to control my money again and I have her." She patted her stomach. "We're going to be just fine."

"I will ring you later and let you know how I get on with Helen." Todd offered.

"Yes, please do and please," Jane stopped him with a hand. "I know you're a policeman and everything, but can you please say thank you to her for me?"

"I can't do that." Todd winked at Jane, "But I'm sure she knows how grateful you might be." He walked away from Jane feeling a bit weird. A man had just been murdered and yet it had allowed a woman to be immensely happy. He should have driven straight to the Hospice and arrested Helen Wood, to question her and ascertain the validity of her letter. He should be checking evidence and CCTV and ensuring that the letter Helen had sent was right, but somehow he knew to just leave Helen alone. She was dying; there was nothing that could ever be done to her which was worse than death. He was going to make his way over to the hospice now, but slowly. He might have a stroll along the Thames and take in the sun which was shining gloriously on this morning, maybe stop for a cup of tea and just appreciate the life he was living. The in and out of the breath as he walked, the heart which beat within him and kept him alive. Helen wasn't going anywhere; nowhere that he could reach her anyhow.

Jane's letter . . .

Brian Knox handed his daughter, Jane, the envelope which he had received at the Max incorporated Offices that morning. As he had never had anything delivered there for his daughter before, he knew it must be something very important and had been looking for a way to break with ice with Jane since Freddie had died. When Jane had told Brian the extent of Freddie's abuse towards her, he had been overcome with guilt so strong; he didn't know how he was ever going to make things up with her.

Brian had adored his daughter when she was growing up, had literally worshipped the ground that she had walked on, but when she became such a spoilt teenager, he admitted to himself that he had been glad when Freddie Farnham had taken her on. Freddie had been like the son he'd never had; a replacement almost for Jane. It had been easy to believe the lies that Freddie had fed him about Jane, easy to believe that she was happy at home and not in need of anyone, actually a little unhinged. So much easier to build a fake life for her in his head, than actually take the time out to be a proper father and even bother to ask her how she was. Brian had promised himself that he would never be that person again. He would never abandon Jane the way he had done in the last few years. He was to be a granddad and he was going to be the best father and grandfather that anyone in the world could ask for.

Jane smiled at her dad; she had already forgiven him his sins. She still blamed herself for the whole Freddie thing and couldn't believe she had allowed herself to become so weak, so quickly.

"What is it?" she asked.

"I have no idea; it was delivered to my office this morning." Brian shrugged. "I haven't opened it. It says 'private and confidential' on it."

"I'll open it later," smile Jane again, this was probably the most they had spoken to each other since before Freddie had died. She looked at every line on his face; she remembered those lines and welcomed the extra ones which added age to her father's face.

"I've missed you daddy," she said quietly.

"Jane, I've missed you too." Her dad grabbed her and cuddled her tightly to his body. "I'm sorry Jane, I'm so sorry that I failed you."

"It's fine."

"No," he insisted. "It's not fine, I let you down. I should have always come to see you, check how you were. I shouldn't have listened to Freddie. He had me believe that you didn't want to see me." Brian shook his head. "I didn't listen to you."

"I never said anything to you."

"Exactly," Brian kissed her on the cheek before letting her go again. "When did you ever not speak to me?" he asked. "We spoke all the time, even when I was at my busiest. Even if you had been losing your marbles, I should have realised that the talking wouldn't just stop. I never listened to the silence. I am sorry."

"I forgive you Dad. You weren't to know."

"When a dog who barks every day, suddenly goes silent, you know something is wrong." Brian said.

"Fitting analogy," Jane smiled; she wasn't going to tell her dad the ins and outs of Freddie's abuse towards her. She could see the guilt on her father's face and loved him too much to put the pain of her past onto his shoulders. "We're going to have a baby, daddy." She laughed, a free laugh, a laugh which released her from the mental shackles in her brain. "You're going to be a granddad."

"I know," he agreed and started laughing with her, she sounded so happy, it was just infectious. "A boy." He hoped, "I'd love a grandson."

"Dream on granddad," Jane laughed patting her stomach. "This is a little girl."

Seven months later . . .

"Here is your baby," the midwife passed a big pink bundle to Jane, who was sitting, sweating in her nightdress. It had been a long and difficult labour, seventeen hours in all, but Jane had enjoyed every minute of it.

Jane's life had completely turned around since Freddie had died. She had made firm friends with the ladies that she had spent that week of counselling with. Alice was working hard at school and had a new boyfriend now, she was happy and getting on with things. At one point, she had voiced a desire to have her teacher arrested, but then had decided that life was too short to be going over the past. Jane had tried to steer her differently, "He shouldn't get away with it Alice," she had schooled, "He could be doing it with someone else right now."

"I can't take responsibility for what he does now," Alice had shied away from the situation. "Maybe when I'm finished school, I will do something about it then." Jane still had the idea to find out where the man was and report him herself, but her love for Alice had kept her quiet.

Verity was busy shagging all of the stable boys, the gardener and even having a lesbian fling with the cook; things would never change with her.

Amelia was working hard on her career, she sometimes lamented the baby that she had got rid of and Jane would talk with her for hours about how she felt. Guilt seemed to be the overriding emotion, but Amelia would often talk about what her baby could have looked like had it been born, was it a boy or a girl? Would it have had dark hair, would it have enjoyed life? These were questions she could never now answer. Jane could see it eating away at her, but Amelia still got on with her life. Maybe one day, when she was ready, she would be able to have another child and the pain of termination would pass.

Lorraine was now Jane's absolute best friend in the whole world. They talked every day and were joined at the hip. A very unlikely pairing, but Lorraine was just the right person for Jane to be around. Whilst she didn't have a sexual attraction to Lorraine, Jane felt safe when she was with her. Lorraine was a very maternal woman it seemed. For all her bravado and machismo, she just loved to love. Jane would often sit for hours in Lorraine's arms, just watching television or talking together. They were in love with each other, Jane could admit that, but she couldn't bring herself to have a sexual relationship with her; it just wasn't what she wanted. Lorraine had been happy to accept the close friendship, she said it left her free to play around with others, so it worked and they were happy.

Lorraine had given her baby to Marc and Eleanor, who were now the proud parents of a little boy called Elijah. He was truly a gift to them. Eleanor was besotted and Marc just as doting. Jane would visit Elijah with Lorraine, who was now 'Aunty Lolly';

Lorraine would cuddle him and kiss him, but then happily hand him back to his parents. She often told Jane that it was the best thing she could have ever done, both for herself and Elijah, so no regrets there. Lorraine was looking forward to also being an aunt to Jane's new bundle of joy and was actually sitting outside in the hospital waiting room, awaiting news of the baby's arrival.

Jane looked at her daughter lying quietly in her arms, now clean from the birth, dressed in a white all in one with little pink mittens over her hands. Her hair was a dark brown but there was only a hint of it. The baby opened her eyelids and two dark little eyes peeked out at the world, not seeing, moving independently of each other. Her mouth opened in a little 'O' and she stretched her arms out above her head, feeling the freedom of the air around her. Jane kissed her on the forehead and smiled down at her newest love.

"She's beautiful," Brian Knox looked down at his granddaughter. "What will you call her?"

Jane continued to smile the smile that had been on her lips since the day that Freddie Farnham had died.

"I'm going to call her Helen," she said. "After the woman who saved my baby."

Helen's letter . . ..

Hello Jane.

By the time you read this letter, I will probably be dead. Hooray, I hear you cry.

So that motherfucker is dead. He deserved to die. He was a bastard.

I wanted to say sorry to you. I am sorry that I was such a bitch. I am sorry that every time you spoke I shot you down. I didn't mean it, I could see that you were hurting, could see you were going through a really awful time and I just didn't know what to do to help you.

I have spent the last six months of my life hating. Hating my mother, hating cancer, hating myself and then I started to just hate everything. Most of all I hated being alone. I would walk into my house and all I could hear was silence. Silence shouted at me and all I could do was sit and listen to it. I hated it.

When I came to the counselling I also hated all of you, you with your perfect lives who just didn't want to have a baby. Of course, that's how I felt at the beginning, but I didn't know any of you, or know your story. The more I sat there and listened to all of you, the more I realised that I'm not the only person in the world who is suffering. Of course I knew that deep down, but it's easy to think you're the only person in the world who is hurting, especially when you are feeling so alone.

LISTEN TO THE SILENCE...

When I listened to you speak and heard what that bastard had done to you, I heard you Jane. I heard your cry for help; I could see the despair in your eyes. You have a baby inside you, who I hope is healthy and a chance of a real life away from that cruel, evil man.

When I saw it on the news, I knew they were going to arrest you, I just knew it. They always think it's the wife that's done it you know? SO I wrote a letter to the police and I told them it was me. I'm not having them arrest you, it's just not fair.

I told them I did it, told them how I run the car over that fucker and then ran over him again just for good measure. I reckon I'll be dead before they get here and if I'm not, then I'll spend a couple of days in prison; that will just be another adventure.

How you thought you would ever get away with it, I don't know; you were the obvious and only killer! I hope I have saved you from even more grief in your life. I free you Jane, go and live your life. Have your baby and be happy.

Helen

p.s. I hope it's a girl.

Printed in Poland
by Amazon Fulfillment
Poland Sp. z o.o., Wrocław